Power Trip

Power Trip

Treasure Malian

www.urbanbooks.net

Urban Books, LLC
300 Farmingdale Road, NY-Route 109
Farmingdale, NY 11735

ISBN 13: 978-1-60162-126-9
ISBN 10: 1-60162-126-4

First Trade Paperback Printing April 2019
Printed in the United States of America

10 9 8 7 6 5 4 3 2 1

Distributed by Kensington Publishing Corp.
Submit Orders to:
Customer Service
400 Hahn Road
Westminster, MD 21157-4627
Phone: 1-800-733-3000
Fax: 1-800-659-2436

Skye

It was the first day of the rest of my life. I was beginning my journey as a law student at Columbia University. I was a bit early for my contract law class, so I grabbed a seat in the first row and began to tap my Christian Louboutin heels against the tiled floor. I waited patiently for the other students, as well as the professor, to arrive. As I watched the students enter the classroom, I became nervous. I felt my hands start to perspire. I couldn't quite understand why I was nervous. I had been an A student throughout my undergraduate career at NYU, but I knew law school was a different ball game. However, I was completely ready for the daunting task that was before me. Finally, the professor arrived. I leaned over and reached into my Louis Vuitton tote bag, which rested on the seat next to me, and grabbed my MacBook Pro. I wanted to be ready in case I needed to jot down notes right away.

I watched attentively as the professor began his spiel about his expectations for the semester and his students. He spoke for twenty minutes before handing out the syllabus and dismissing us. Seeing as it was the first day of class, it was unlikely that professors kept the students for the entire class time. I couldn't be happier about that. The entire class got up and made a quick exit through the door located at the back of the classroom. I, on the other hand, moved a bit slowly, because I had received a text from my best friend, Ariana, and was texting her back. As

I was immersed in the text conversation she and I were having, I didn't notice the guy standing by the door, that is, until I walked right into him.

"Oh my. I'm sorry about that," I said, looking up from my phone.

I thought to myself that this guy was fine. He looked to be about six feet one, give or take an inch, and he had nice smooth caramel skin. He reminded me of Derrick Rose. He rocked a low cut with waves that made me want to go swimming. Being a fashionista, I had to scrutinize his attire. I must say, the man could dress. He looked dapper in the YSL V-neck, the slacks, and the Ballys that adorned his feet. I had to get out of my own thoughts when the stranger flashed me the sexiest smile I had ever seen, showing a perfect set of pearly whites.

"It's a'ight, beautiful. I'm not made of glass."

There was suaveness in his tone, which piqued my interest. I was far from a thirsty chick, though, so I smiled back and walked away. We had a class together, so we definitely would cross paths again.

As I walked past him, I could feel him staring, or more like burning a hole in my back. It was expected, though, because I was bad. I had gorgeous, exotic features, including a set of hazel eyes that mesmerized anyone who looked into them, even if only for a second. I was shaped nicely. I could definitely be one of them chicks in a Lil Wayne video or something, but I was much classier. I was equipped with a flat tummy, thick thighs, a big butt, and a set of 36 C boobs that were perky and sat upright. How could I blame him for staring?

As I walked across campus to where I had parked my BMW M5, I thought about the stranger. There was something about his smile and his demeanor that made me want to know more. My thoughts were interrupted by the ringing of my cell phone. I had to push the thoughts about the stranger to the back of my mind—well, for now at least. I slid my finger across the screen of my iPhone to answer.

"Hey, Mom. Wassup?"

My mother and I were extremely close. We spoke every day about any and everything under the sun.

"Hi, baby girl. How was your first day?"

I could tell my mother was extremely happy that I had decided to follow her path into the law field. She couldn't hide the enthusiasm in her voice as she waited to hear about my first day of law school.

"Mom, it went pretty well. I'm looking forward to the rest of the semester. The classes I'm taking this semester seem really interesting, so yeah, we'll see how it goes."

I had finally reached my car when I felt a hand tap me on the shoulder. I turned around and was pleasantly surprised that it was the stranger. I put up one finger, signaling him to give me a minute to wrap up my conversation. I had completely missed the last thing my mother said, but I knew it wouldn't be smart to let her know I was no longer focused on what she was saying. So I thought it would be a good idea to just end the conversation.

"Mom, it's still early. I'ma drop by your office so we can grab lunch. Love you," I said, quickly ending the call. Then I focused my attention back on the mystery man.

I gave him the once-over before speaking. "So, you following me?"

He let out a smooth chuckle and smiled. Damn. I really wished he would stop giving me that sexy-ass smile.

"Nah, it's not even like that. I'm just the type of nigga that goes after something that I want."

Who did this nigga think he was? Better question, who did he think *I* was?

"Oh, I see. So what's your name, and what exactly is it that you want, huh . . . ?" Here he was declaring that he was after something, and we didn't even know each other's name.

"Cameron. Just Cam is cool."

I extended my hand for him to shake it. "Nice to meet you, Cameron. I'm Skye."

The electricity that shot through my body the moment our hands touched was mind boggling. What was it about this man? Whatever it was, I was ready to find out.

"So wassup? I was hoping we could exchange numbers and get together tonight—"

I had to cut him off. "Tonight? You don't waste any time, do you?" After realizing my hand was still in his, I slowly pulled it out of his grasp.

"I told you, Skye, I go after what I want. I already know that I'm interested in getting to know you, and obviously, we on the same page, because you're still here."

I had to admit that he was right. I was definitely interested in getting to know him. Without any further inquiry, we were swapping numbers. I handed him his phone back after saving my number in it. What he did next was shocking, and it left my heart racing. He moved closer and kissed me on the forehead.

"Drive safe and don't forget to call me." With that said, he walked away.

I watched him go for a few minutes, until he disappeared back into the university's courtyard, and then I jumped in my car, heading downtown to my mother's job.

My mother was one of the top criminal attorneys in the state of New York. I admired everything about her: her strength, her determination, her resilience, and her success. She was a perfect example of "Started from the bottom, and now we here!" She grew up in Brooklyn, in

Marcy Projects, to be exact. No one had expected her to be where she was today. However, she had refused to let the negative opinions of a few people, and the experience of the drug-infested housing projects, determine who she would ultimately become. Once she got her working papers at the young age of fifteen, she hit the ground running. She was on her grind day in and day out, doing any odd job she could snag, and still managed to keep way above average grades in school.

While girls her age were out partying and turning up, my mother was working or had her nose in her books. It paid off too, because she graduated high school at the age of sixteen and started her college career that following fall at Howard University. To this day she would tell you that leaving Brooklyn to attend school in Washington, D.C., was one of the best decisions of her life. Not just because of the opportunities she was presented with at Howard, but also because that was where she met my father, Harvey Lewis.

Yes, *that* Harvey. Three-time NBA champion, four-time MVP Harvey Lewis. He and my mother met during a visit he paid to Howard with his fraternity brothers. My parents loved to tell the story of how they met and fell in love. Don't get me wrong. It was a beautiful story, but their version was also a little too long. I preferred the short version. They met and knew they wanted to be together, and although he went to Duke, in North Carolina, and she was in D.C., they made it work. They came from different walks of life. My father was also born and raised in Brooklyn, but his circumstances were different. He was from Park Slope, an uppity neighborhood, and he came from a home with two parents who were pretty well off, seeing as they were both doctors. He never let the difference in their upbringing come between what he and my mother shared. It worked out well, because I came into the world four years later.

My parents adored me. As far back as I could remember, I had never wanted for anything. I had been their princess and had been treated accordingly. Still was. I had had the best of everything: I'd gone to the best schools, rocked the best designers, you name it. I would be forever grateful for my parents and the life they had provided for me. I had turned out to be a mixture of both of them. I had got my exotic looks from my mother, as well as my drive and my ambition. My father had blessed me with this fiery attitude and no-nonsense personality. He was never one to be fucked with, and neither was I. I hated that people saw a pretty face, designer clothes, heard a soft voice, and then assumed I was soft. Let's not get it twisted. I may have been raised with a silver spoon in my mouth, but I was far from oblivious to the things that went on around me.

I reached my mother's office building, parked the car, and hurried inside. Once I reached her office door, I knocked, but there was no answer, so I walked in. Every time I visited my mother's office, I reflected on our life. The photos she had strategically placed around her office were like a time line of all the major events and points in her life. I looked at all the photos, as I'd done a dozen times, before she finally came waltzing through her office door. She walked over to me and embraced me before stepping behind her desk.

"Hi, beauty," she said to me as she dropped a thick manila envelope on the desk and took her seat.

The sunlight coming through the window illuminated my mother's smooth caramel complexion. She was a very pretty woman, and she didn't look a day over twenty-five, although she was forty-one. I prayed that I looked as good as she did when I reached her age.

"Hey, Mommy. We still doing lunch, or are your swamped?"

She gave me a face that answered my question. It was rare that my mother had time for anything other than her cases, because she was just that good. I had figured she wouldn't be able to leave the office for lunch. It was cool, though. I respected her grind.

"Don't even worry about it, Mommy. Rain check?" I smiled at her to reassure her that it was okay.

"You should come over tonight. Your dad and I would love to have dinner with our only child."

I wanted to take her up on that offer. The time I spent with my parents was invaluable, and I loved to get with them every chance I got. However, I had already told Ariana I would go with her to Green House for some party that Brooklyn rapper Fabolous was hosting.

"Tonight I'm heading out with Ari, Mom, but tomorrow for sure."

She was about to respond, but her phone started ringing.

"Go ahead, Mom, and get that. I'm going to head out. I'll call you later on."

We sent each other air kisses, and then I left.

I hadn't had a bite to eat all day, so my first stop was Habana Outpost. I absolutely loved their Cuban sandwiches and margaritas. I had to pass on the margarita this time since I was driving, but I definitely enjoyed my Cuban. I had some time to kill after lunch, so I decided to hit Fifth Avenue and do some shopping for the night that was ahead.

Cameron

There I was, trying to get through this meeting with my pops, and my thoughts kept drifting to shorty, the chick I'd met at my school. I was in no way, shape, or form a nigga that chased bitches, but there was something about shorty. I wanted her, and I was gonna have her.

"Yo, Cam, pay attention."

I guessed my pops could tell that my mind was elsewhere. Not that I really needed to hear him out. I knew what he was saying, and I personally felt the shit didn't apply to me. He had a bunch of little niggas working for him who needed to be reprimanded, and I definitely wasn't one of them.

"I hear you, Pops." I had to say something so he would think that I was listening. To keep it trill, the only thing on my mind at that moment was shorty. *Why though?* That shit was tripping me out.

My pops went on for a good two hours, which was expected because this was the monthly meeting, where everyone who was somebody in the organization got together to catch up and touch base. I looked around at the familiar faces and smiled to myself. These niggas were my family, and they had proved themselves to be loyal on more than one occasion. Majority of them had had shit on lock with my pops since before I was born, and they were still riding. I had put a few of my niggas on too, just because any real nigga would make sure that his niggas was eating. That was me, as real as they came. Niggas knew not to let my suit and tie fool them. I was good at gunplay when my hand was forced. It rarely ever came to that, though. That was what I had all those niggas for.

I thought about how shorty might react to my lifestyle. Not every day did you meet a nigga in law school who was knee-deep in the drug game. I was a different type of dude, though. The day I'd graduated from high school, my pops was ready for me to dive headfirst into the game. Shit, one day I would have the reins to the entire operation. I had had no problem with that, but I'd had a few stipulations of my own. I'd told my pops I was going to college and, ultimately, law school. Don't get me wrong. I'd never been able to really see myself as a nine-to-five nigga, but I'd known the advantage that having an education would give me in this game. A legal education at that. I knew shit now, and I continued to learn shit, that niggas wouldn't even think about until they were standing before a judge, getting the book thrown at them.

I had to laugh at myself, though. Nobody outside this organization knew that I had any involvement in it, and I wasn't about to change that for a chick. I no longer needed to think about how she would react, because she would never find out. Shit, not even my moms knew about the shit I was into. Speaking of my mother, I missed her, and I made a mental note to head out to Long Island as soon as my schedule permitted to spend some much-needed time with my favorite lady.

The meeting finally concluded, but niggas just lounged around, kicking it. I had some loud that I was in the mood to blow, so me and my nigga Ty rolled up and got bent. We were on the forth blunt when my iPhone started vibrating in my pocket. I pulled it out and watched as shorty's name flashed on my screen. As badly as I wanted to talk to her, she was gonna have to wait. I sat my phone on the table and enjoyed my high.

"My nigga, what you doing tonight?"

I heard Ty talking, which made me open my eyes and sit up. "Hopefully, I'ma be doing this badass shorty I met at school today."

We laughed and gave each other dap. Ty was my nigga, more like my brother. We'd been niggas since we came out of the womb. Our pops were right-hands. We did everything together: fought, fucked bitches, got money, you name it. I knew that besides my pops, this was the only nigga walking the earth whom I could trust with my life. My phone vibrated again, but this time it was a text.

Hey, wassup? I know you wanted to meet up tonight, but I promised my best friend I would roll with her to Green House. You're welcome to come if you want. Talk to you later.

"Yo ,Ty, you want to mob to Green House tonight?" I tapped this nigga, who looked like he was about to pass out and shit.

"Yeah. I heard Fab hosting some shit there. You know wherever that nigga at, a shitload of bitches will follow."

I laughed at the truth behind his statement.

"I thought you was tryin'a see shorty, though," he said as he switched positions in his seat. That nigga always wanted to get comfortable and sleep when he was high.

I laughed again. "Yeah, she the one who told me to come through. She going with her best friend."

Hearing shorty had a friend put this nigga on full alert again. "Her friend better be bad. You always get the A-one chicks and leave me with the ugly-ass friend."

I couldn't say much to that, since it was true.

As we pulled up to Green House, I knew I had made the right decision by having my driver bring us. Finding parking would have been impossible, and I didn't have the patience for that shit. When the Range came to a complete stop, I secured my nine, which was tucked in the small of my back. I doubted highly that niggas would need to pop off at the venue, but I didn't take chances with my life. I hopped out of the whip with Ty and my muscle, Rick and Max. Those niggas were the definition of *loyal*. They would bust shots and take shots for me if need be, so I made it my business to keep them close.

"Cameron!"

As we got closer to the entrance, I heard someone call out my name. I already knew who the voice belonged to. Two people on Earth called me Cameron: my mother and Skye. I knew my mother wasn't there to see that nigga Fab, so it had to be the latter. I looked in the direction the voice had come from and saw her standing at the entrance, with the bouncers and another shorty. The sight of shorty made my dick jump. She had her hair up in one of them messy buns that bitches seemed to love so much, but the shit looked perfect on her. I really got to see her features, and she looked better than she had earlier that day. Her friend wasn't bad looking, either. I smiled at shorty and pulled her close to me once I reached her.

"Wassup, beautiful?" I said as I wrapped my arms around her for a hug.

"Hey. This my best friend, Ariana," she answered, introducing me to her homegirl.

"What up? This my brother, Ty, and my niggas Rick and Max."

Her homegirl's eyes fell on Ty, and she blushed. I looked over at him, and that nigga was in a trance too. Ole "love at first sight"–ass nigga.

"I know we not getting in these long-ass lines," I said, looking at the lines, which seemed to wrap around the corner.

Skye and her homegirl laughed, but I was dead-ass serious.

"No, Jay, they with us," Ariana said to one of the bouncers.

He nodded his head and let us walk in.

Oh, they got some clout and shit, I thought to myself.

We followed the ladies to their section and took our seats. I ordered bottles to jump-start the evening.

"You look good, Ma." I had to let Skye know she was definitely killing the game tonight. "Thanks," she said, standing up. "Come dance with me."

Did I hear shorty right? Do I look like a nigga that dance?

"I'm straight, Ma. Go ahead, though. Let me watch you."

She turned to walk away with Ariana as Rich Gang's "Tapout" came blaring through the speakers. I watched as she sang the hook along with Future and danced.

"She is bad, son," Ty said, throwing back his Patrón.

"I told you, fam. Her homegirl a little cute too." I had to throw that in there since he'd complained that he always got stuck with the ugly bitches.

I turned my attention back to Skye. Watching her dance made me wanna just fuck her on the dance floor. When French Montana's "Pop That" came on, I watched her twerk and bounce her ass. I couldn't help myself; I found myself creeping up behind her and grabbing her waist. She turned her head, and when she saw it was me, she continued to bounce, this time on my dick.

"I thought you didn't dance," she remarked, giggling.

I palmed her ass and said, "I didn't wanna miss out on this."

The rest of the night was straight. We got drunk, danced, and talked. By the time we dipped out of the spot, it was almost 4:00 a.m. I wanted to take shorty back to my crib, but something told me to chill and let shit between us run its own course. I was really feeling her. She wasn't just a pretty face. She was mad cool, smart, and didn't seem thirsty. You could tell she was feeling the kid, but she wasn't being overly obvious, like some of these chicks were nowadays.

"I had a good time, Cameron. Thanks for coming to chill with us," shorty said when we were out in the parking lot. Yo, even her voice was sexy.

"I did too, and it's nothing, Ma. Thanks for the invite. You drove?"

I looked around for the white M5 she had hopped in earlier, but I didn't see it.

"Nah, I knew parking would be disastrous. I took a cab," she answered.

I looked at her sideways. "A cab? It's almost four in the morning, Ma. You not about to catch a cab home. I'm not with that."

I walked over to where Ariana and Ty were talking, with Skye on my heels.

"Yo, Ariana, you drove here?" I questioned.

"Yeah, I did. I'ma take Skye home. Don't worry."

I was gonna interrupt, because I had a better idea, but Skye beat me to it.

"Y'all acting like I live far. I can—"

I cut her off. "Nah, it's too quiet for that. Ty, what you about to get into, bro?" I had a feeling Ty was sliding off with Ariana, and I was never one to cock block.

"I'm straight, bro. I'll hit you later on," he told me.

That was my nigga. I was a proud big bro. I wanted to see if I would be as lucky.

"A'ight, son," I said. "Yo, Ari, it was nice meeting you, Ma. Skye, my driver can take you home."

I waited to see if she would object, but she didn't. She hugged her homegirl, said goodbye, and followed me, Rick, and Max to the car.

***

When we pulled up to the address shorty had given my driver, it was the Waldorf Astoria. Shorty must have really been caking to live like that. Who was that girl? I hopped out of the truck and held the door open for her.

"This how you living, shorty?"

She smiled. "It seems that way. Thank you for the ride, and for tonight. I had a good time. Get home safe."

I hugged her and said, "No problem, shorty. Oh, and I'm not going home yet . . . I'm gonna find a spot for some food, 'cause a nigga starving. Good night, though."

I turned around and walked back to the car, and she called after me.

"Cameron, I mean, if your boys don't mind waiting or coming back for you, you can come up. I can cook."

She didn't need to tell me twice. I dismissed my boys and followed behind Skye as we headed to her place.

Shorty's crib, a whole apartment at the Waldorf, was dope; she definitely had taste. She told me I could look around and make myself comfortable while she jumped in the shower, so that was what I did. I looked at the pictures she had hanging up in her living room. Seemed like she came from a cool family. I spotted a picture of her and Harvey Lewis.

Damn. Shorty mess with old ballplayers? Fuck this picture shit. I should go jump in the shower with shorty. Nah, let me chill.

I walked over to the cream sectional and sat down. I sat back, with my eyes closed, and relaxed. Shit felt good, 'cause a nigga was low key tired.

Skye

That shower was everything I needed and more. I stepped out, feeling like a new person, dried off, and walked into my bedroom, which was adjacent to my bathroom. I slipped on a pair of Victoria's Secret lace panties and applied some Dove lotion. I sat on the bed and rubbed my legs for a minute, just because I loved how smooth they were. Then I remembered I had left Cameron waiting. I slipped on a pair of boy shorts and a wifebeater and pranced into the living room.

Really? I thought when I caught sight of Cameron. Did this boy really fall asleep? I stood in front of the couch, shaking my head. He was fine as fuck, even when he slept. I smiled to myself. I grabbed the throw blanket that was folded across the arm of the couch, and put it over him before heading back to my room and retiring to my bed.

The next morning, I woke up feeling rejuvenated. I glanced at the neon numbers on the cable box, which read 10:13 a.m. I felt like lying there for another hour or two but then decided to get up and make breakfast, since the original plan was for me to cook. I climbed out of bed, stretched my five-foot-four-inch frame as high as it could go, then entered the bathroom to wash my face and brush my teeth. After brushing my jibs, I looked myself over in the mirror. My bun was extremely messy but still cute, so I left it as it was and headed to the kitchen to start breakfast.

As I opened my bedroom door, the aroma of good cooking hit me, and my stomach growled.

Did he make me breakfast? I wondered.

I headed to the kitchen and found Cameron fixing our plates on the center-island top. Wow, that was really nice of him. I stood and admired him for doing his thing.

When he finally sensed my presence, he looked up and flashed his panty-wetting smile, and said, "Good morning, Ma. I was gonna wake you up in a few. I figured you would be hungry when you woke up, so I found my way around your kitchen."

I got closer and saw he had made pancakes, eggs, and bacon. I took a seat at the island, across from where he was standing, and he placed one of the plates in front of me, along with a napkin, silverware, and a bottle of pancake syrup.

"You didn't have to, but thanks," I said. "I really appreciate it. And sorry for not waking you up last night. I thought you were tired, so I left you alone. Well, obviously, you were, because you were passed out."

He laughed, sat down to join me, and we ate. After breakfast I gave him a washcloth and a toothbrush and let him go handle his business while I cleaned up the kitchen. I was sitting at the island, drinking a bottle of water, when he came and joined me.

"I called Ty. He'll be here in a minute to get me, and you'll have your space back," he announced as he stood a few feet from me.

I looked up at him and rolled my eyes. *Damn.* I hoped he hadn't noticed that.

"Dang, you acting like I'm kicking you out," I commented. I kind of wanted him to spend the day with me.

"Nah, it's not like that. I need to change and shit. I can come back, if you want."

I thought about it for a second. Hell yeah, I wanted him to come back, but I wasn't about to seem that eager.

"I mean, it's whatever," I said nonchalantly. "I guess we'll catch up another day or something."

He shook his head from side to side and sighed. "Come on, Skye. You can keep it trill with me, Ma. If you want me to stay, say that. No need to hide how you feel and shit."

He was right. I didn't need to, because he was either gonna respect it or not.

"Yeah, I want you to stay. I mean, you slept in my house, and I barely know anything about you. However, I do understand that you want to go home and change, and that's fine," I told him.

I stood up and put the water bottle in the recycling bin before walking out of the kitchen.

Call it being a brat if you wanted, but I was used to getting everything my way. If he knew I wanted him to stay, that was what he need to do. I went into the living room and sat down in the La-Z-Boy, my favorite chair ever, because it was just so comfortable and big. It swallowed me up when I sat down, and that was what I liked most about it. I grabbed the remote off the coffee table and turned on the TV. I started flipping through the channels, wondering when he was going to come into the living room after me, but he didn't until he came to say bye because Ty had arrived.

Since that day at my house, I hadn't really talked to Cameron. Of course, I saw him during class, but that was about it. I guessed he wasn't feeling that I had been a brat about him leaving, but whatever. That was me, Skye, all day, every day. I kept telling myself, *Never change, just like Jay-Z says in his song.* If Cameron was going to deal with me, he had better learn to get with it. Besides, I hadn't really had the time to think about him. It was only week three of classes, and I had already become a bit overwhelmed. Law school was really no joke. Seemed like the only thing I had time for nowadays was school and seeing my parents. I hadn't even hung out with Ariana, but that was not because of schedule conflicts. It was because she and Ty had been connected at the hip since the night we went to Green House. I was not mad, though. He was a cool dude, and they seemed to really enjoy each other's company.

Tonight was turning out to be no different than the past few nights. There I was, sitting on my living-room floor, surrounded by books, in a pair of boy shorts and a baggy off-the-shoulder T-shirt. I didn't care how it sounded; I was comfortable. I kept looking back and forth between my legal writing textbook and my contracts textbook. Those classes were going to be the death of me. How had my mother done this? Shit, not only had she finished law school with honors, but she'd done it while also raising a baby. I'd been, like, four when she graduated.

I flipped back and forth between my textbooks continuously, becoming more restless as the minutes seemed to get away from me. I was at the point where I was ready to toss my textbooks aside and hit the bed when my doorbell started ringing. I definitely wasn't expecting anyone, so it startled me a bit. I figured that maybe it was Ariana stopping by. Other than my parents, she was the only one with permission to come over whenever she wanted. I got up from the floor and walked to the front door. I opened the door and was in for the shock of my life when I saw Cameron standing there with orange roses. I honestly didn't like roses, because they stunk to me, but orange was my favorite color. How did he know that?

I stood there looking at him for a minute before he spoke, breaking the silence.

"You going to let me in or not?"

I didn't answer, just moved to the side, giving him space to come in. Once he was inside, I closed the door and turned to him. He handed me the flowers and went to kiss my forehead, but I moved back.

"Thanks!" I said as I headed to the kitchen to put the flowers in some water.

I didn't expect him to follow me, since he hadn't the last time he was here, but surprise, surprise, he did.

"You don't want to be bothered?" he said.

Did he really just ask me that? I thought. After all, we had had class together for three weeks, and *he* had chosen not to speak one word to me.

"I never said that. But wassup? What brings you by?"

I put the flowers in a vase and filled it with water. Then I sat on one of the stools at the island, and he sat down across from me and stared into my eyes. I felt myself blush, so I turned my head.

"I just wanted to see you. I know I should have reached out or spoken to you when I saw you in class and shit, but it's just that—"

I cut him off. "You don't really need to explain yourself to me. It's cool." I could care less why he hadn't spoken to me, because to me, regardless of what his reasoning was, it was petty as hell.

We sat in silence for a few minutes, until he decided to speak again.

"I just want you to keep it trill with me all the time. I'm not a regular nigga, Skye. Don't tell me shit because you think it's what I want to hear, or because you afraid of my reaction."

Whoa. Afraid of his reaction? This nigga got the game fucked up.

"First off, Cameron, it wasn't even like that. I wasn't telling you what I thought you wanted to hear, nor was I afraid of your reaction. I just didn't deem it necessary for

me to tell you that I wanted you to stay. You knew that! I
guess you just wanted to hear me say it, but that's neither
here nor there. Not speaking to me over that was petty."

By the time I finished my rant, he was behind me. He
spun my stool around. Now we were face-to-face.

"You're right, Skye. My apologies. I handled it wrong."
He kissed me softly on my lips. "You forgive me?"

I was unable to answer. The kiss had left me feeling
some type of way. His lips were so soft and moist. Not
moist where he walked around with slobber all over his
mouth, but just right, which was good, because I would
never tolerate dry lips. He lifted my chin with his finger
and looked me in my eyes. I looked back, feeling like our
souls were speaking to each other.

I finally was able to speak. "Yes, I forgive you, Cameron."

He smiled and stepped away from me. "What were you
doing before I got here? In bed?"

I stood up and headed toward the living room, and he
followed me. I stood next to my textbooks and pointed.
"This! Story of my life."

He chuckled. I wanted to know what was funny. This
school crap was stressing me out.

"You look stressed," he observed. "Take a break. Let's
kick it before I have to run. We can finally talk, get to
know each other, and shit."

I sat Indian-style on the floor and picked up a textbook.
A break wasn't going to help me pass those classes, but I
could multitask.

"What do you want to know?" I asked as I turned the
pages of the textbook. I looked up and watched as he sat
down on the sectional and got comfortable.

"How old are you? How you know Harvey?"

I had to stop his interrogation. "Damn! Are you inter-
rogating me? I'm twenty-one, and he's my father."

He had the same reaction everyone else had when I said Harvey was my dad, but I didn't get it. My dad was an ex–NBA player, not the president of the United States. "Yeah, so tell me, Mr. Cameron, What are you about?" I shifted my focus to him, so he could see I was interested in really knowing who he was.

He shrugged. "I mean, what you see is basically what you get. I'm twenty-three, last year at Columbia, and I'm from Harlem . . . regular shit."

I made a face, which must have told him that the little information he'd volunteered wasn't going to cut it, so he went on. He told me everything, at least I felt like it was everything. He had grown up no differently than me: his dad was a businessman, and his mom was a stay-at-home wife and mother. I mean, my mother didn't stay home, but in terms of coming from a good home and being well provided for, we had that in common. He spoke about his little sister, and I could tell that she meant the world to him. A family man . . . That was a plus. He had a soft side to him, and I liked that. Yeah, having a tough exterior was cool and all, but what female wanted a guy whom she couldn't connect with on an emotional level? He didn't really dabble too much in the lives of his parents, which was fine.

My intent was never to pry; I just wanted to know who I was dealing with. You couldn't learn everything about a person in one night, and I didn't expect to. However, what I did learn helped me make the decision to keep seeing him.

When he was done talking about himself, I opened up to him, which was shocking. I normally kept my life story under wraps, but I felt comfortable with him. Just as he had, I shared with him a bit about my life while I was growing up and a little about my family. He was clearly as interested in me as I was in him. I was definitely looking forward to seeing where this relationship would go, if anywhere.

Ty

Every year, Cam's parents had this nice-ass Thanksgiving dinner party at their crib on Long Island, and this year was no different. My pops was coming through, and Ariana and her parents were too. I had to admit, I was really digging shorty. I was at the point where I wanted to let her in completely, but I couldn't. I didn't want to fuck up what my nigga had going on with Skye, because he wasn't ready to tell her about his other life. As his boy, it was my job to protect his secrets at whatever cost. I didn't understand what was taking him so long, though. Cam and Skye had been seeing each other for as long as I'd been fucking with Ariana, which was, like, three months and shit. Everything seemed cool with them. They were always together— between classes, during date nights, during all-night phone calls. In fact, they were damn near inseparable. Whenever they weren't together, it was because he was in the street with me, grinding. Seemed serious enough, so why wouldn't he just be one hundred with shorty? Not my place to judge, though.

I snapped out of my thoughts when I heard Mama Mariah calling me.

"Tyquan. Hello, Ty!" She almost had to shout to get my attention.

"Yes? Sorry, Mama. Wassup?" I answered, looking in her direction as I sat on the living-room couch.

"Your guest Ariana and her parents are here."

"Okay, I'm coming now. Thanks, Ma."

As I stood up, I saw the look on Cam's face. He was tryin'a hide the fact that he was wondering where Skye was, but I knew him. I walked into the foyer and approached Ariana and her parents as they waited patiently by the door. Ariana's face lit up when she saw me, and even her mother smiled. She had never met me before, but I figured anyone who could make her daughter happy deserved at least a smile from her.

"Hello, Mr. and Mrs. Morgan. Hey, Ari. You look beautiful," I said in greeting.

I shook her father's hand, hugged her mother, and gave Ari a hug as well. They were cool. Her pops spoke to me as if he already knew me. I guessed Ari had been talking about me. I took them to the den, where Cam's parents were waiting, and introduced them. All the parents seemed to hit it off and began to engage in conversation. Ariana and I decided to dip back into the living room and join Cam. As we were walking through the foyer, the doorbell rang. We were right there, so I went to answer the door. I opened the door and saw that it was Skye and her parents. *Damn.* Skye's mom looked like she could be her twin. I thought Skye was bad, but her moms could get it. If I wasn't feeling Ari, and if Skye's mom wasn't married . . . nah, even if she was married . . .

"Hey, Ty," Skye said and smiled at me as I moved to the side so they could come in the house.

By now Cam's parents were approaching the front door.

"Wassup, Skye? Hi, Skye's parents," I said. "Let me get Cameron for y'all." I took Ariana's hand in mine, and we walked off to get Cam.

Cam must have been listening with his bionic-ass ears, because that nigga was already walking toward us when we reached the edge of the living room. I nodded my head at him as he walked past us. Once Ariana and I were seated on the couch in the living room, I texted my pops to see where he was at. Then I slid my phone back in my suit pants pocket and focused my attention on Cam's little sister, Victoria, who was sitting in an armchair on the other side of the coffee table.

"Yo, sis," I called and took Victoria's attention away from whatever she was doing on her phone, which was probably texting.

"Yes, bro? Wassup?" she said, lifting her head.

"This Ariana. Ari, that's Vic, Cam's little sister."

As the girls were exchanging hellos, Cam came back into the living room and signaled for me to follow him.

I kissed Ariana on the cheek. "I'll be right back, Ma."

I got up and followed Cam. We walked to the west wing of the house and then took the elevator down to the bunker. I knew it was serious, because we never went down there. Once we were inside the bunker, Cam walked over to the floor-to-ceiling safe that had been built into the wall. I knew to stand back until he had opened it. He performed a few steps that I couldn't see, then punched in a code and opened the safe.

He looked over his shoulder and called out to me, "Come on, bro."

I took a few steps, and as I got closer, I could see that the safe was full of weapons: different types of guns, grenades, knives, you name it.

"What happened?" I almost regretted asking that question the moment the words fell from my lips.

"They hit the warehouse in Red Hook and bodied Rick."

His words hit me like a ton of bricks. Rick had been like an uncle to us ever since we were little niggas. Whoever had done this was about to feel the wrath of a lot of hurt people.

"Who the fuck is *they*? And what was there?" I paced the floor as I waited for answers.

Niggas like me didn't cry, but losing Rick was a hard pill to swallow. Even thugs cried, right? *Fuck it, though*, I thought. I didn't have time to shed tears.

"That dude called Man and those niggas from Cypress Hills. Crazy shit is that nobody knows about that warehouse except a very limited number of people. So, somebody close is on some snake shit. As far as the loss, we took . . . ten keys, and a half a mil."

Did I hear that nigga correctly? *Ten fucking keys and a half a mil?* Nah, shit was about to be ugly for them East New York niggas.

"How we know who was behind it?" I asked.

Cam leaned over and picked up a weapon. When he stood up straight, I saw that he was holding a MAC-11. This machine gun happened to be his weapon of choice.

"My pops set up security cameras at all the spots, but the only ones who know about the cameras is him, your pops, me, and now you. Max made it out, and he called my pops a little while ago. Then he sent your pops to the other spot out there to check the cameras."

That was probably why my pops hadn't texted me back yet. It was fucking Thanksgiving. Who did this shit on Thanksgiving? I thought about what was to come next while Cam kept talking.

"No cops showed up, as expected. The warehouse is so out of the way, so no one could pinpoint where the shots were coming from. The cleanup crew should be there now, handling Rick's body and whatever mess is left."

I didn't need to hear anything else. I stepped into the safe and grabbed two .45s.

"What's the plan?" I looked over at Cam as I waited for an answer.

"Max on his way to pick us up. We gonna ride through Cypress and send a little message. That nigga picked the wrong team to fuck with. I know he not gonna be out and about, but the good thing is that I know where his parents stay."

I knew it was on, and I was ready. Somebody had to pay for us losing a family member. If we had to put everybody in Cypress in the ground before we got to Man, so be it.

The ride to Cypress Hills was mostly silent. Occasionally, Cam cursed, because Skye was blowing up his phone. I understood he was in a different place, but he could have told shorty he had to run out. He had just left her completely in the dark. Ariana wasn't blowing up my phone, because I had texted her a bullshit story about my pops's car not starting and him needing a ride.

"You ready, son?" Cam said, taking me out of my thoughts.

I looked out the window and noticed that we were already in Cypress. Max pulled the car into a parking spot in front of an apartment building, and we all hopped out with hoods and ski masks on. We followed Cam into the building, then up to the third floor. We lined up on both sides of the hallway, behind Cam, and he knocked twice on the apartment door, with his hand covering the peephole. Seconds later, an elderly lady opened the door. Her eyes nearly popped out of her head as she watched five masked men rush into her apartment. We discovered four kids, three boys and a girl, in the living room, and we now had their attention.

"If anyone moves or says a word, Granny right here dies," I heard Max say.

I hoped they believed him. Max was a straight killer, and he would kill his own mother if she crossed him. We weren't in the business of murdering old ladies or kids, so I really did hope they played by our rules. Cam rushed to the back of the apartment, and when he came back, he had a look of disappointment on his face.

"Where the fuck is Man?" Cam barked, flipping over the coffee table.

I looked over at the three frantic kids. Cam saw what I saw, then looked at JR, another one of his dudes, and barked orders.

"Yo, take them in one of them rooms in the back."

JR quickly motioned to the kids to get moving, but the girl and one of the boys simply ignored him. He walked the two obedient boys toward the back of the apartment. Cam walked over to the couch and grabbed the boy who was still sitting there by his shirt.

"Yo, when my brother catches y'all niggas, it's going to be a wrap," the boy yelled, trying to sound tough.

Cam turned his head and looked at the boy sideways. He had made the wrong move by declaring he was Man's brother. That meant only one thing: collateral damage. Cam let go of the boy's shirt, stepped away from him, and looked at Max, who then raised his .45 and put a bullet in the middle of the boy's forehead. The elderly lady and the girl broke down and started screaming and hollering. We didn't pay that shit no mind. Man had taken the life of one of ours, and that kid was the price he had to pay.

We had to get low fast, because the neighbors had definitely heard the shot, and we weren't in any position to be dealing with those kids tonight. We had enough shit that needed to be handled.

"Yo, bro, let's get low," I said before I walked to the back of the apartment to get JR.

When JR and I stepped back into the living room, Cam had the girl by her throat.

"Tell that nigga Man that he's next!" he snarled at her.

We backpedaled out of the apartment and down the stairs. We concealed our weapons as we weaved through the housing project, back to the car. We headed to one of our spots in Brownsville and ended up staying there till the sun started to rise.

Skye

I squinted as my eyes tried to adjust to the sunlight that was streaming through my windows. I thought about last night and reached over and took my phone off the nightstand. I was disappointed that I didn't have a call or a text from Cameron. He had just up and left the dinner last night without a word. I knew he was okay, because his dad had said he went to help Ty's dad, but he still could have called or texted me. *Whatever*. I was not about to dwell on that. Aside from his little disappearing act last night, my parents had had a good time. They had clicked really well with his parents, which was a good thing.

I sat up in bed and looked around the room. I had decided to stay the night at my parents' house since I rode with them to Cameron's house. They hadn't wanted me going home alone. As I looked around, memories flooded my thoughts. I missed home; I missed this room. I had lost my virginity in here and had dealt with my first heartbreak in here. This was my sanctuary. I didn't really know why I had opted to move out last year, because I hadn't had to. If it was up to my parents, they would have me living under their roof forever, but I wasn't with that.

I fell back onto the bed. I didn't have anything to do right now, so I was going to take advantage of my opportunity to stay in bed. As I got comfortable, my phone started to vibrate. Thinking it was Cameron, I answered without looking at the screen.

"Hello!" I yelled into the phone.

"Hey, *chica*."

It was nice to hear from Ariana, but I had wanted it to be Cameron so bad.

I masked my disappointment. "Hey, girlie. What you doing up this early?"

"Ty came over at, like, eight something this morning. He's in the shower now, though."

I was going to ask about Cameron, but the beeping on my other line interrupted me. I looked at the phone and saw his name flashing on my screen.

"Ari, that's Cameron on my other line. Let me call you right back, girl." I hung up before she could respond.

"Now you know my number, Cameron!" I barked into the phone. I was irate and planned on letting him know just how pissed off I was.

He didn't speak, and that pissed me off.

"Hello . . . ?" I said. I was ready to hang up, but he spoke up just in time.

"Where you at? Why you not home?"

What the hell? Why was he questioning me like I was the one who had disappeared for the night? I wanted to be mad, but something in his tone made me soften mine.

"I stayed at my parents. Are you there now?" I climbed out of the bed and walked into the bathroom.

"Yeah. I need to see you." The sincerity in his voice made my heart melt.

"I'll call the front desk and have Jacob come up and let you in. I'll be there soon."

I ended the call and called Jacob. I knew it was totally against policy, but he was a friend and would do a favor for me. As expected, he agreed to let Cameron in my apartment.

***

When I got home, I found Cameron sitting on the couch, staring into space. When he finally realized I was there, he managed to show me his smile, which I loved so much. I sat next to him and rested my head on his shoulder.

"I'm sorry I didn't call you. A lot went on last night. Rick was murdered," he told me.

I sat up straight and faced him. The look on his face was one of intense sorrow. I could see the pain he was trying mask.

"I'm sorry for your loss, baby, but I'm here for you if you want to talk, or if you need anything."

He kissed me and shook his head. "Nah, I'm straight. Don't want to talk about it at all."

That was what I didn't like about him. He felt he needed to be tough about everything and to everyone. He didn't have to be that way with me, but he didn't understand that.

"Okay. We don't have to talk about it."

But I wasn't going to sit there in silence. I had on yesterday's clothes and wanted a shower badly. I got up and headed to my bedroom, stopping at the hall closet to hang up my peacoat. Once I was in my room, I stripped. Then I stepped into the bathroom and got in the shower. I stood under the spray, allowing the water to beat on my body. It felt amazing and reminded me how badly I needed a spa trip. I suddenly felt a cool breeze, so I turned around to find the glass shower door pulled back and Cameron standing there. I tried to hide my excitement, but I couldn't. I slowly looked down and had to gasp at the size of his dick.

"Can I join you?" he said.

I smiled and stepped back, giving him space to step into the shower with me. I had started to lather my sponge up with soap when I felt Cameron kiss my shoulder. I dropped the sponge and turned to face him. After a few seconds of looking into each other's eyes, we let our lips meet. We kissed with fervor, and before I knew it, my back was against the shower wall. In one swift motion, he lifted me up and began to slide his rock-hard manhood into my now dripping wet box.

"Damn, Skye. You so tight, Ma."

As he inched in farther, my body tensed up. He was big.

"Want me to stop? I don't want to hurt you," he told me.

It was nice that he cared, but hell no, I didn't want him to stop. I let out a soft no, and he went deeper.

After a few strokes, the slight pain I felt was erased and replaced with complete pleasure. I dug my nails into Cameron's back as I felt him hit my spot over and over.

"Cameron," I moaned as I felt an orgasm shoot through my body.

He put me down and turned me around so I was facing the wall. I was glad he was still holding me up, because my legs felt like jelly. As he entered me slowly from behind, I bit down on my lip and arched my back.

"Ya pussy feel mad good," he said in a low voice.

I wanted to yell duh, but I couldn't formulate any words, just moans and oohs and aahs. He slapped my ass, then gripped both cheeks as he pumped in and out. I felt another orgasm coming and noticed his breathing had got heavy and short, so I knew he was on the verge of busting. I threw my ass back, and he pumped faster.

"Shiiit!" Cameron called as he busted his nut inside me.

I released my juices all over his dick. I couldn't believe we had just had sex without a condom. Don't get me wrong. The shit had felt good, but that wasn't something I was into. I didn't want to ruin the moment, however, so I said nothing. I simply picked up my sponge, washed, and got out of the shower. I headed into my bedroom and was in the middle of slipping on a T-shirt when Cameron came walking in with a towel wrapped around his waist. Damn, that nigga was fine. He walked over to where I was standing and kissed me. I felt a tingling between my legs, but I had no intention of having sex with him again, not right now at least. I walked away as I put my wet hair up into a ponytail, using the hair tie I had on my wrist.

"Skye—" he called after me, but his sentence was cut short by the ringing of his cell phone.

Thank goodness, because I wasn't trying to converse at the moment. I walked into the living room and flopped down on my couch. I knew I should have gone over some work before now, since class would be back in session in a few days. Ugh! Thanksgiving break was entirely too short. I turned around when I heard footsteps approaching.

"I gotta go. I'll come back later or something," Cameron announced hastily.

Or something? *Is that nigga serious?* We had had sex, and then he had just decided to up and leave? I was not about to be one of them chicks who let a dude do whatever because he was cute and had a good dick game. I was good on that.

"Okay." I kept it short. He could go ahead with his little disappearing acts. At that point, I was feeling like Sweet Brown: ain't nobody got time for that!

We shared no more words that day. I heard his footsteps, then the front door closing. I decided not to dwell on the little situation with Cameron. I called up my girl Ariana to see what she was up to. She said Ty had just left, so we agreed to meet up for lunch and do some shopping.

Ariana

When my taxi pulled up to Koi Restaurant, I paid the driver, then stepped out into the brisk air. The cold and I had never got along, so I put my Ralph Lauren riding boots to the pavement and quickly walked to the entrance of the restaurant. When I entered, I was greeted by a hostess. She was so polite, and that was another reason why I loved that place, besides the bomb-ass sushi they served. Once I told her someone else would be joining me, she showed me to a nice intimate table for two. I removed my coat and got comfortable. I glanced at my no-label watch and wondered why Skye wasn't here yet. When I looked up, I saw the hostess leading her over to where I was seated. I smiled as I stood up and hugged my best friend.

Skye was my girl. We'd been friends since birth basically. Our fathers were fraternity brothers, so our families were extremely close. I felt a little bad that we hadn't really been hanging out much lately. Between my job at the radio station and my time spent with Ty, I rarely had a moment for anything else. Then I figured that since she'd been kicking it heavily with Cam, the time apart hadn't bothered her.

"Girl!" she yelled as she got comfortable in her seat.

I knew she had some tea.

"Yes, honey?" I chuckled as I picked up the menu and scanned it.

"This boy is driving me crazy."

Suddenly, she had my undivided attention. I hadn't had a clue that there was trouble in paradise. Yeah, it had been too long since I'd kicked it with my right-hand.

"What's going on? I thought things were going well." I was confused.

She sighed and began to give me the rundown. "Things were . . . Well, I guess they are going well. I just get the feeling like he's keeping something from me. He keeps playing these disappearing acts, and the shit is getting old quick!"

She was frustrated. I could tell, so I let her get everything off her chest.

"I feel like maybe he has a girl, and if he does, that's cool, but keep it real with me. I would be pissed, because we had sex, but I would definitely get over it. You know me. I can deal with a lot, but being lied to is not something I am fond of."

Wait, did this chick just said they had sex? She had to be really feeling dude, because Skye was definitely one of those "ninety-day rule" chicks that Steve Harvey talked about in *Act Like a Lady, Think Like a Man.*

Before speaking, I took a sip of the water that the waitress had just placed on the table. "*Chica*, I know that can be frustrating, but I also know that you cannot speculate on what he is keeping from you, if he's keeping anything from you at all. The best way to find out what is what is to flat out ask him."

The look she gave me told me that she agreed with what I had said. It was true. The quickest way to lose a nigga was to accuse him of shit he was not doing. I didn't want my girl to go down that road.

"You're right, but enough about the Cameron and Skye soap opera. How are things with my day one?"

We placed our orders before I began to give Skye my spiel about how things were between me and Ty. Man,

I had to admit, I was really feeling him. He was considerate, real, and his dick game was one hundred. I could
definitely see us on some long-term shit, and he had
expressed to me that he felt the same way. No, I wasn't in
love, but I was heavily in *like*. Yeah, that was how I would
put it. Skye listened attentively as I ran down all that
had been going on, and of course, she offered her advice.
Once our food arrived, the talking ceased. We were in
shape, but we loved us some food.

Lunch was great, but then it was time to tear up the
shops on Fifth Avenue. Catching a taxi was easy since
hundreds of them filled the streets of New York City
at all hours of the day. Once we got to Fifth Avenue, we
hit all our favorite spots: Bergdorf Goodman, MAC, Gucci,
Christian Louboutin, and a heap of others. Shopping
with my girl was always an all-day thing, which was why I
didn't head home till about 8:00 p.m.

As I walked through the door of my condo, I felt my
cell phone vibrate. I dropped my bags on the living-room
floor and grabbed my phone out of my purse. I smiled
when I saw Ty's name on the little screen and answered.

"Wassup, handsome?" I may have sounded a bit to
chipper, but whatever. I didn't mind my man knowing he
was missed.

"What you doing?"

I sat on the couch and held the phone between my
shoulder and ear as I took off my boots. "I just got home,
babe. I went to eat lunch and shop with Skye."

His background was noisy as hell. I almost wanted to
tell him to call me back, but I decided against that.

"Pack a bag. We gotta run to Atlanta, and we just gonna
stay there and kick it till Sunday."

Did he just say, "Run to Atlanta," like it was the next
borough or something?

"What you going to Atlanta for, babe?"

I didn't really need to ask that, because I was going no matter what he said. A weekend in the A sounded good to me.

"Just to chill and shit. You coming?"

Shit. He definitely didn't need to ask me twice. "Yeah, baby, I'll go. I'ma pack now. Are you on your way to get me?"

He yelled at someone in the background to turn the music down before he shifted back to our conversation. "Yeah. Be ready in an hour."

After getting off the phone with my babe, I gathered all my shopping bags and headed to my bedroom to figure out what I would be taking on my weekend trip and to pack. I walked back and forth between my closet and the dresser, grabbing everything I thought I would need for a weekend. Once I had out about a week's worth of things, I sorted through it all and narrowed it down. I had a bad habit of overpacking, but I was trying hard to keep it simple for once. I decided on a few outfits and, shockingly, only two pairs of shoes. If for some reason I needed something else, I could hit up Lenox Square or something. Who was I kidding? I was going to hit up Lenox, anyway. A trip to that mall was a ritual whenever I was in the A.

I had finished packing everything in a duffel bag and was in the middle of putting my boots back on when my cell phone started ringing. I grabbed it off the coffee table and answered. It was Ty, letting me know that he was downstairs. I was excited to be going away with him for the weekend. I didn't want to waste any more time, so I put on my coat and grabbed my duffel bag. I needed to let my parents know I would be away for the weekend with Ty, so I texted my mom the information while I was in the elevator.

When I got outside, I saw Ty standing near a black Range Rover, and I headed over to him. Damn, my man looked good. He reminded me of the singer Tyrese. I was totally into dark chocolate, so Ty was just my speed. I stood on my tiptoes and kissed him before sliding into the backseat of the Range. Ty stowed my duffel bag in the back, then slid in next to me.

"Hey, Cam," I said when I saw him sitting in the driver's seat.

Hmm . . . if Cam was coming, why hadn't Skye been invited? I thought to myself. I thought back to the conversation I had had with her earlier, and figured something definitely was up.

"Wassup, Ari? I don't think you met this nigga, but this our boy JR." He tilted his head toward the guy in the front passenger seat.

I said wassup to their friend before grabbing my phone out of my purse and texting Skye.

Wassup, chica? Ty invited me to go to Atlanta till Sunday with him, and Cameron going too. I'm definitely going to find out what's going on with this dude. No worries. I got you.

I slipped my phone back in my purse before getting comfortable and laying my head on Ty's shoulder as we started our journey to the airport.

Cameron

I turned on my phone as soon as we exited the airport. I looked through my text messages to make sure I hadn't got an important message. I saw that Skye had texted me, so I opened hers first.

Honestly, Cameron, I'm good on your bullshit. Really? A trip that my best friend was invited on, but I wasn't? I'm not even tripping on the fact that you didn't invite me. The fact that I wasn't important enough for you to tell that you were going out of town is what bothers me. Especially after you dipped from my house right after fucking me. But it's cool. Like I said, I'm good on it. Enjoy your time in Atlanta, and don't think to hit me up when you're back home, either.

I felt bad for not inviting Skye to Atlanta, but this wasn't a social trip for me. It was business. Ty had me tight. I didn't understand why he had to invite Ariana to come along, but I couldn't really be mad at him for it. He was doing enough by keeping our business dealings under wraps, because I didn't want this to get back to Skye. I really needed to make some decisions about that girl if I wanted her in my life. I would definitely have to put her on game soon.

My thoughts were interrupted by Ty tapping me to get my attention.

"What happened?" I asked, turning around to face him.

"Our ride is here."

I followed him and Ariana over to where our homeboy Matt was waiting for us in his truck. Matt had been our boy for a while. We'd met him back in seventh grade, when he first moved to Brooklyn. We'd lost touch right before we went to high school because his grandmother got sick, and he and his moms had to come down to the A to take care of her and shit. I'd been kind of surprised when he reached out years later. He had been going through a tough time and needed some homies to lean on. I had never been in the business of letting my homies starve, and I wasn't going to start with Matt. I'd set him up with a team and some weight, and he was eating good because of it.

I climbed in the passenger seat to give the lovebirds some space in the backseat.

"What up, boy?" I said, bumping fists with Matt.

"Same shit, different day, man."

I nodded at his nonchalant response as he pulled off. I sat back and stared out the window as we rode through the streets of Atlanta.

Although I wanted to call Skye and apologize for not keeping her in the loop, I couldn't. This trip was important; we had been sent here so that I could meet with our connect Miguel Alvarez. Miguel was the current Mexican drug lord of the notorious cartel Los Jefes. They were ruthless and were known for their involvement in human trafficking, gun trafficking, and racketeering, and for supplying niggas like my pops with the purest white girl known to man. My father had been dealing with those niggas for as far back as I could remember, back when Miguel's father, Ricardo, was boss.

So it was pretty safe to say things should go smoothly, because our track record with them had been nothing short of impeccable. However, fucking with those crazy Mexicans, you didn't really know what to expect, so I had to be on point. After the loss we had taken during the hit on our warehouse, who knew how this meeting would play out? It was their money that had been taken. I wasn't too worried about that, though, because we weren't no crab-ass dudes who came with a boatload of excuses. We came ready to pay back every cent that was lost.

When we got to the hotel, all I wanted to do was shower and hit the bed. It was a little past two in the morning. Usually, I was a night owl, but since the shit with Rick had gone down, I just felt drained. Don't get me wrong. Though it was fucked up, losing homies really came with the territory. This was my reality. But Rick wasn't just a homie; he was as close to an uncle as I had had, since both my parents were only children. Losing him had really taken a toll on me, not to mention that I had to see his wife and kids soon. How the fuck was I supposed to face them?

After the shower, I wasn't in the mood for anything. I climbed in the bed buck-ass naked. A nigga just wanted to relax. I lay there, awake, for a minute, thinking about Skye, wishing she was next to me. Then I succumbed to sleep.

The next morning, I was awakened by the sound of someone banging on the door to my room. I sucked my teeth and climbed out of bed. I had totally forgotten that I slept in my birthday suit, but that shit felt good, though. I walked over to where I had left my duffel, and rummaged through it, looking for something to throw on. I pulled out a pair of Ralph Lauren sweats and threw them on before walking over to the door. I looked through the peephole and saw that it was that nigga Ty.

"Why the fuck you banging on the door like you them boys, bro?" I barked, aggravation seeping into my tone, as I opened the door.

If anyone knew that shit annoyed me, it should have been him. We slapped fives and bumped shoulders before he walked through the door.

"Son, why you not ready? You know the meeting at twelve, right?" he said.

I looked at the Presidential Rolex that I had on my wrist, checking the time. It was already 10:45 a.m.

"Fuck. I told myself to set my alarm and shit last night, but a nigga was beat."

I grabbed my duffel and flopped down on the bed to pick out an outfit. When it came to my clothes, I was an indecisive-ass nigga. All my shit was fly, but it didn't matter. I had to love the fit, or I wouldn't feel right. Too bad I didn't have the time to be picky. I settled for a Balmain shirt, a hoodie, and a pair of Nudie Jeans. I got off the bed and headed into the bathroom, leaving Ty to whatever he was doing on his phone.

Even though I had showered before I went to bed, I was a morning shower type of nigga, so I brushed my teeth and jumped in. That shit felt good, but I knew I was working on borrowed time, so I had to make it quick. When I got out, I dried off and got dressed. When I walked back into the room, Ty was on the balcony, smoking. As bad as I wanted to get high, I made it my business to go into all meetings sober, especially when I was fucking with these crazy-ass Mexicans. I tapped on the balcony door and signaled Ty to come in.

"Yo, did you get a burner from Matt?" I asked.

I prayed that he had remembered, because although I couldn't go into the meeting with a piece, I felt much better knowing my nigga was packing and waiting out front.

"Yeah, he dropped the shit off this morning and left me keys to one of his whips for us to use."

I should have known. My nigga was always on his shit. We left my room, and as we waited for the elevator, I remembered he had Ari out here with him.

"Where you told shorty you was going?" I asked him as we stepped onto the elevator.

"I told her I was going to the gym with you, and I left her some money to go shopping."

I laughed, because that nigga was a clown. "The gym, though, bro?"

He knew it was a dumb-ass lie, so he joined me in the laughter. "It worked, so fuck it."

I nodded my head, because he was right.

Once we got outside, we walked around the block to the parking lot where Matt had parked his car. When I saw the shit he had left for us, I had to shake my head. Out of all cars, that nigga had left us a Prius. Did we look like Prius- driving cats? Ty must have been thinking the same thing, because we looked at each other and burst out laughing.

"A Prius, son? Nigga could have left us the truck," I said as I climbed in the passenger seat.

I couldn't really complain, though, because he had provided us with wheels to handle our business. We had to be thankful for that.

When we pulled up to the little Mexican spot on Piedmont Road, I mentally prepared myself to deal with whatever bullshit they was going to throw at us. I looked over at Ty, and no words needed to be shared. I knew that nigga would never let anything happen to me if he could help it, so I wasn't even worried. I slapped fives with my brother and hopped out of the car.

As I entered the restaurant, I took in the scenery, just to make sure nothing seemed out of the ordinary. I had been here often enough to know what was routine and what wasn't. I spotted the owner's daughter, Lisa. She was bad as fuck. I had never been into dating outside my race, but I made an exception for this half Mexican–half black chick. I wouldn't really call what we had done dating, though. Today she was rocking jeans that hugged her fat ass, which made me stare a little. When she saw me, she smiled and walked over to me.

"*Hola*, stranger." She playfully slapped my arm.

That was her "I miss the dick" gesture. Yeah, I smashed shorty during every trip I took to the A, and as bad as I wanted this trip to be the same as the others, I had a shorty at home now.

"Wassup? Can you tell Miguel I'm here?"

She looked at me, confused. I knew she was expecting me to flirt and shit, but I wanted to see where things could really go with Skye, so I was going to try the monogamous thing.

"Oh, I see. Just business this trip, huh?"

I nodded, and she turned away to let them know I was here. I tried to help it, but I couldn't help it as I watched her ass with every stride she took. I waited a few minutes before Aurelio appeared in the doorway of the back room and signaled to me to come over. I headed in his direction, avoiding eye contact with Lisa. Once I reached the door he was standing at, we shook hands, and then he moved over so I could enter the room. I took a few steps and came to a stop. As usual, six heavily armed Mexicans stood there while Aurelio searched me. Once he saw I was clean, he nodded, giving the guards the okay to let me pass. As I walked farther into the room, I spotted Miguel, who was sitting at a table with two chicks, eating. He must have felt my presence, because he looked up from his food and smiled.

"Young Cam, how are you today?"

I hated when he called me young Cam. I was a grown-ass man, but of course, I had to bite my tongue and suppress the annoyance I felt from being called that dumb shit. He stood up to shake my hand and then signaled for me sit.

"Wassup Miguel? I'm cool. How are you?" I said as we both sat down at the table.

He sighed and shook his head. I already knew where this was going. "I was doing pretty well, my friend. That is, until I got a phone call about your spot being hit and me losing five hundred thousand dollars. You could understand why I would be in a not so great mood, right?"

He stared at me and waited for me to respond. I was just making sure he had said his piece before I said mine, because I knew those other Mexicans wouldn't hesitate to shoot if they felt I had disrespected their boss. I knew that because it was exactly what any nigga on my team would do if my father was disrespected.

"Miguel, I understand your frustrations, but you have nothing to worry about."

His eyebrows went up. That nigga wanted to raise his own damn blood pressure, because nothing I had said should have put him on edge.

"So you telling me that I should not be concerned when it comes to my money?"

If he had just shut the fuck up and let me speak, he would know the answer to that dumb-ass question.

"Yeah, my father didn't ask for this meeting for me to come at you with excuses as to why the money's gone. There was a problem, and I'm here with the solution. You weren't due to get paid for another week, but I'm prepared to pay you back what is owed, with interest, for the hassle *now*!"

I had to emphasize the word *now* so he would understand I wasn't there on some bullshit.

"I see why my father had no issues when dealing with your father for so many years. I appreciate the way you guys do business. How much interest are we talking about here?"

I sat up straight and looked him directly in his eyes. I wanted him to see how serious I was. My eyes dared him to try to play me for some rookie-ass nigga as my next statement fell from my lips.

"Name your price, Miguel."

This was the ultimate test this nigga was engaged in right now. He was getting what he was owed a week early, with extra. I wasn't one to be played for a fool, because I wasn't new to that shit. He sat back and pondered my statement. I could tell he was battling the idea of taking me to the bank or doing the right thing and keeping shit civil. When money was involved, niggas tended to get greedy. I hoped for everyone's sake that Miguel wouldn't go there. He clasped his hands together and leaned forward.

"I like y'all, Cam. The numbers we pull in monthly dealing with your father are astronomical. With that being said, I'll just take what is owed."

Was that man testing me? Why couldn't we just handle shit straight up? What was with the mind games?

"Nah, on behalf of my pops and our organization, we feel it's only right to give you a little bit extra. How's seven hundred fifty thousand dollars?"

I had gone in with the intention of giving those niggas a whole extra five hundred thousand dollars, but since he wanted to play mind games, that had got cut in half.

He smirked. I knew that nigga was fishing, but I wasn't about to bite the bait. "Seven fifty sounds good. I hope you didn't travel with that type of cash."

I didn't like being underestimated. Who the fuck would travel on a plane with $750,000 in dirty money? Not anyone with a fucking brain. That nigga annoyed me, and I was glad that this meeting was almost over. We discussed plans for the money transaction to take place back in New York in the next few days, and then I dipped.

Ty

When I saw Cam coming out of the restaurant, I let out a heavy breath, because you just never knew what would happen when you were dealing with those Mexicans. To say those dudes were crazy would be an understatement. I started up the car as Cam got in, and once he was situated, I pulled off. I glanced over at him and could tell he had some shit on his mind.

"How'd it go, bro?" I said.

He shook his head from side to side and rubbed his temple. "Man, it went cool, but dealing with them cats is a headache. Everything is a fucking mind game or a test."

I could honestly say that this was part of the job description I was glad I didn't have to deal with. I didn't trust the Mexicans at all, but our supply of grade A shit was basically endless, so I couldn't really complain.

"What you trying to get into the rest of the time we out here?" I asked him.

I had a few things on my mind, with fucking the shit out of Ariana at the top of the list.

"Bro, you can just drop me off at the hotel. I brought the books a nigga need to get in some studying. Back to school on Monday, and I haven't picked up a book the entire vacation."

I respected that. I mean, how could I not? My nigga was waist deep is this business but still managed to keep school first. I wished I had the willpower to do the same, but school wasn't my thing. It was a dub after high school.

"A'ight, bro."

The rest of the ride was silent, aside from the hip-hop that blasted through the car stereo system. I wasn't really feeling this music, though, since I was not a big fan of country rap. The rapper 2 Chainz was my hitter, but I had to listen to that nigga's music in moderation because I got tired of that shit after a while. When we pulled up to the hotel, Cam and I gave each other dap and he got out. I wondered if Ariana was still in the room or had gone out, so I stayed in the Prius, pulled out my phone, and called her.

"Hey, baby," she answered on the first ring.

I loved that she always was happy to hear from me.

"What's good, love? You still in the room?" I asked. Then I heard some nigga trying to get her attention, and I got a mad. "Yo!" I barked into the phone.

"Yeah, baby, my bad. This nigga pulled my arm, trying to get my attention, and I had to check his ass. But nah, I'm at Lenox. You meeting up with me, or you still with Cam?"

That nigga had better be glad I wasn't in the vicinity. "Yeah, I'm on my way."

When I pulled into the Lenox Square parking area, I drove around for about fifteen minutes, trying to find parking. I was relieved when I saw a blue Honda pulling out of a spot. I quickly swerved into the spot before anyone else could snatch it. As I walked toward one of the mall entrances, I texted Ari to see where she was. She replied, telling me to meet her at the Louis Vuitton store. I hadn't been to this mall in a minute, so I had to grab one of them brochures with a map on it to find the store.

Ariana

When I saw my man walking into the store, I smiled. I couldn't believe how totally smitten I was with him. He was everything I could want in a dude. He had time for himself, and he managed to have time for me. He was clear about his feelings and where he stood with me. I didn't ask for much, just a loyal nigga with good dick. Ty gave me that, so your girl didn't have any complaints.

He walked over to me as I looked at the pocketbooks in the glass case, and stood directly behind me, kissing my neck. I felt my panties moisten. Why did his touch have that effect on me? I turned to face him, and he playfully bit his lip.

"I missed you too," I said as I turned away to look at the bags again.

I couldn't decide between the Deesse GM and the navy blue Alma GM. After a few minutes of debating, I decided on the Alma. The navy blue would go fine with a pair of jeans on a regular day. After paying for the bag, Ty and I walked hand in hand through the mall, stopping at stores we liked on the way. After a few hours of tearing up the mall, we stopped for food, and then we were ready to retire to the hotel. I was so happy his friend had let him borrow a car, because getting a taxi to take me to the mall had been hell for me. I had to remember this wasn't New York.

As Ty put the shopping bags in the backseat, I got in the car and decided to call Skye. She had to be bored out of her mind. I mean, we had tons of friends, but when it came to kicking it and going out, it was just us two. So I knew that with me out of town, my girl was in her crib, drowning in them textbooks. The phone rang four times, and I was ready to hang up when she finally answered.

"Hey, bestie," she croaked.

Ew. She needed to clear her throat, as she sounded like a sick little boy.

"Yuck, trick. Clear your throat," I said, laughing at her.

She laughed with me. "Shut up. I was knocked out. But thanks for calling me. I need to get up and get some studying done."

See? I knew it. School, sleep, and no play. Her lifelong ritual.

"Oh, I was just calling to see what you were up to. Ty and I are on our way back to the hotel. We went shopping at Lenox."

I was waiting for her to—

"Tell Ty I said hey. And where's Cameron?"

I laughed to myself. She had interrupted my thoughts, but that was what I had been waiting for. I knew Skye better than she knew herself sometimes.

"Ty, she said hey, and she wants to know where Cam is," I said. Then I turned to him and waited for his response.

"Wassup, Skye? He at the hotel. He said he needed to study."

I didn't need to repeat that, because I had held the phone near Ty's mouth so she could hear his answer. I put the phone back to my ear as she started to talk.

"Oh, okay. Well, thank you for checking on me doll. Enjoy your time there, and call me when you touch home."

We said our goodbyes and ended the call.

When we got back to our hotel room, my intention was to fuck my nigga's brains out till we went to bed, but there were some things I needed to discuss with him first. While

he was on the balcony, I jumped in the shower, using that
time to get my thoughts together. My approach needed to
be correct if I had any chance of getting the answers that I
wanted. I washed and thought hard. When I stepped out
of the shower, I put on my robe and tied it as I walked
into the room. He was looking extremely good, sitting on
the edge of the bed in nothing but boxer briefs and socks.
I sat next to him and rubbed his shoulders. I wanted him
relaxed for when my questions started pouring out. He
looked up at me and smiled.

"Why you didn't get me so I could shower with you?"

Shit. I hadn't even thought about that.

"I didn't want to bother you, baby. Plus, you will have
plenty more opportunities to shower with me."

He nodded his head in agreement and said, "True."

All right, Ariana. This is your chance. I had to be my
own cheerleader.

"Baby, wassup with Cam?" I said.

The look he gave me almost made me regret that I had
asked. I should have figured out a better way to start the
conversation, but I wasn't about to turn back now. I had
told my girl I would get to the bottom of this shit for her,
and that was what I planned to do.

"What you mean?" he asked me.

I might as well just put it all out there. This beating
around the bush shit wasn't my speed at all. "Look, baby,
I know that it's not really any of our business what goes
on between them, but Skye is my best friend. Nah, that's
my sister, and her best interest is always first to me. She
feels like Cam's not really feeling her or he's keeping
something from her."

I paused to give him a chance to speak, but he said
nothing. I could see that he was listening but had decided
to stay mute. That was fine. I wasn't going to stop.

"I also just feel like if he isn't feeling her. He needs to just be honest with her, instead of stringing her along. We grown, right? She's tired of him dipping on her without any explanation. Shit, I would be tired of it too. As females, we don't expect y'all to give us a complete rundown of your daily agenda, but be considerate. For example, he out here in Atlanta, you invited me, but he couldn't invite Skye? Put not inviting her aside. He didn't even tell her he was going out of town, and that's beyond fucked up. Skye isn't an ugly, weak broad, so she don't need to put all her chips on a nigga who don't want her."

Finally he spoke up. And just in time, as I was honestly running out of shit to say.

"It's not even like that."

Wow. Was he serious? After everything I had said, he replied with that bullshit? Nah, that wasn't going to cut it.

"So what *is* it like?"

He sighed, then gave me all the answers I wanted, plus more. He revealed to me that he and Cam were both major players in an illegal operation run by Cam's dad. He spared me the details, which I was thankful for, because I didn't have time to be an accessory to anyone's bull. I was shocked, though. Cam had my girl over there thinking that he was some law-abiding citizen who was going to law school and shit, when the whole time he was living this other life. It explained the disappearing acts, but it didn't explain the dishonesty. Skye could forgive a lot, but lying wasn't one of the things on that list.

I, on the other hand, was much more understanding. Living that life wasn't really something you just flat out told people. However, if you had the intention to deal with someone on a serious level, some info needed to be shared. I had never asked Ty what he did for a living, because quite honestly, it didn't matter to me. I mean, I saw that he was able to provide for himself, so I knew he wasn't a broke nigga. Plus, he wouldn't be the first hustler I had dated, and if things didn't work out, he wouldn't be the last.

When he was done telling me everything, I promised I wouldn't tell Skye, but I was giving Cameron only till Tuesday to come clean with Skye. Keeping secrets wasn't something I felt comfortable with when it came to Skye, because we shared everything, but this was something that was truly Cam's place to share. After that conversation, a girl was beat. I had plans on putting Ty to bed, but I was no longer in the mood, which was why when he headed into the bathroom, I got comfortable and dozed off.

Cameron

Damn. I couldn't fall asleep for shit. I'd been lying there, tossing and turning, for, like, an hour. Skye crossed my mind when my phone started vibrating, and I low key hoped it was her. It wasn't, though. Just a text from Ty.

Yo, bro, it's about time you have that conversation with ole girl if you serious about her. Ari pressed me about how Skye feels you dissing her and shit. If shorty worth you being with her, she gonna ride. If she not, she'll dip, and that would be doing you a favor. So just let her know, fam. I'm going to bed. Nigga, don't oversleep and make us miss the flight.

As much as I didn't want to admit it, Ty was right. I wasn't saying I wanted to marry shorty or nothing like that, but I did want to be with her. If she wanted to be with me, she was going to understand what I did, and if she didn't understand, it was whatever. Chicks came and went, so that was something I would never stress about. It didn't change the fact that I wanted her to be the one for me, though. I knew what I had to do. I scrolled through the phone book on my phone till I found her name. I contemplated calling her but opted out and decided to just text her.

Wassup, beautiful? You probably asleep and shit, so I hope this don't wake you up. But I just wanted to apologize about how I been handling shit lately. I wanna see you tomorrow and talk to you. If you with that, come pick me up from JFK. Our flight gets in at 2:00 p.m. If you not there, I'll know what it is. Good night, Ma. Sleep tight.

Something told me she would be there tomorrow. The feeling that came over me made me smile. I was still trying to figure out what it was about shorty that had me ready to break all the rules and let her in. That was the last thing I thought about before I fell asleep.

Skye

I hated the fact that I couldn't sleep when sunshine was streaming into my bedroom. For some reason, I kept forgetting to close my blinds before I went to bed. I looked at the time; it was only nine o'clock in the morning. It was Sunday, and I had absolutely nothing to do.

"Thank you, Mr. Sun!" I said out loud to no one.

I let out a huge sigh before grabbing my phone. My morning ritual was to check missed calls and text messages as soon as I got up. Although I was pissed, I still smiled as I read the text message from Cameron. He wanted me to pick him up from the airport at 2:00 p.m. so we could talk. I didn't know if it was my curiosity or me just genuinely wanting to see him that had me excited. Maybe a bit of both. Regardless of the reason, I decided that I was going to pick him up for sure. I sat my phone down and headed to the bathroom to brush my teeth and shower. While I was in the shower, I sang Olivia's "Walk Away." I knew I had a voice that only a mother would cheer on, which was why I was singing in the shower when no one else was around. I laughed out loud, thinking about what anyone would say if they heard me singing.

After my shower, I dried off and headed, naked, to the kitchen to have some food. I was comfortable in my skin. Plus, I was home alone, so who did I need to cover up for? I searched through the refrigerator for something that was already cooked, because I didn't feel like making anything. I spotted a big salad that I had from yesterday, and did my happy dance, which was similar to Michael Jackson's moonwalk. I grabbed the salad and a bottle of water before sitting down at the island and getting my grub on.

Man, that salad hit every spot possible. I must have been really hungry, because I ate every bit of that salad. My tummy was satisfied, and it was time to "get my life," as Tamar Braxton liked to say. I headed back to my bedroom and fixed the bed before going into my walk-in closet. I searched through the racks that held my jeans and settled for a pair of black Burberry jeans.

Simple enough, I thought to myself.

I shifted a handful of hangers to the other side, and the first top I laid eyes on was a black Burberry sweater.

"Today is going to be a good day," I said out loud.

It was rare that I was able to decide on an outfit that fast. Maybe because I wasn't trying to be extremely fancy today, since I was only going to pick up ole boy from the airport. I applied lotion to my skin before putting on my panties and bra, and then I got dressed. I needed something to do to waste time since their flight wouldn't be getting in until 2:00 p.m. I glanced at my textbooks and sighed. Might as well get some studying done since I had free time.

I arrived at the airport at 1:40 p.m. I had expected there to be way more traffic than there was. It was cool, however. I sent Cameron a text, letting him know where I was parked, and then I sat back and listened to music. A little bit after two, I saw Ariana, Cameron, and Ty headed toward my car. I had to admit, I got a little bit happy seeing him. I'd missed him, even though I didn't want to admit it. When they got close to the car, I hit the button on my door that unlocked the other doors so they could hop in. As soon as Cameron was seated up front, he leaned over and kissed me. I wasn't surprised, but what did surprise me was the fact that I didn't pull away. I wanted to be mad at him, but my mind wouldn't let me.

"Hey, Ari, Ty. Where am I taking you, Ty?" I turned around in the seat and waited for him to answer.

The look he gave me said I should already know the answer.

I shook my head. "Never mind. Arianna's house, it is."

We all laughed as I pulled off.

After we dropped off Ariana and Ty, Cameron and I grabbed some food from Amy Ruth's uptown and then headed to my place. I was really anxious to know what he wanted to talk about. It had better be good, because at that point, I was ready to declare us just friends so that I would not have to deal with Cameron at all. At least that was what I was trying to make myself believe.

When we got in the house, we wasted no time. We headed straight to the kitchen, washed our hands, sat at the table, and started on our food. I guessed that salad I'd enjoyed earlier wasn't the huge meal I had thought it was, because in my head I was singing, "R.I.P. I'm about to kill this food," in my best Young Jeezy voice. That made me chuckle to myself.

"What you smiling about?" Cameron asked me.

Oops. He had seen me.

"Nothing. But wassup?" I said as I scooped up a spoonful of rice.

"I don't really want to ruin the moment right now."

He didn't even bother looking up at me while he spoke. That was bullshit. *What is he hiding? A chick? A baby? Was he gay? All of the above? What the fuck?* Now my mind was racing a mile a minute, and I was trying to catch up with it so I could formulate what I needed to say next.

"Cameron!" I didn't shout, but I said his name as sternly as I possibly could, because he needed to hear and understand the seriousness in my tone. I guessed he heard it, because he finally had the balls to look me in my face.

"Say whatever it is that you need to say," I said calmly.

He sighed, dropped his shoulders a little bit.

Damn, I thought. *What could be so bad?* He was acting like he was about to tell me he had killed my puppy or some shit.

"A'ight. Skye, look, this is not easy for me. I never felt like I wanted to have the type of relationship with a female where I would need to tell her the shit I'm about to tell you." He paused.

I hoped he wasn't waiting for me to respond, because I had nothing to say until he got whatever it was he was about to say off his chest.

He went on. "I'm really feeling you. I mean, I'm sure you know that, but at the same time, I haven't really been doing my best to show you that. I want to, though."

That nigga could really beat around the bush. To say I was uninterested in the pre-pep talk would be being nice. *Like get to the point already.*

He continued. "I haven't been completely honest with you, but I haven't been dishonest, either. I would just say that I been omitting information."

I could never have prepared myself for what he said to me next.

I thought, *Like, really, dude? A drug dealer or supplier, or whatever your position is in the whole thing? That is not something you keep from your girl.*

I was not one to judge, but I couldn't help thinking about how this nigga had been preaching that "I'm a real nigga" and "I'm a different breed" shit. *Nah, bro, you the same.* What did I even say to that shit? Part of me wanted to kick the nigga out, but part of me wanted to be there, to be with him. I was built to handle this. I knew that for sure. My only worry was whether it would all be worth it. And I naturally wanted to know if there was a possibility that a nigga would kidnap me or worse just because of my association with him.

"Can you say something, anything, even if you just wanna yell?" he said in a small voice.

Hearing his voice turned my attention away from the rant that was taking place in the back of my mind.

"Cameron, what do you want me to say?"

If he wanted to hear me say it was okay, I wouldn't hold my breath if I were him, because this shit wasn't okay in the least bit.

"Anything, Skye."

I looked him in the eyes, which I should not have done. Seeing how sincere he could be when talking to me always made me weak and made me forget why I was even mad. Unfortunately for him, it wouldn't be that easy this time.

"I mean, it is what it is," I said. "How do you manage? I mean, you really are living a double life. To think that I thought this shit happened only in movies. Let me be clear, though. I'm not mad because of the things you're involved in, Cameron. I'm mad because you didn't keep it real with me. I mean, I understand that some things you're not at a liberty to discuss with me, but to just keep me totally in the dark? That wasn't fair. It's been almost four months that we been kicking it, Cameron, and I was always honest and up front with you. Why couldn't you be the same way with me?"

That was a ridiculous question, because I didn't want to hear his excuses. I was happy this guy was smart, because he didn't even fix his lips to give me any.

"I'm ready now," he answered. "I'm willing to tell you whatever you want to know. I want us to work, Skye. I really want to see where this could go."

I couldn't deny the fact that I wanted the same thing. I would only be lying to myself if I told myself this relationship didn't matter to me, so I listened some more.

Matt

I was glad those niggas were out of my city. I almost hadn't been able to control the urge to kill them the minute I picked them up from the airport. I would have fucked the bitch first; she was cute. Ultimately, I would have had to kill her ass too, though. I couldn't stand that nigga Cam. I didn't give a fuck if he was my brother or not, and it ain't like he knew he was. Our bitch-ass father, Hassan, had kept me a secret because he already had his little man. Ty, on the other hand, would have been collateral damage. He would have got it just because he was so close to Cam. It was fucked up, because he was actually a cool dude. *Oh, well, though. It's just the way the cookie crumbles*, I told myself.

I sat back, smoking my blunt and listening to music. I was in my zone. Shit was coming together nicely. It was fucked up that shit had to go this way, but desperate times called for desperate measures. I remembered the shit like it was yesterday, man. I was in, like, seventh grade or some shit, and my moms had lost her job. Shit was rough. It had always been me and her. I'd never met my dad, and as far as I was concerned, the nigga was dead. So when my mother told me we were moving to New York so that my dad could help us out and shit, I was shocked. I was mad at first too, because he hadn't been there all them years, but at the same time it felt good, like I was finally going to get the piece of me that was missing. I was a naive-ass little nigga.

When we got to New York, we learned that one of my grandmother's friends had got us a room in a shelter. A fucking shelter! At that time I didn't feel any way about it, because, like I said, we was in a fucked-up place. So I was thankful just to have a roof over my head. All that changed on the day I met my father. He rolled up to the park where he was meeting me and my mother in a decked-out-ass Benz. The nigga had security and shit, so I knew he had to be my dad. I was young, but I had grown up in the Bluff, one of the most dangerous places in the A. To say my hood had a high crime rate would be putting it lightly. I was on game from the time I was a youngin', so yeah, his swagger and demeanor told me what he was about before he even opened his mouth. But I ignored that, since I was thrilled to meet my dad.

Here I was, a little nigga, getting a little hype that my pops was somebody, and not just some weak-ass dude, until he said the words that changed my life forever.

"What the fuck you call me for? Why did you even come back to New York?" he snarled at my moms.

Just reliving the moment made me cringe. I remembered them arguing back and forth for a good thirty minutes, and not once during that time did he acknowledge me. Finally, he tossed my mother a hundred-dollar bill and bounced.

That was the last time I saw or even spoke to him for a while. My moms finally got this waitressing job, and we were able to afford a decent place. It wasn't in the best area, and she wanted me to have a fighting chance, so she sent me to middle school across town. That was where I met Cam and Ty. I was a bum nigga: couldn't make friends for shit, and chicks didn't wanna be bothered with me. The ones who did speak to me did so only because they felt bad for me. One day, Cam and Ty rolled up on me in the locker room before gym and gave me two duffel bags full with brand-new gear. Fly shit too. From that moment on, we hung together. I had no idea that Cam was my brother, although I looked at him as such because of the way he and Ty held me down.

It wasn't until we graduated from middle school that I found out who Cam was. After he crossed the stage to receive his diploma, I watched him run to his family. And there was my bitch-ass sperm donor. I didn't say anything to anybody at the graduation ceremony, but when I got home that night, I told my mother. That was when she finally told me the whole story about her and my dad. She had been one of his workers and had taken trips up and down 95, transporting drugs and money. One night they'd been drunk and they'd fucked, and nine months later, I'd made my entrance. She knew that he had a wife and that his wife had given birth to a son just a few months prior, so my moms didn't want to stir up any beef. My mother wasn't the confrontational type. She reached out to my pops, who gave her fifty thousand dollars and told her to bounce. She felt it wouldn't be smart to go against his wishes, so she left and never looked back.

The summer before high school, I heard rumors around how Ty and Cam were doing little jobs for my and Cam's pops and shit, so I felt like my pops should let me get down. I mean, I was entitled to everything Cam was entitled to. The only difference was I didn't want shit for free. I didn't even want to be acknowledged as his son. I just wanted a little job to keep myself fly and to entertain my lady friends. I had to be patient, though, because I couldn't just run up to him at any given time. Luckily for me, Cam and I ended up playing in the same summer league, and I caught up with our pops after one of the games. That nigga gave me one hundred dollars and told me to go cop a pair of the new Jordans.

At that moment, the resentment I had for him exploded. I didn't know how to control my anger, so I started acting out. I linked up with some niggas I had met in Cypress, and started getting into all types of shit. Before long my grandmother got sick and I had to move back to Atlanta. I kept in touch with my Cypress niggas, though, and that was how I found out they were beefing with Cam and his team. My nigga Man and them had the upper hand, however, because they had an inside man. Shit sounded like an easy come up for me. All my ill feelings resurfaced, and of course, I agreed to get down. You heard people preach about that "a woman scorned" shit, but what about little boys who were neglected and rejected by their own fathers? Hell had no fury like a boy rejected.

I was out for blood.

Skye

Ever since the heart-to-heart Cameron and I had had the other night, things had been great. I really didn't have any complaints. Other than the few nights after Rick's funeral, he had made more time for me, and he had made it his business to have breakfast and dinner with me every single day. He had done a complete 360 in terms of being honest and not disappearing. The lines of communication for us were open and clear. When he was in the street, he even checked in, on some "Baby, just letting you know I'm safe"–type shit. As a result, we had been getting closer and closer by the minute. Oh, and let's not forget about the sex. It was fabulous.

Most people would probably say we were moving extremely fast, but it was a good thing we weren't most people. We were grown and knew what we wanted. I didn't see a problem with that.

I sat up in the bed and looked over at Cameron. He was sleeping peacefully, but he wouldn't be for long. I made a mental note to thank him for being a back sleeper. It made what I was planning much easier to execute. I pulled the covers back, slid off my Victoria's Secret thong, and straddled him. He didn't budge. . . . Damn, he could sleep through anything. I didn't feel defeated yet. I leaned over and planted soft kisses on his chest, rubbing his abs in the process. I worked my way up and kissed his lips before softly nibbling on them. I felt him palm my ass, and he opened his eyes.

In between kisses he managed to get out, "Why . . . you . . . stealing . . . kisses?"

I didn't consider it stealing; those lips were already mine. Before I could respond, he turned over and placed me on my back. I loved the aggressiveness he expressed when we had sex. Shit turned me all the way on. He nibbled on my left nipple while he played with the other.

"Mmm, baby," I moaned.

The throbbing I felt between my legs was becoming unbearable, and it was like my body was yearning for him. He knew that, but he wasn't about to give me what I wanted so easily. He rarely ever did. He put one of my legs over his shoulder as his kissed down the center of my stomach to my inner thigh. My body jerked when I felt him slip his tongue into my leaking opening. Shit felt too good. The way he worked his tongue felt like he was spelling his name on my shit. He was marking his territory, I guessed, but a chick wasn't complaining. He penetrated me with two fingers as he nibbled and sucked on my clit simultaneously. I couldn't take it. At that point I was trying to scoot away from his mouth, but he wasn't having it. He pulled down on my thighs to hold me in place.

"Stop . . . trying . . . to . . . get . . . away," he said in between sucks.

I felt pressure start to build within me and knew a climax was coming. I grabbed his head and held it as my legs began to shake.

"Fuckkk! I'm comin', baby." I let out a long, hard breath as I released all on his tongue.

Like the good nigga he was, he cleaned up his mess, licked and slurped every drop of my juices. That nigga had a sexy-ass smirk on his face when he stood up and came out his briefs before lying back on the bed.

"Come ride Daddy."

I didn't need to be told twice. I straddled him and slowly slid down on his piece. I had to give my pussy the chance to adjust to that nigga's size. It didn't take long, though, before I was slamming up and down against his thighs.

"Damn, baby," Cameron called out.

I was on a cloud, and his words went in one ear and out the other. He grabbed my waist and bounced me faster. Before I knew it, I was comin' again.

"Yesss, Cameron. Fuck this pussy, baby."

Once he let go of my waist, I turned around and rode him in reverse cowgirl. He slapped and grabbed my ass as I went to work. Before I knew it, he had pushed me onto my knees, into the doggy-style position, and was sliding in from the back. He pumped in and out, slowing down only to slap my ass. I threw my ass back to match each of his thrusts.

"Whose pussy is this?" he called out.

I gripped the sheets and moaned, "Yours, baby. This . . . pussy . . . belongs . . . to . . . you."

He grabbed my ponytail, not too rough, but rough enough to turn me on even more. I arched my back a little more, and he continued to hit my spot over and over. That nigga's pipe game took me to places I had never been before. He had me on clouds I didn't know I could reach. I felt another orgasm building up.

"Ohhh . . . cum with me, baby," I called.

On cue, our bodies released at the same damn time. That had to be the best feeling in the world. I fell face-first onto the bed, and Cameron fell back. We lay in silence for a few minutes, waiting to catch our second wind.

"I'm going to shower, baby. You coming?" I said as I got up and stood on the side of the bed.

"Yeah, beautiful. Give me a minute, and I'll be there."

I spun around on my heels and headed to the shower. By the time Cameron came into the bathroom, I was already getting out of the shower. I hoped he didn't think I was going to stay in there till I turned into a prune because he took forever. I kissed him as I walked past him and headed into the bedroom.

After slipping into some comfortable clothes, I changed the sheets on the bed, then sat down and rolled him a blunt. He had taught me how to roll a few days ago. I wasn't a smoker, but I didn't mind having my man's blunts ready for him when he wanted one. I left the blunt on the night table, next to his cell phone, so he would be sure to see it, and then I headed to the kitchen to make breakfast.

As I was standing over the stove, making Cameron an omelet, I heard him scream out, "When I catch you, I'ma fucking kill you, your mother, and your seed, you bitch-ass nigga."

I turned off the burner on the stove and rushed into the bedroom, where I found him cursing out loud at no one in particular and getting dressed.

"Baby, what happened?" I walked up to him and grabbed his arm.

He said nothing. Just continued to get dressed. He was in the process of slipping on his construction Timberlands when I stepped in front of him.

"Cameron, please don't start this. We been doing so well and being open with each other. Let's keep that up."

He didn't seem fazed by my words as he grabbed his Moncler coat off the chaise that sat in front of my window. Then he stormed out of the bedroom and headed to the front door. I stayed on his heels. Before he walked out the door, I gave it one last try.

"Cameron, stop please!"

He turned around, and I saw a look on his face that I had never seen before. I saw fear. He pulled me close and hugged me before passionately kissing me.

"I will call you and fill you in the first chance I get, Skye. I just can't right now. I'm sorry. I love you."

And then he was gone. My heart was racing. He had just told me he loved me for the first time, but the way things seemed in that moment, I worried it would be the last time. I became frantic and paced my living room, until I decided to call the only person other than my parents and Cameron who could provide some comfort.

"Ariana!" I screamed into the phone as soon as she answered.

Matt

When I got the call that this nigga had been caught slipping, I almost hit some black flips on my Olympics shit. The day I'd been waiting for was there. For the first time ever, I felt like things were going to work in my favor. I was on the first thing smoking back to the Big Apple. I wasn't missing that moment for nothing.

Man was busy at the spot, so he sent his uncle Max to pick me up from the airport. That was cool with me, as long as I didn't have to catch a taxi. I know them shits were convenient, but trying to catch one as a black male was hard as shit.

When we pulled up to the location, I became anxious. This was my moment. I had always been the underdog, but not on this day. Niggas was about to learn that you couldn't just shit on people and expect to have no repercussions. It was time for that nigga to pay up. I hopped out of the whip and followed behind Max as he walked toward a house that looked to be abandoned. I felt a little uneasy because I didn't have a burner on me. I mean, I was cool with those niggas and all, but still. Shit, look at Max. That nigga was one of my father's top niggas, and he was partaking in taking his life. There was no loyalty in this business, and I was surprised my pops had lasted as long as he did.

When we got inside the house, I had to cover my nose with my coat, because the shit reeked of piss and all types of other shit. I was glad when Max opened a door that led to the basement. As we descended the stairs, the smell began to fade, and I moved my coat from my nose. When we reached the bottom of the stairs, the sight I laid eyes on was beautiful. Shit made me feel like a little kid in a candy store. I mean, any other nigga probably would have shit on himself upon seeing this shit. They had that nigga tied to a chair, butt-ass naked. He looked pretty bruised up, and blood was leaking from everywhere on the nigga's body.

"Y'all went to work on this bitch," I said before hawk spitting on him.

"I was itching to kill the nigga, because they bodied my little brother! But I agreed to let you do the honors. My word is my bond. So I just whupped his ass every time I got the urge to kill him," Man said as he threw water on him in an effort to wake him up.

"Rise and shine, Pops," I said as I let out a demonic laugh.

All the niggas in the room was looking at me like I was crazy, but at this point, I didn't give a fuck. Those niggas didn't know my struggle, so I didn't expect them to understand.

"You not my son, you bitch-ass nigga. Your mother was a ho! Maybe I would have claimed you if she had got the DNA test, like I asked. But her ho ass knew you wasn't my kid. So fuck you. Fuck all y'all niggas. Cam gonna—"

Not only had this nigga disrespected my moms, but he had also had the nerve to mention his bitch-ass son who wasn't around to save his poor daddy's life. I snatched the 9 mm that was in Max's hands and put a bullet right straight through his head, instantly ending his life. I watched his brain matter splatter, but that shit didn't faze me. In that moment I felt good, and I was ready to dead that nigga Cam too, but not before I found out who his connect was. I soon would be the nigga who was calling the shots.

"Damn, son! Why you had to kill him that fast?" I heard Man say, snapping me out of the celebration I was having in my head.

"Fuck that, nigga. He thought I was about to listen to him talk shit. I didn't come here for that," I answered.

As I was ranting, I looked over in the corner and saw duffel bags against the wall. I walked over and unzipped one of the bags. Inside it, I found neatly stacked bills.

"Where this come from?" I said.

Max walked over to me and picked up one of the duffel bags. "We were supposed to be heading to meet their connect to pay him some money and get some more work."

"You know who their connect is?"

I watched Max shake his head no. "This would have been the first time he took me with him. Usually, he took Rick."

Damn. I was a little disappointed, but it was all good. I didn't mind putting in a little more work to get the results I wanted.

"This is seven hundred fifty thousand dollars, and there's five hundred thousand in each of those. Once we get to a safe spot, we can split the shit evenly," Max said.

I had never been around so much money in my life. I had the urge to kill all those niggas and keep the bread for myself. I was smarter than that, though. I needed these niggas, for now at least.

Man walked over to us with a lighter in his hand. "Let's burn this shit down."

I had a better idea. I walked over to my dad's dead body and got his phone out of his pocket. I scrolled through his phone book until I found the person I was looking for. I hit CALL and listened as the phone rang. When he answered, I pointed to Man.

"Wassup, Pops?" I said.

Man smirked and got closer to the phone.

"Not your daddy, fuck boy," Cam said. Then the line went quiet.

"Cat got your tongue, bitch?"

Cam finally spoke up. "When I catch you, I'ma fucking kill you, your mother, and your seed, you bitch-ass nigga."

He sounded tough, but I knew he was shitting bricks.

"Oh yeah? Meet me on the corner of Georgia and Linden. Blue house."

Once he hung up, we burst out laughing. We was gonna let this nigga find his daddy with his brains blown out. He would be next, that was for sure.

Cameron

When we pulled up to that house, I didn't know what to expect, but I was taking whatever risk was necessary. I didn't give a fuck. That was my pops's life we were talking about. I would die in a heartbeat for that man. It was just me and Ty, because I hadn't had time to reach out to anyone else. I could have made time, but that was the last thing I was worried about. We hopped out of Ty's car and approached the run-down blue house that sat on the corner. We looked up and down the street before pulling out our guns and entering the house. The first level was quiet and empty. We trailed along the wall as we cautiously went up the stairs. We searched each room on the second level, but there was nothing and no one.

"Fuck!" I yelled out in frustration.

"Calm down, bro. We gotta be missing something."

He was right, but what was it? Then it hit me. We headed down the stairs and opened every door on the first level until we found the door to the basement stairs. I took a deep breath and looked over at Ty. He gave me a reassuring look, letting me know silently that regardless of what was to come, he had my back. I knew that. I hesitated, dreading finding out what was down there, waiting for us.

"I'm right here, bro. I'm with you every step of the way. Go ahead," Ty said.

I started down the steps, with Ty behind me. When I reached bottom of the steps and scanned the basement,

I felt like my life had been sucked out of my body. I fell to my knees and looked on in disbelief. Ty was speaking, but I couldn't hear shit that was coming out of his mouth. I was trying to process the fact that my pops was gone. Brooklyn was about to feel like Iraq, with the heat I was about to bring to the streets.

I felt like screaming. I was never one to cry, but in that moment, I could have cried a river. I had to hold it together, though. I refused to look weak in front of anyone, even if it was just Ty. I saw Ty kneel down beside me, and I felt his arm go across my shoulder.

"Cam, I swear to you, son, we will get everyone responsible for this shit. I'ma go as far as to include anyone who shares the same last name as Man. You got my word, bro!"

I appreciated how genuine Ty sounded. I was very aware that niggas really couldn't be trusted in this game, but I trusted him wholeheartedly. I didn't doubt that he would follow me to the end of the world to get these bitches back. I just hoped he was ready.

"I appreciate it, bro."

What the fuck was I going to do about my father's body? I didn't want to leave him there like this, but I couldn't call the cleanup crew.

Think, Cameron. Think! I told myself.

I had to yell at myself to remind myself that I had to keep it together. I still had an organization to run. My time to grieve would come, it just wasn't right now. I stood up and paced back and forth as I gathered my thoughts.

"A'ight, do me a favor, Ty. Go pick up Skye and take her to my mother's house. I promised her I wasn't going to keep her out of the loop anymore, and I'm trying to stick with that. Don't tell my mother and Vic anything, except that I will be on my way."

Ty looked at me like he was confused. I wasn't in the mood for this nigga to get dumbfounded.

"Bro, are you fucking crazy? These niggas just declared war. We don't know who we can trust anymore, and you think I'm about to leave you?"

He was right. What the fuck was I thinking?

"Cam, let's go. From the car, we can call the cops and say we heard shots, and we can let them find him. I know you don't want to leave him like this—and believe me, neither do I—but we don't have a choice. If you don't want a funeral and all that shit, we can bring in the cleanup crew. But we're not doing that to your moms. Let the boys get him to the morgue and shit, and we'll go from there."

Everything he was saying made sense, but I couldn't come to terms with leaving my dad like that. But I knew that I had to. I walked over to his body and kneeled down.

"I got you, Pop. I promise, man. I love you."

I felt a tear drop, and I knew I had to get out of there before I had a complete breakdown. Before turning to go up the stairs, I grabbed my father's cell phone, which was lying on the floor. Then I went back upstairs, with Ty following behind me. We left the house, and once we got in the car, I instructed Ty to pick up Skye and take me to my mother's house. Before he pulled off, I read the house number so that I could give it to the police.

I was scrolling through my pops's phone book when I came across the person who could help me: Detective Harris. I didn't really fuck with cops, but my pops had a few of them on the payroll. Harris reminded me of myself, which was why I didn't mind dealing with him. He was a street nigga who became a cop just to stay ahead of shit. Smart man, but at the same time, the dumbest nigga in the world. What street nigga was willing to put himself around a bunch of pigs all day? It worked for him and our operation, so I couldn't complain about that. I hit CALL on my pops's phone, and when Harris finally answered, I told him everything, starting with the phone call I'd received. Of course I left out the fact that I knew who had called me. I mean, even though Harris was a dirty cop, he was still a cop, and that shit would still be considered snitching. I just needed him to handle my father's body. He said that he would contact me when they needed someone to come down and claim the body.

I really couldn't believe that shit had happened. I must have been in denial all these years, thinking niggas on my team were loyal. Never would I have expected niggas to cross my father like that. It was cool, though. I had a surprise for those niggas. I was putting heat to every nigga who I thought could be a suspect. If they had ever looked at my pops wrong, disagreed with him, or mumbled under their breath in his presence, that was their ass! I didn't give a fuck at this point. Niggas was going to pay.

Skye

When I got the phone call from Ty, telling me to come downstairs, I flew out the door. I was happy that I was already dressed; however, I wished I would have taken the time to mentally prepare myself for what was to come. As I approached the car, I saw Cameron sitting in the front passenger seat. He didn't even acknowledge me, but that was not what stood out to me. As I looked into his eyes, which were once full of life, I saw emptiness. What the hell had happened? I climbed in the backseat of the Jeep truck and sat quietly. An eeriness flowed through the car, sending chills up my spine. Something was terribly wrong. There was no music playing, no conversation, no eye contact, nothing! I was left with no choice but to remain quiet as we headed to wherever it was that we were going.

When we pulled up to the house, I remembered it from Thanksgiving. We were at Cameron's parents' house. I instantly got nervous; I hoped everything was okay with his parents and his sister. Those were the most important people in the world to him, and I didn't even want to imagine how he would handle anything happening to any of them. We had been parked in the driveway for a good ten minutes before Cameron decided to climb out of the car. He opened my door and reached for my hand. I slowly placed my hand in his as I got out of the Jeep. With our hands clasped, I felt bound to him. It was a very satisfying feeling, but at the same time, it was extremely scary. I had never felt connected to anyone other than my parents and Ariana. This was on a different level, though, as he was hurting and I could feel his pain.

As he moved toward the front of the house, he dragged his feet, as if he carried the weight of the world on his shoulders. Something told me things were about to take a drastic turn. I didn't know if it was going to be for better or worse, but I knew that I was going to have to ride it out. Was I ready? was the question I asked myself repeatedly.

When we finally walked into the home, we were greeted by Cam's mother. Mariah was such a sweet lady. I had spent time with her only on Thanksgiving, but we frequently texted each other, and sometimes we even talked on the phone. She had a heart of gold, and you could tell she went above and beyond for her family. She reminded me of my mother in that sense. I knew that if I could be at least half the mother to my own future kids that these two women were to their children, I would be all right.

Her warm welcoming smile turned into a worrisome frown when she saw the look on Cameron's face. She walked right up to her only son and hugged him while saying, "Hello, Skye and Tyquan. Baby boy, what's wrong with you?"

Cameron said nothing. Instead, he pulled out of her embrace and headed toward the staircase. I needed to know what was going on, so I followed him as he went up the stairs and into a room, which I figured was his old bedroom. It was extremely tidy to be a boy's bedroom, but I guessed that was because he didn't live here anymore. I glanced around the room before closing the door and sitting next to Cameron on the edge of the bed. There was so much I wanted to say, but I was afraid that saying the wrong thing would send him over the edge. *Fuck it*, I thought. I couldn't take sitting there in silence for another minute. I turned my body at an angle so I could attempt to look him in the eyes, but he wouldn't acknowledge me. I still needed to find out what had happened.

"Cameron, baby, what happened? You're scaring me."

I prayed that he would answer me. It took him a minute, but finally, he spoke slowly.

"They killed my pops, baby."

Nothing could have prepared me for that moment. I literally felt my heart break into pieces. I hadn't known his dad for a long time, but time didn't matter. All that mattered to me was my man had lost his father, an amazing woman had lost her husband, and a young girl had to go the rest of her life without her father.

What do I say? What do I do?

No amount of words would be able to ease the pain he felt, so I didn't even try to talk to him. I knelt in front of him and pulled him close. The minute we embraced, he broke down. I knew he was fighting back tears, and I felt good knowing that he trusted me enough to allow me to see him in such a vulnerable state. I rubbed his back as he sobbed. I knew he was crying not only for his father but also for all the friends he had lost and had been unable to mourn.

When his crying stopped, I planted soft kisses on both of his cheeks, then on his lips. I knew he needed me, even if he didn't tell me.

"I love you, Cameron."

He looked at me and smiled. It wasn't the big smile that I was used to, but it was still sexy.

"I love you too, Skye. Look, I need you to understand that shit is going to be crazy from now on. My pops is gone, so not only do I have to handle the niggas who are responsible for this, but I have to run this organization. Let's not forget there's a fucking snake running loose that needs to be beheaded as well. I love you, and I want to be with you, but I'm not asking you to go through this with me."

Was he kidding? It was obvious that this was where I wanted to be. I could have walked away a long time ago. It was time for him to realize that I was still here and that I didn't have plans to go anywhere.

"You don't have to ask me, Cameron. I'm where I want to be. What type of woman would I be if I left you when you needed me most?"

Before he had the chance to speak, his phone started ringing. He looked at it, and sadness fell over him once again, but that didn't stop him from answering.

Cameron

Although I was expecting Harris's phone call, it didn't make the shit any easier. Ty and I were gonna head down there and verify the identity of my pops's body. But first, I had to tell my moms and Vic. That was going to be the worst part of dealing with his death. I had to make sure my sister and mother were straight, and I knew they were gonna take it hard. I found a little comfort in knowing that I had a shorty who was going to stick with me through this shit. I just hoped that when shit really did go down, she would stand by her decision to ride.

"Go downstairs and take my mother into the living room. I'ma go get Vic from her room, and I'll be down there," I said to Skye before I kissed her forehead. Then I headed out of the room.

I dreaded every step I took toward my sister's room. She and my pops were extremely close. She would definitely take losing him the hardest. When I got to Victoria's room, I tapped on her door.

She took a minute but finally said, "It's open."

I opened the door and walked in. She was sitting at her window with her laptop on her lap and her phone in her hand. She was probably on them social sites, because that was all she did.

"Wassup, big bro? I didn't know you were coming over today," she squealed as she stood up to hug me.

My baby sister was my life. We were extremely close. We didn't have the normal brother-sister relationship, because we never argued or disagreed. I could be dead-ass wrong, but Vic was standing by me, and vice versa.

"What's good, mini me? Come with me downstairs. I gotta put you and Mommy onto some shit."

I turned around and headed out of the room, and she followed. When we got to the living room, we found my moms, Ty, and Skye chopping it up. Victoria took a seat next to Moms on the couch. I had the most important people in the world in that room, and I made a vow right there and right then that I wasn't losing none of them. Losing my pops was enough.

"You feeling better, baby boy?" my moms said, smiling up at me when she noticed me standing in the archway.

I took a deep breath and moved an inch closer. "Mom and Vic, I need to tell y'all something about Dad."

Moms's smile instantly evaporated and was replaced by a pained expression. It hurt my heart to see my moms's mood shift like that. Seeing her now made me want to break down, but I couldn't. I had to be strong for my family. I was now the man of the house, and I had to maintain our life.

This is all me! I can't be weak . . . I can't be weak, I told myself.

Once I convinced myself that I could handle my new responsibilities, I continued. "I just got a call . . ." I felt like shit that I had to leave out pieces of information, but I figured the less they knew, the better. "Dad was found in an abandoned house . . ."

Victoria got up from the couch and stormed out of the living room. Without me even having to ask her, Skye got up from the armchair she occupied and followed Victoria. I sat down on the couch next to my mother, who was completely shaken up. She had been with my father since she was fifteen. He was her first, her only, and her everything. I knew she felt like her world had just come crashing down around her. She had me, though, and even though I couldn't bring my pops back, I had her. I was going to make sure she was good. I wrapped my arms around her and held her as she cried. Only God Himself understood the physical pain I was enduring by trying to suppress my cries, screams, and anger. As my mother calmed down, I explained that I had to go to the morgue. I hated that I had to leave her, but I had a load of shit to take care of. I left the house, climbed behind the wheel, and texted Skye from the car, letting her know that I needed her to take care of my moms and my sister until I got back. I felt a little better knowing that she would help console them any way she could in my absence.

When Ty and I pulled up to the coroner's office, I had to reach deep within to drag myself out of the car. Part of me didn't want to have to say goodbye to my father, but I knew I needed to get it done and over with so I could handle everything else. Once I stepped inside the building, a chilly feeling flooded my body. Nah, it wasn't because the air was on, even though that tripped me out, because it was December. I guessed the bodies needed to stay cool or some shit. Knowing that building was probably filled to capacity with dead bodies creeped me the fuck out, but I was on a mission.

After signing in, I had to sit and wait to be called. It felt like I was there forever, but in actuality the whole process took only fifteen minutes—fifteen minutes too long, if you asked me. I was escorted to the door to the room where my father's body was being held, and the attendant said I could either go in or remain outside the room and look through the glass. Since I knew it was him, and I was just doing this shit as a formality, I opted for the glass. I watched as the mortician pulled the sheet back from my father's face and chest. Seeing my father lying there, with his eyes open and with a tiny bullet hole in the center of his head, enraged me. I had to get out of here. I nodded my head so the mortician could cover him up, and then I waited for the attendant to give me paperwork to sign. I signed those papers with lightning speed and dipped.

Ariana

When I got the text message from Skye about Cam's dad, a sense of guilt filled my veins. I felt like I should have spoken up when I realized what was up. How could I have, though? What would I have said? And if I had said something, would Ty still be involved with me? He was the first guy I'd been with in a while that really showed me that he cared and that he just wasn't in it to hit and split. I hadn't wanted to lose that. I knew that if Ty and Cam found out that I had known something was going on and hadn't shared it, it would be the end not only of my and Ty's relationship but of my life as well.

It was not like I had had anything to do with it, I reasoned. If I explained to Ty and Cam what had happened, maybe they would understand the position I'd been in.

I cursed out loud. "Shit!"

Why was I wasting time trying to convince myself that this wasn't going to end badly any way I put it? I had fucked up, and I probably would suffer dire consequences because of that. I wished I could go back to that day. If only I could go back to that day . . .

I paced the floor as I thought about everything that had taken place that day. It all started when I was leaving the radio station after my shift. I hosted the late show and usually didn't drive to the station. It was a little after eleven o'clock, and I was standing outside the radio station, trying to flag down a cab. Suddenly, a car pulled up, and I was surprised to see my ex, Man, hop out of his whip. He approached me and told me that he understood that I had a man, and that he respected that, but he just wanted to see me and have dinner as friends. It was freezing outside, and I didn't see a yellow cab in sight, so I took him up on his offer.

We ended up hitting this bar uptown for wings and drinks. It was cool. We kicked it about our brief relationship and why it hadn't worked. I had never been one to dwell on the past, but Man felt the need to tell me that he still felt like I was the one that had got away. He could have told that story walking, though. It didn't stir any sense of regret in me whatsoever. He had had his chance, and that chance had passed.

We were laughing, joking, and enjoying the music and shit when he got a phone call.

He took the call and then kept yelling into the phone, "Unc, chill. I got it covered."

I already knew the shit he was involved in, so that didn't faze me.

When he hung up, he told me, "My uncle Max be on some scary shit."

Of course, at the time I didn't really put two and two together. It wasn't until Ty told me that he, Cam, and their team were beefing with Man and his boys from Cypress that I had an inkling of what was going on. It was then that I remembered that Cam's guard was Max.

"Why the fuck didn't I say something!" I screamed now, as if someone was there with me and could explain my misstep to me.

Cameron

After visiting the coroner's office, Ty and I headed to one of the warehouses we had in Brownsville. I needed to pick up the video recording from the cameras, as something had told me to scrutinize that shit, because I was sure we had missed something. I had learned a long time ago to go with my gut, and at this point, my gut was screaming at me, telling me to look at the recording.

When we got to the warehouse, everything seemed in its rightful place. The only people who knew about this spot were Ty, his pops, my pops, and me. So if something was out of place, I would have definitely had to step to Ty, but nothing was, so I could relax, at least for now.

After we left the spot, we headed to the city. I needed to hit up a few stores in SoHo to get Skye some clothes and shit. I wanted her to stay with my mother and Vic until I got to the bottom of this shit. I felt better knowing that they were all safe and in the same spot. Only a select few people knew where the house was, so my moms, Vic, and Skye should be good there.

As we headed back to Long Island, I thought about reaching out to some other niggas that worked for my pops. I felt like there were other niggas I could probably trust. But as I mulled over the idea, I concluded that truth be told, I wasn't trying to risk it. Ty and I would handle this shit on our own, at least until his pops touched down. He was out of the country at the moment, handling some shit in Panama, but he would definitely be ready to lay down a serious murder game when the news hit him about my pops. We decided to wait till he was back in the States to let him know, because he needed to be focused on the shit he was dealing with down there.

Skye

We were all laid out in Mariah's California king–size bed. I looked over at Mariah and Victoria as they slept. Instantly, a wave of sorrow went through me. I felt extremely bad that I couldn't do much to ease the pain that Victoria and Mariah were enduring. I had done the best I could so far, though. I had made them some food and some tea, and then I had comforted them in this bed while they cried themselves to sleep.

I really couldn't imagine dealing with the death of my father. The thought alone made me feel sick to my stomach. I needed something to take my mind off the madness that was going on around me. So I quietly reached over to the nightstand, picked up my phone, and went to my Kindle app. I remembered that I hadn't finished reading *Love, Lies and Obsessions*, by Demettrea, this new author. I thought about going downstairs to read but decided against it. I wanted to be here, in case one of them woke up and needed me. After propping up a pillow, I got comfortable and dived into the book.

That lady was ill with the pen. I was so wrapped up in the story line that I forgot about what was going on around me, that is, until Cameron came bursting through the bedroom door. I raised my finger to my lips quickly, signaling to him to hush, before he had a chance to wake up his moms and Victoria. I was happy to see him. I had no clue what he'd gone out to do, and at the moment it didn't matter. I was just glad he had made it back safely. I slowly got out of the bed and then walked out of the room behind my man.

Once we were in the living room, I reached out and pulled him by the back of his shirt, stopping him in his tracks. When he turned to face me, I pulled him close and hugged him. Being in his arms felt so right. If I could have stayed in that moment forever, I would have.

He used his index finger to lift my chin and kissed me. "I love you, Skye."

I felt tears well up in my eyes, and as soon as they began to fall, he wiped them away.

"Don't cry, Ma. I'm straight."

He was back to being the Cameron with the tough-ass exterior. I knew better, though. He was far from straight. I followed him into his bedroom, where I saw a bunch of shopping bags on the floor. I was confused, because he was supposed to have handled some business while he was out.

"Baby, you went shopping?" I asked, walking over to his bed and sitting down.

"Nah. Those for you. I need you to stay here for now. Just until I—"

"No need to explain, babe. I'll stay. And thanks for the stuff," I said, cutting him off. He didn't really need to explain to me. I didn't want to be anywhere but near him, in case he needed me. I also didn't mind being there for his mother and his sister.

He stood in front of me, leaned over, and kissed me again. I wanted him, right then, in that moment.

"Baby, I gotta go downstairs and discuss some shit with Ty. Are you hungry or anything?"

Damn. So much for the quickie I wanted to have. It was okay, though, because I understood he had a lot on his plate. It was my job to be understanding, so that was what I planned on doing.

"No. I made us something to eat before they went to sleep. I'ma jump in the shower and just relax. Probably finish reading. I'm here if you need me."

He smiled at me. I was happy that through all of this, he could still manage to smile. I admired his strength.

"I love you, beautiful," he said.

I blew him a kiss and watched him walk to the bedroom door.

"I love you too."

Ty

While Cam was upstairs checking on his moms, his sister, and Skye, I was able to have my moment. I knew not to cry or show how hurt I was in front of Cam. I had to be strong for my nigga, but truth be told, I was hurting like shit. Hassan had been like a second pops to me. He was the true definition of a real nigga, and he'd been a straight leader. He had made sure everybody ate well, and he hadn't treated the cats who worked for him like peasants. He was well respected, which was why that shit was so shocking. Who had big enough balls to cross him at this magnitude? Stealing from him was one thing, but killing him? There was no rock on Earth that the culprits could hide under. Cam and I were gonna hunt those niggas down and drop them one by one.

Just thinking about that shit hurt my heart. As I sat on the couch in the living room, I felt tears well up in my eyes, and I didn't even attempt to hide them. I let the tears fall. But when I heard footsteps approaching, I wiped my eyes and sat up straight on the couch.

"Yo, bro, come downstairs," Cam called.

I looked up and saw him standing in the archway. I really had to give it to that man. The way he was holding his shit together was shocking. I didn't know if I would be able to function if it was my pops who had been murdered.

"A'ight." I got up off the couch and followed him down to the bunker.

Cam turned to me once he had shut the door, and said, "Son, we gotta watch this video recording from the Brownsville warehouse, and I mean *really* watch it. Those niggas are not that smart. They had to have slipped up. I just have a feeling the answers to everything are on this tape."

If my pops had watched that shit and hadn't see anything out of order other than the robbery itself, I doubted that we would spot something. But I decided to watch the tape to satisfy my brother's curiosity.

I nodded. "A'ight. Put it on."

In the bunker a red leather sofa sat across from a fifty-two-inch TV that was bolted to the wall. I walked over to the sofa and sat down, then propped my feet up on the coffee table. After Cam put on the DVD, he took a seat on the other end of the sofa. We focused intently on the DVD that was playing. We watched as Max and Rick unloaded the money and the product from the car. Rick took everything inside to put away, while Max stood guard outside. There was nothing out of ordinary, except that somebody was always supposed to be on the lookout while the other stashed the product and the bread. Max made a phone call before joining Rick inside. Why didn't he stay outside? Cameron must have been thinking what I was thinking, because he sat up straight and really focused on what was going on, on the TV screen.

Minutes after Max went inside to join Rick, a black SUV pulled up, some old-ass Durango. Four guys hopped out, and all of them were wearing masks except Man. *Dumb niggas*! I thought. After a few minutes of prepping their weapons, two of them headed inside, and that was when the shots started. We saw Rick run out of the warehouse. He was stopped dead in his tracks by the tip of Man's piece. We saw the gun flash and Rick drop. As painful as that was to watch, we couldn't stop. My mouth nearly hit the floor as we watched Max walk out of the warehouse with the other two dudes, carrying the bags that were filled with the money and the product. I turned to Cam, only to find him pointing his nine at me, with tears streaming down his face.

Cameron

"Son, what the fuck is your problem?" Ty asked.

Was that nigga about to sit here and try to play me for a dumb nigga?

"Fuck you mean, What's my problem? Son, your pops watched this video. He saw all this shit go down," I snarled.

I watched as a shocked expression covered Ty's face as the truth behind my statement hit him like a ton of bricks. I wanted to believe that he had no idea about the snake shit his father was on, but at that point, everybody was a suspect. *Fuck that.*

"Cam, you my nigga, my brother, son. I would never cross you or your pops."

A part of me wanted to lower my gun, because we was family. Why did it have to come to this? Why? I was battling with just letting him live until I got to the bottom of it or just killing him off on GP. He kept trying to plead his case.

"Cam, son, why the fuck would I watch this with you if I knew the shit would implicate me? Think! I'm just as shocked as you, bro."

He had a point, but I wasn't ready to put my gun down.

"Call your pops and tell him I sent you to review the tape from that night again. Ask him why he lied," I said.

I could see him contemplating what I had just asked him to do. He knew that if his father said the wrong thing, either both of them would be dead or I was gonna kill his pops. Either way, it was a lose-lose situation for Ty. But I hoped he would attempt to spare his own life.

"He still in Panama."

I looked at Ty sideways. "You trying to play me? This nigga getting money that he stole from my pops. I'm sure he can afford the fucking roaming charges. Call him!"

Good thing we were in the bunker, because the way I was screaming would have definitely woken up my moms and them. I watched as Ty pulled out his iPhone and called his pops. I prayed my boy didn't cross me. The phone on the other end rang four times before Jeff finally answered.

"What up? You straight, son? Why you calling me while I'm out of town?"

Ty hesitated, so I had to reposition my gun to remind him what was gonna happen if he didn't cooperate.

"Pops, I gotta ask you something, and I need you to keep it one hundred with me. Hassan was bodied today, my man—"

Jeff cut him off. "I know you not calling to ask me if I had something to do with it when you know I'm in Panama."

There was all the proof I needed. That nigga didn't even seem fazed that his best friend had been murdered.

"Nah, Cam sent me to the spot to check video from the night of the burglary. I watched the whole thing. Pops, tell me you didn't have shit to do with this. Why you lie about what you saw on the tape?"

The line went silent for a minute. "Fuck them niggas, Ty. That nigga Hassan wasn't built to be no leader. He had us doing all the legwork, while he reaped the benefits. Fuck that nigga and fuck Cam. You that nigga's lapdog. He don't see you as his equal, but ya head too far up his ass to see that, though."

I didn't want to hear anymore. I wanted to kill Ty because his father was scum, but he was my brother. I lowered the gun and sat back on the couch as he wrapped up the conversation with his pops.

"What now?" I heard Ty say after he ended the call with his father.

That was the same shit I was thinking. I mean, this was the ultimate test of our friendship. His father had to die.

"Ty, you already know. I'm going to kill Jeff. Either you can live with that and just not deal with me or you can kill me right now. Wait. Nah. That's not an option, because your piece is in your car. So you can live with the fact that your right-hand man's going to kill your father or you can go to war with me at a later date. That's on you."

Ty

I couldn't believe it had come to this. For anyone else, the choice would have been easy. Blood was thicker than water, right? It wasn't that simple, though. My pops and Hassan had grown up together, so how the fuck could he cross the man that had always had his back? Then he had turned around and preached that loyalty shit. I was disgusted and embarrassed that I had to call that nigga my father. I didn't share his same views about the situation. As far back as I could remember, Hassan had been a team player. Yeah, he may have had little niggas putting in work, but he was the boss. How did niggas expect that shit to go? It was too many chiefs and not enough Indians. Everybody wanted to be the boss.

Cam, on the other hand, was just like his pops. He looked out for everyone around him and kept his niggas straight. We had never bumped heads, though you would expect that we would have since his pops was the boss man. You would think Cam would be on some "I'm above everyone else because my pops is that nigga"–type shit, but he wasn't. He was in the streets with us, and he put in work with us. I couldn't even force myself to agree with what my pops had said. One thing my pops had always told me, which was something that Hassan used to say all the time, was that "snakes needed to be beheaded." It was fucked up that the snake in this situation was my pops, but I knew what had to be done.

I looked over at Cam, who looked as if he was deep in thought, just as I was.

"Yo, Cam."

I waited for him to look up at me. I was glad it took him a minute, because it gave me a chance to prepare my words in my head.

"I'm not tryin'a go to war with you, bro. My pops went against the grain, so he gotta pay the price," I declared.

Cam's eyes almost popped out of his head. He hadn't expected me to side with him. *Shit.* Honestly, I hadn't thought I would side with him, either. That was my pops we were talking about, but that didn't change the fact that he had fucked up.

"Nah. I'ma keep it trill with you, Ty. I respect that you picked me over your pops. That's loyalty, and I wish all niggas had that shit flowing through them like you. But I'm not gonna let you agree to me killing your pops. I would never do to you what your pops did to me. I tell you this, though. He better stay where he at. There's not enough space in the States for both of us. If we cross paths, shots will be exchanged. Either he gonna kill me or I'ma kill him."

Cameron

I really did respect that Ty was willing to ride for me. He knew his pops had to get it, because he had done the unforgivable, but I knew that Ty and I would never be able to overcome me killing his pops, even if we tried. I couldn't have that tension with him right now. Putting aside the bullshit with his pops, Ty was still the only nigga I could trust, and I still had problems that needed to be solved. Max was at the top of my list. When he'd started working for my father, that nigga was homeless. His baby moms had put him out because he wasn't working, and she had got tired of providing for the nigga. My pops had cleaned him up and had given him a job. *Never bite the hand that feeds you.*

Man was next, and his death was going to be slow and painful, but first, I was going to kill everyone that he loved: his mother, his sister, and his daughter. He had to be last because he had to see how it felt to lose people that you loved. I guessed losing his brother wasn't enough. I wondered how he would feel if he knew that Max was the one who had pulled the trigger, sending his brother to an early grave. Niggas really didn't have an ounce of loyalty when money and power were involved. I had known that before, but now I was feeling it in the worst way.

I looked over at Ty, who was sitting still on the couch, deep in thought. He hadn't said anything since I told him that I was gonna let his pops live. I was fine with my decision, because I knew that I would see Jeff again, and when I did, it was on sight. How had my pops done this shit on a daily basis? I wondered. I was physically and mentally drained already. I just wanted to lay up with my shorty and exhale.

"Yo, Ty, I'm ready to take it down for the night. On some real shit, I just want to relax, get my mind right and shit. I'll get at you tomorrow to discuss our next move."

I didn't even wait for him to respond. I just got up and headed toward the elevator. He got the message and followed behind me. After letting him out on the main level, I headed upstairs to Skye. I had some frustrations that I needed to release, and I knew her pussy would be the best therapy. I walked into my old bedroom and found her passed out in the bed. I contemplated waking her up but decided against it. I needed to figure out a way to show her how much I appreciated her. She had been living a pretty normal life, and then I'd come along and shaken up her world. But instead of dipping, she was still here for me. I walked over to the side of the bed and lightly kissed her cheek. I was about to walk away when I noticed a rolled blunt sitting on the nightstand.

I chuckled low. I loved shorty. She knew I was gonna need this shit after the day I had had, and she had it ready for a nigga. I couldn't wait to blow that L, but I needed a quick shower first. After the shower, I smoked my L, climbed in bed with my shorty, and got some much-needed sleep.

Since the day of my pops's death, I had put everything on hold. All the niggas who worked for my pops had reached out to me once they heard about his death, but I had brushed them off. I didn't want sympathy or help or nothing! Even Max had called me. That nigga had some nerve, but I had kept it together, because before I dealt with him and everyone else, I needed to make sure home was together. Christmas was a week away, and the women in my life deserved to have a semi-normal Christmas. It would never be normal again for my moms and my sister because my dad wasn't there, but I would do my best to make it a special holiday.

Skye had been a big-ass help around the house the past few days. She had cooked, cleaned, and decorated the house, in hopes of getting us all in the Christmas spirit. On top of that, she had had two finals she had to take the other day that she didn't get a chance to study for. I prayed she did well. She had worked so hard last semester and still had managed to hold me down. I, on the other hand, had skipped finals. School was the last thing on my mind.

My alarm went off, shaking me out of my thoughts. I'd been up for a minute, but I had just forgotten to turn the alarm off. I grabbed my phone off the nightstand, turned it off, and lay back down. It was the day of my pop's funeral. I wasn't ready, and I hadn't the slightest idea how I was going to get through it. I knew I had to hold it down for my moms and Vic, but telling myself I needed to do that and actually doing it were two different things. I lay there, deep in thought, until Skye turned over and kissed me.

"I heard the alarm go off, baby. Get up."

Damn. I wasn't trying to wake her up, because I really wanted her to sleep as much as she could. I low key had a feeling she was pregnant, because every time we had fucked recently, she couldn't take the whole thing, and usually she handled the shit like a pro. Not to mention she hadn't needed those pad things for a minute. I didn't know, though. Maybe her cycle was fucked up, or maybe she had some other female issue that chicks went through. I was sure she would tell me if she was pregnant, and just in case she was, I was trying to keep her stress free.

"A'ight, beautiful. I'm getting up," I said as I sat up in the bed. "What time your parents going to be here?" I asked her while I looked through the messages in my phone.

"They are going to meet us at the church, because they are going to pick up Ariana. Speaking of Ariana, when I last spoke to her, she was asking about Ty. She said that he been calling her, but he didn't want to see her, and that isn't normal. You know wassup with him, babe? It is kind of weird that he hasn't even been over here in the past few days."

Shit. I hadn't even told Skye the shit that went down and how I found out that Jeff knew that Max had set Rick up and was working with the Cypress niggas. Why did she have to ask about Ty? I had been keeping my word about not keeping stuff from her, but I didn't want to divulge this particular stuff at the moment. However, I decided to tell her, anyway.

Skye

I couldn't believe the shit Cameron had told me about Ty's father and Max. I had planned on taking a shower with him, but I couldn't get up. I had to lie there and really process it. That shit was real. When Cameron had told me about his lifestyle, I hadn't anticipated it would get this messy. It appeared that everybody wanted to be in a position of power. I was really starting to question everything. Was it even worth it anymore? I had to shake that feeling. Regardless of whether it was worth it or not, I had told Cameron I was going to stick with him, and that was what I planned to do.

I climbed out of bed finally and headed into the bathroom to join my man in the shower. Seeing him in there, with the water falling off his body, reminded me how much I loved him. When I stepped into the shower, he turned to face me and kissed me.

"I thought you wasn't going to come."

I didn't respond; no words were needed. I took the washcloth out of his hand and washed him. When I was done, he did the same for me. I lived for those moments. And this moment was essential now because it helped me answer the questions that I'd asked myself earlier. Life with Cameron was definitely worth it.

After the shower, we dried off and headed into the bedroom to get dressed. I was sitting on the bed, applying lotion to my skin, as I watched Cameron put on his Tom Ford suit. My baby cleaned up nice. Once he was done getting dressed, he left the bedroom. I assumed that he was going to check on his mother and his sister. I was moving extremely slowly now because suddenly I felt sick. I figured it was because I knew I was headed to a funeral, so I brushed it off and continued to get ready. I slipped into the BCBGMAXAZRIA dress that Cameron had picked out for me. I then stepped into my black Christian Louboutin Daff pumps and made my way downstairs.

As our limo arrived at the church, I kissed Cameron and whispered, "I got you, baby," in his ear.

It was important that he understood that I had his back and that he wasn't going through this alone. Yes, he had his mother and his sister, but they were in no position to comfort him. I was there for all of them. I watched as he stepped out of the limo first and then took his mother by the hand. Victoria and I exited the limo next and followed Cameron and his mom into the church. I held Victoria's hand as we walked down the aisle to the front row, which was reserved for family. Once everybody was seated, I kissed Cameron on the cheek and hugged the ladies. I didn't plan on sitting in the front with them, since I was sure they needed their privacy at this difficult moment. I was going to find my parents and Ariana and sit with them. But when I went to walk away, Mariah stopped me.

"Where are you going? Please sit with us, Skye. You are family."

Her words meant a lot to me. I didn't protest. I quietly took a seat next to Cameron.

The service was amazing. They sent Cameron's dad home in a very classy manner. Everything was breath-taking, from the flower arrangements to the songs performed by the choir, right down to the speeches given by

Cameron and his mother. During the service, I couldn't help but notice the number of people that had come out to say their final goodbyes to Hassan. You could tell that he was heavily respected.

After Cameron and his family conversed solemnly with some of the folks, we filed down the aisle and stepped outside. The limo was waiting for us where it had left us off. Just as Mariah and Victoria were getting into the limo, I noticed something odd. A group of about six or seven guys who looked Mexican were watching our every move from their spot a stone's throw from the church doors.

"Baby," I said, tapping Cameron on the shoulder.

"Yeah? What happened?"

I looked in the direction of the men and said, "Do you know them?"

When he saw who I was referring to, his face turned sour. He spun on his heels and headed in their direction. I contemplated getting in the limo but decided that I was going to stand beside my man. I walked quickly so I could catch up with him. When I reached him, I took his hand in mine and squeezed it. I had to remind him we were in this together.

"Young Cam," one of the guys said as we approached. He looked to be of Spanish descent. Maybe he was Mexican.

"Miguel," Cameron said when he reached the guy.

Miguel looked at me and licked his crusty lips. That shit made my skin crawl. "Who is this pretty lady?" he asked. His voice sent chills up my spine, but not chills that meant I was turned on. They were ones that made me want to run back to the limo to get away from his ass.

Cameron's nostrils flared as he spoke. "My girl."

Miguel smiled. Before he could speak, Cameron spoke again.

"Thanks for coming to pay your respects. We gotta head out, though, and get to the cemetery."

We had turned to head back to the limo when Miguel stopped us in our tracks. "Cam, we didn't come to make trouble," he announced. "As you stated, we wanted to pay our respects and to let you know we are now owed two million dollars."

Cameron turned right around to face Miguel. His cheeks were red now. He started to say something, but Miguel interrupted him.

"No need to object," Miguel said, stepping closer to him.

Cameron didn't back down.

Miguel continued to speak. "You lost my money once, and I allowed you the opportunity to pay it back with your little interest. Now the money is late, and you didn't reach out to me. I see you have been dealing with a lot, but that doesn't have shit to do with my money. So as I stated, two million dollars, and you have two days. I would say tomorrow, but I'ma give you a day to regroup after having to bury your father. But only because I like you. I must warn you that if I have to take this trip again, it won't be this civil."

Miguel turned to walk away, and the guys who were with him followed. Cameron said nothing. He just escorted me back to the limo, and we headed to the cemetery.

Cameron

When we got home from the cemetery, we were joined by some of the guys who were really close to my pops. Max was among the men, but that was for my own reasons. Ty also joined us. Things had been awkward between us, and I made a mental note to address that before the night was over. Even Skye's parents were there to show support, along with Ariana. I didn't want anything like that, but my mom wanted to have them all over for dinner. After days of trying to convince me, I had given in to her wishes. As she, my sister, Skye, and Ariana went to work in the kitchen, I gathered all my niggas, and we headed to the bunker.

"I thank y'all for coming to pay respects to my pops. I appreciate it," I said as they all settled in.

Most of them were familiar with the bunker, because, like I said, they were really close to my pops. As I walked over to the TV to start the recording from the Brownsville warehouse, I heard some of them tell me that thanking them wasn't necessary and shit. I nodded at their comments and pressed PLAY on the DVD player.

I didn't need to watch the recording again. Instead, I watched Max as he focused on the recording and began to sweat bullets. Everyone except Ty, Max, and me was confused as to why I was playing the recording, but they would soon understand. As they watched Max on the TV screen walk out of the warehouse, helping them Cypress niggas with the shit they stole, they all simultaneously drew their weapons and aimed it at their target.

Max looked over at me. "I can explain, Cam. It ain't even like that."

I walked over to him and punched him in his mouth. He grabbed his jaw and winced in pain.

"Speak when I ask you a question," I barked.

I looked over and saw that Junior's piece had a silencer on it. I smiled at him. Knowing why I was smiling, he handed me the burner.

I glared at Max. "So riddle me this. How you know Man? Why you set my pops up? *And* who else is in on it? You got one chance and one chance only. Make it count," I growled.

I looked around at the other guys in the room and saw that they were looking around at each other. I silently hoped that the name of no one in that room would come out of his mouth.

Max remained silent.

"Answer me, bitch!" I shouted.

He gulped before opening his mouth to speak. "Man is my nephew."

That nigga really was a snake. He had killed Man's brother, his other nephew, and I hadn't even asked him to.

He went on. "Nobody here knew what was up. Actually, no one else on the team knew. Rick started fishing, and that's why he got killed. And as far as your pops goes, Man's plan was to take him out, take you out, and take over Brooklyn. I was going to be his underboss. Cam, nobody wants to be a driver or a security guard they whole life."

The fuck? Who would say some dumb shit like that when they were about to see the light?

"Max, you a dumb nigga. You were muscle and a driver, but you ate like a king and got greedy. Niggas like you don't deserve to run with real niggas, son. What happened the day my pops got bodied?"

I didn't know why I even asked that. The facts surrounding the murder didn't matter, because they weren't going to bring him back. I was curious to know, though.

"I picked him up so that we could go pay the connect, but instead I took him to that spot to meet Man. Man sent me to the airport to pick up some other nigga, and I took him back to the spot. Your pops and the nigga said words, and he killed him. We took the money and dipped."

Some other nigga? Who the fuck would kill my pops for Man? That shit was bigger than I had fucking imagined.

"Who's the other nigga, and what the fuck he had to do with it?" I quizzed.

Everything that Max did now proved exactly why he was muscle and a fucking driver. Any real nigga would have taken his death like a real nigga. That bitch was in there singing like Beyoncé.

"He not from here. His name is, uh . . . Matt . . . Matthew, or some shit."

Ty and I looked at each other, and our eyes did all the talking as Max went on.

"I don't know what he had to do with it or why he wanted your pops dead. All I know is that when he got there, he called your pops 'Dad,' or some shit like that, and Hassan went off, telling him how he wasn't his son and that his moms was a ho. That's when he shot him."

I had heard everything I needed to hear. I raised the gun, aimed directly between Max's eyes, and got ready to end his life, but Ty stopped me.

"Not like this, Cam."

I looked at Ty strangely. What the fuck did he mean, not like this?

"We about to go upstairs and have dinner with your moms, your sis, your girl, and her parents," he reminded me. "You want to do that with bloodstains on your suit and gunshot residue on your hands? I know you ready to end his life—shit, we all are—but not like this."

I hated that he was right. I was ready to off that nigga right there and right now. This was one of the many times I was reminded why I was lucky to have Ty on my team.

"A'ight. We'll go have dinner. Everyone, keep your eye on this nigga. Don't let him . . . Matter of fact, I wouldn't want this bitch calling for backup!" I reached in his pocket and snatched his cell phone. "But yeah, if he moves, somebody better follow him. If he tries to leave, shoot him where he stands. I'll just have to deal with my moms and Skye's parents, but he's not living through this night."

I watched as everyone shook their head in agreement, and then I dismissed all of them except Ty. They all headed upstairs.

"What happened? We good?" Ty asked me once they were gone.

Damn. Shit had gotten so sour between us that the nigga was acting all jumpy and shit.

"Calm down, bro. I'm trying to find out from you if we're straight. Since that night, shit been different. You don't trust that I'ma leave your pops be, unless we bump into each other, or you think I'm mad at you? Wassup?"

I needed to know where his head was at.

"Nah, bro, it ain't even like that. I know your word is your bond. So when you said you gonna let my pops rock, I didn't second-guess that. It's just different. I mean, now we know my pops didn't have anything to do with the murder, but he still was disloyal, and that shit doesn't sit well with me. And I do feel like you may feel some resentment toward me because of him."

Did I feel resentment toward him? Nah. For what? His pops had made his decisions, and Ty was his own man. I couldn't hold him responsible for another man's actions.

"It's different because we making it different. You my nigga, Ty. I don't feel no way toward you over that shit. If we going to get those niggas, we gotta put that shit behind us, bro, for real. We even got heat coming down on us from Miguel and them niggas, and I need you, bro."

His face scrunched up when I mentioned Miguel. He knew going to war with them Mexicans was a recipe for disaster—hopefully, for them.

He stuck his hand out, and we gave each other dap as he said, "I got you, bro."

We headed upstairs, and on the way I told him what had gone down at the church with Miguel.

Dinner went well. Even Max pretended to be enjoying himself. I guessed he wanted his last few hours on Earth to be peaceful. I was glad Skye's parents were over. I knew she missed them, and I felt bad that I had been taking up so much of her time that she didn't get to see them. They were understanding and felt that she was just trying to be supportive while we dealt with the loss of my dad. I mean, that wasn't a lie, but it wasn't the entire story.

After dinner, Skye's parents left, and then my niggas and I headed to the spot in Brownsville. I wasn't trying to be out there all night. I wanted to get this shit done with and go home to my favorite girls, which was why as soon as we got to the spot, I ended that nigga's life. *Why waste more time*? I thought. I watched the cleanup crew do their thing, and afterward, Ty took me home.

Matt

After the nigga Hassan's funeral, I spotted Cam talking to some Mexican niggas. I knew they had to be his connect. Those niggas looked like big money and moved like bosses. Not the type of bosses that was running around the hood, but more like the niggas you saw on TV. I knew that approaching them would mean taking a huge risk, but I had to take my chances.

Once I seen Cam's limo dip, I caught up with the Mexicans. Of course, they didn't want to hear shit I had to say, but I had some information that would make them listen. I told them about the money we had taken when I killed Hassan. Of course I told my version of how shit had gone down, leaving out the fact that I had killed Hassan. Actually, I left the incident out altogether.

The bullshit-ass story I made up must have sounded believable, because they told me to take a ride with them. Of course, I was hesitant at first. Mexican niggas ain't shit to fuck with. They were the epitome of seven thirty. During the ride they told me how they were going to handle the Cam situation, and they offered me his position once he was out of the picture. Shit was sweet. Not only were they doing the dirty work, but I was also still getting everything I had wanted when I set out on this mission. Shit was coming together nicely. I was feeling like Lil Wayne, with his line "I ain't got no worries."

Skye

I was jolted out of my sleep when my alarm started blaring in my ear. I managed to stop it quickly before it woke up Cameron as well. He had got in late last night, so I knew he wanted to get some rest. I rolled over, frustrated that I had been woken up out of such a good sleep. I contemplated going back to bed, but I knew I needed to get hopping soon if I was going to keep the early appointment with my doctor today. The last week or so, I'd been feeling extremely crappy. I hadn't had energy for anything, nor had I had an appetite, and my boobs had been sore as fuck. Not to mention the last time we tried to have sex, it had hurt like hell.

All those were pregnancy signs, I knew, but I'd been in denial about it, even though I had missed my period twice! Don't get me wrong, I was happy as hell about becoming a mother, but I just wished the timing was better. With all that had been going on—the beef with the Mexicans, and not being able to catch Man—I already had to worry about my safety when I was in the street, but now I had to worry about my child too.

I glanced at the time again and decided that I needed to get up right now and get ready, because Ariana would be picking me up soon. We hadn't had any time together since before Cameron's dad's death, so I had reached out to her and had asked her to accompany me to the appointment. She was excited as hell and had jumped at the opportunity to go with me. I couldn't front; I was excited too.

I climbed out of bed stealthily, so as not to awaken Cameron, and made a beeline to the bathroom. The entire time I was in the shower, I thought about my baby. How was he or she gonna look? What were we going to name him or her? How was I going to be as a mom, and how would Cameron be as a dad? As I was getting dressed, my phone vibrated on the bathroom counter. I picked it up and saw that I had a text message from Ariana.

I'm outside, bestie. Hurry up. I hope your ass is ready and you won't have me sitting outside forever.

I had to laugh at her, because she knew me too well. I was indeed still getting dressed, but after getting her text, I moved faster. Once I had slipped on my Uggs, I wrote Cameron a note, telling him that I was running out with Ariana, and then I left. When I got outside, I hopped in Ariana's car and I instantly hugged her. Even though we spoke every day, it wasn't the same as seeing her in person. I had truly missed my best friend.

"Hey, bestieee!" I said, stretching the word *bestie* to add dramatics.

She laughed. "Hey, *chica*."

As she pulled off, I frowned when I realized what was playing through her car speakers. I hadn't ridden in her car in so long, I had forgotten that she listened to classical music in the morning. Don't get me wrong. I did love to relax to Bach, but in the morning I needed some hype music to help me start my day right.

"You know this not gonna work, girl," I said as I pressed the radio feature on the console and switched to Power 105.1 FM. Monica's "Love All Over Me" was playing. I sang along, thinking about Cameron.

When we arrived at my doctor's office, I felt butterflies in my stomach. I didn't know why I was nervous. I already knew what it was that was ailing me. I just wanted my doctor's confirmation, as well as a checkup to make sure everything was going as it should. After I signed in, Ariana and I sat down and waited. I had picked up one of the brochures on pregnancy and had started to read through it when I felt my phone vibrate. I took it out my pocket and saw that I had got a text from Cameron. I smiled, knowing that he was checking on me.

Wassup, baby? Why you didn't wake me up before you left? Are you okay? Did you eat?

Seeing that I was right, I laughed. Then I texted him back.

You came in late, and I wanted you to get some rest, babe. And yes, I'm okay. I will grab food before I head back home. I love you, Cameron.

When I was finally called to see the doctor, my nerves started to get the best of me. Maybe I should have brought Cameron along with me, after all. Nah, it was okay. He would be able to come to every appointment after this one, so I wasn't worried. My ob-gyn was a sweet lady. She had a personal touch with her patients; she didn't treat us all the same and tended to our individual needs. That was what I loved about her. When I entered her office, she decided to talk about life, school, and everything else before jumping right to the reason I was there.

The pregnancy test she then performed confirmed what I already knew—that I was pregnant. I was going to be a mommy. No words could express how I was feeling. I was on a cloud, and in the face of all the shit that had been going wrong lately, I now had something to smile about every day, regardless of what was going on, and Cameron did too.

In addition to having lab work done, I got a Pap smear. I had mentally prepared myself for that stuff. I just hated needles. After the exam was done and the blood was drawn, the doctor and I had a discussion about my medical history, and then she gave me a bunch of information about what I could expect. The best part of this visit was finding out my due date, which was August 13. I looked forward to the day I got to see my precious baby's face. It was such an amazing feeling.

After the doctor's appointment, Ariana and I headed over to Beauty and Essex for some food. It was a new spot that my mother had told me about, so we had decided to check it out. It was a nice place, and we loved the atmosphere. It was somewhere between a bar and a restaurant. The food was good, and we would have loved to try their drinks, but I was pregnant and she was driving. I definitely would be trying them in seven months.

I had to admit that today was a much-needed day out with Ariana. I had a chance to take my mind off the madness, even if it was only for a few hours. I just needed a minute without having to think about pissed-off connects, ungrateful-ass snakes, revenge, and all the other shit that was going on. I was not saying I had a problem being there for my man, because I didn't. I just missed normalcy. I missed my damn condo, for sure. I loved being at Cameron's mom's house with them, but I missed my space. I couldn't express these concerns to Cameron, though, because he already had a lot going on. It felt damn good to express them to Ariana. As always, she was a shoulder and a listening ear.

Cameron

While Skye was out, I had a chance to make some phone calls. I had a fucking manhunt going on. I had put 250,000 racks on each of them niggas' heads, yet no one had any new information on Man and Matt. If those niggas was after my spot, I knew they hadn't disappeared. They wouldn't, not until they had completed their mission . . . or until I had killed them. Which was my intent.

"Where the fuck are these niggas?" I asked out loud to no one, since I was alone in my bedroom.

The shit was aggravating me. My organization needed to move forward. Niggas were hitting my phone, complaining about how they were getting low on product left and right. To top it off, I was out of a connect. Could shit get any worse at this point? I had Skye there like a fucking hostage. I didn't let her go back to her crib, and she rarely saw her parents or went out. I knew that shit was eating away at her, but she was trying so hard to show me that she was a rider that she didn't say anything. I sensed it, though.

I was in the middle of smoking a blunt when Skye walked in the bedroom. She didn't even come all the way in; she just waved at me from the doorway and then turned around. I figured she was going to chill with Vic. They had become extremely close since Skye had been staying here, which was good. Who wouldn't want the most important women in their life to get along?

When I was finished smoking my blunt, I left the bedroom, went downstairs, and stepped into the living room, where I found all my ladies on the couch, watching a movie. I sat next to Skye and pulled her close to me. I loved the shit out of that girl. It had only been five months since we got together, but she was riding with a nigga like we was married and shit. A basic bitch would have been left. I knew there was something about that girl when we first met.

Skye

The past few days had been good, with the exception of morning sickness kicking my ass and me trying to hide it from Cameron. I wasn't trying to hide it because I was afraid of his reaction to the pregnancy. I just wanted to surprise everyone with the news when they came over for Christmas, which was only a few days away. I think Cameron knew something was up, however, because before I found out I was pregnant, I would roll his blunts and chill with him when he was smoking, but now I would exit the room fast every time he lit up, giving him some lame excuse for my departure.

When Christmas Eve rolled around, Victoria and I had to head out to shop for last-minute gifts, while Cameron and Mariah went food shopping. Victoria and I went into four stores, trying to find something for Cameron. He had everything, so it was tough trying to find things that I knew he would love.

"Skye, this is the last store we looking in for that fool. It's a shame we couldn't find something faster," Vic said as we walked into the Hermès store.

I laughed and nodded my head. "Okay, Vic. This is the last stop for Cameron, but, girl, honestly, I was pressed to come here so I could get me a bag."

Victoria looked at me and burst out laughing. "Me too."

I joined her in the laughter as we slapped fives. We had so much in common. We liked the same music and had the same fashion sense. The fact that we agreed on everything made shopping with her much easier.

We browsed through the men's section, and I ended up getting Cameron a bunch of things that I knew he would look good in. When I noticed Victoria lingering in the women's department, I went and purchased the bag she'd been looking at minutes before, along with the matching belt. She was going to be surprised, and I wanted to make her smile. After leaving the Hermès store, we had to quickly decide on things for my parents, her mom, Ty, and Ariana, because we had to beat Mariah and Cameron home. They didn't know we had gone out to get more gifts.

When we got home, we didn't see Mariah's car anywhere, so we knew they weren't back yet. We were in the clear. We didn't have any wrapping to do, because the stores we had gone to did gift wrapping before they packed up the stuff. All that was left for us to do was put everything under the tree, and we did that in no time.

Victoria wanted to bake cookies when we were done, but I really felt a little drained. I promised to keep her company while she made them. She moved around the kitchen, getting the ingredients together, then sat across from me at the table. As soon as she prepared the cookie dough, I got sick to my stomach, and my lunch threatened to come up. . . . Nope, it *was* coming up, so I got up and ran to the nearest bathroom.

I was standing over the toilet, holding my hair up, as I threw up the food I had consumed earlier. I felt like shit. I didn't think I could get with seven more months of this sickness shit. When I was done, I turned around to go to the sink and saw Victoria was standing in the doorway, staring at me.

Please don't ask me. Please don't ask me, I thought to myself.

"You pregnant, Skye?"

Of course she would ask me. Why couldn't a person have a stomach bug rather than a pregnancy? Vic was smart, though, so I couldn't even try to fool her.

I smiled. "Yes. You're going to be an auntie!" I said, stepping over to the sink to rinse my mouth out.

She hugged me so tight that I thought she was going to squeeze the life out of me. "Oh, my gosh! Congrats, Skye. Does Cam know? How far you? When did you find out? Like, tell me everything."

I had to laugh at her. Her intentions were good, and I knew she was excited, but she had to slow down.

"Slow down, Vic. Cameron doesn't know. I planned on telling everyone tomorrow. I just found out a few days ago, and I'm two months."

She was smiling from ear to ear. I was happy she was excited, and I knew that she would be a great auntie.

"Vic, is it okay if you make the cookies alone? I want to lie down for a bit, until my parents get here."

She nodded her head up and down. "Of course, girl, and I won't tell anyone. I think the Christmas announcement is a good idea."

I hugged her. "Thank you."

My intention had been to lie down for a little while, until I got my second wind, but I ended up falling asleep.

"Wake up, baby," I heard Cameron say as I was opening my eyes.

"What time is it?"

He looked at his watch and said, "Nine thirty."

Damn. I had slept the whole day away.

"I would have let you sleep, but I wanted you to get some food in your system."

His mention of food make my stomach turn. "I'm not really hungry, baby. I'm going to get in the shower. Are you coming?"

He leaned over and kissed my forehead. "Nah. I'm going to finish helping my moms, but when you done showering, come eat."

I brushed him off, climbed out of the bed, and went to shower. I didn't know if it was the showerhead, the water pressure, or a combination of both, but this shit felt good on my muscles. After I was finished washing up, I wanted to stay in there and enjoy the water massage, but I knew Cameron would come get me out of the shower so I could stuff my face. It made me smile, though, because he really cared about my well-being. I imagined how he was gonna act when I told him about the baby.

I stepped out of the shower, and after drying off, I slipped my feet into my fuzzy slippers and put my robe on. As soon as I walked in the bedroom, I saw a salad and a bottle of water on the nightstand. He must have known that I was getting right back on the bed. Since he had gone out of his way to bring the salad upstairs, I decided that I would try to eat it. I prayed that it sat right with me, because that throwing-up shit was for the birds.

Surprisingly, that salad hit the spot, and it stayed down, so that was a plus. I took my empty dish back downstairs and then went right back upstairs and climbed in the bed. Cameron, Mariah, and Victoria were in the kitchen, slaving away, and I was in the bed, watching Lifetime movies. I felt myself getting sleepy, so I texted Cameron.

I'm getting sleepy, and I want to lie in your arms. Can you come to bed?

He didn't text me back, but he was upstairs in a minute flat. I waited up while he took a shower, and as soon as he joined me in bed and cuddled me, I was out.

"Merry Christmas, *chica!*"

I knew that was Ariana's voice, but why was I dreaming about her? I felt someone shake me softly, and I slowly opened my eyes. Then I laughed.

"Merry Christmas, Ari. I thought I was dreaming, girl. Y'all here early."

She sat on the edge of the bed. "I knew your mother and my mother wanted to be here early to help Mariah cook and stuff."

I loved that our mothers got along so well. We had really become one big family, which would be totally official once baby was born. I smiled and rubbed my tiny belly.

"Ty here already too?"

She nodded up and down. "Yup. Him, your dad, and Cameron outside playing basketball."

Now, when my father came in complaining about knee pain and shit, he was on his own.

"Oh, and Mariah said we doing gifts after breakfast, so get up and get your life, *chica*."

When Ariana left the room, I got up out of the bed, feeling refreshed, and got myself together before heading downstairs and having breakfast with the family. When I walked into the dining room, everyone was there except me. Even the guys had wrapped up their basketball game. I spoke to everyone before sitting in the empty seat next to Cameron. There were so many breakfast foods on the table, I was silently praying that the smells didn't make me sick. So far I was good.

Everyone made their plates; then Mariah said grace, and we dug in. After breakfast, we all gathered in the family room and exchanged gifts. Mariah got all teary eyed when she opened the Hermès bag and belt I had got her. I was happy to see her smile, because she deserved it. Everyone else received extremely nice gifts as well and was happy. Once everyone had opened all their gifts, I was ready to make my announcement. I stood up and placed my things on the floor and on the couch next to me.

"I have a gift for the entire family, one that we can all share for years to come," I declared.

The room fell completely silent.

I started laughing, because they were all confused, except Ariana and Victoria, of course.

"I'm pregnant."

Whoa. Everyone began talking at once. They was more excited than I was, and it was my baby. The amount of support and encouraging words I received from everyone was overwhelming. I even started tearing up, but I blamed that on hormones.

"Mariah, we're going to be grandmas!" I heard my mom say as she hugged Mariah.

Cameron hugged me and didn't want to let me go.

The rest of the day was so awesome. Everyone had a wonderful time as we played family feud and Pictionary, ate some more, and just enjoyed each other's company. It was truly what we all needed.

Ty

Wow. Skye was really pregnant. I was happy for my niggas Cam and Skye. Becoming parents had to be about the best thing that could happen to you in your lifetime. I was not a father yet, but when I became one, I knew it was going to be the best shit I had ever experienced. Their baby was coming at a good time, because they needed the joy in their life right now. Well, Cam definitely did.

Sin City was having a Christmas bash, and it took a lot, but I convinced Cam to go with me and Ari that night, since we had spent the whole day with the family. He needed to get out of the house, because you could see stress and worry all over his face, and that wasn't like my nigga at all. A nice outing around bad bitches and fat asses should do the trick. Of course we couldn't touch the hoes, but we could watch and spend a little money.

When we pulled up to Sin City, the lines were long as fuck. Good thing we knew the niggas throwing the shit, because we didn't do lines. We walked into the spot like we owned the shit. It felt good to be out on the scene with my right-hand and my girl. It was a much-deserved night out. Even though Cam wasn't trying to leave Skye at home without him, I was glad he had decided to come out. Him going to be a father definitely called for a celebration. What was a better way to celebrate than to ball the fuck out at the strip club?

The spot was packed with wall-to-wall people. We were barely able to get through to get to our table in

VIP. In addition to the spot being crowded, people were stopping Cam left and right, giving him condolences for his pops or praising his pops. It was appreciated, but it wasn't the time or the place. My nigga just wanted to chill and celebrate the journey he was about to embark on. As his right-hand man, I was gonna make sure he had a good time.

"Son, what bottles you want?" I yelled in his ear as we settled in our section.

"Get whatever."

I could tell by his voice that he wasn't really feeling being out. He was on edge since we now had beef with the Mexicans. I understood that and shit, but you couldn't stop living. I tried to tell him that we were gonna see them Mexicans. We were going to see Man and Matthew too. Them niggas were gonna get theirs, but in the meantime, we were celebrating the creation of life.

Fuck it. YOLO! I thought.

"Baby, I'll be right back," Ariana yelled before she walked down to the other section of the club.

I watched her every move until she caught up with some chick. I assumed she knew her by the way they hugged and were laughing. I tapped my pockets and remembered that I had a pound of kush and was ready to roll up. Time to get smacked. This nigga needed to cheer up.

"Yo, Cam. Roll up. I'ma go to the bar," I said as I handed him the fronto leaf and the bud so he could roll up while I went to order bottles.

I intended to go straight to the bar, but French Montana's "Freaks" came on just then and made me wanna rub up on some ass, so I set out in search of Ari. When I found her, she already knew what I was coming for. She walked over to me, turned around, and started grinding her ass on me. My dick got hard.

"Damn, Ari."

She was lucky we was in the club, because I felt like fucking her pussy up. When the song ended, I gave my shorty a kiss and left her chilling with her friend. As I got closer to the bar, I noticed six niggas standing around, sticking out like sore thumbs.

"Mexicans?" I said out loud to myself, in disbelief.

Suddenly, a burst of gunfire erupted, and the club went bananas. I had already pulled out my piece, so I was ready to bust back, but suddenly it felt like time had stopped and everything was moving slowly. I looked toward the VIP section, where I had left Cam, then toward the dance floor, where I had left Ariana. I had a choice to make: go to my brother, have his back, and make sure he was straight or get Ariana to safety.

I said a short prayer for Ariana as I maneuvered through the frantic crowd, trying to get to Cam. It was a hell of a task to dodge bullets and push through the crowd, but I had to make sure my brother was good. I ran backward at one point, letting off shots in the direction of the Mexican niggas.

"The fuck, man?" I yelled, as if someone could hear me over the screams and cries of those around me.

These niggas weren't letting up. I had to take cover for a second behind one of the booths to switch the used clip to a fresh one. Once I was good, I was up and on the move again.

Cam, where are you? I kept saying to myself.

Suddenly, the gunfire ceased, and the Mexicans ran out of the club as quickly as they had come in. I had made it to the VIP section by then. I caught sight of Cam.

"Nooo!" I yelled as I watched Cam choke on his own blood.

I fell to my knees next to him and tried to see where he'd been hit. I tried to stop the bleeding, but it was too much. He had been hit at least six times.

"Stay with me, fam," I told him. "We going to get you out of here."

Fuck the not crying thing, I thought frantically. That "be strong" shit went out the window. I gathered Cam in my arms and rocked my nigga back and forth and cried.

"You gonna be good, Cam."

It was not supposed to happen like this. I rarely called on God, because I felt I wasn't deserving after the shit I'd done, but I had to now.

"God, not him. He got a family he has to be here for and a baby on the way. Not Cam please."

I hoped God would help me out. *Do me this one solid!* I pleaded silently. A minute later, I decided I couldn't sit there waiting and hoping any longer. I got up and held Cam up by putting one of his arms around my shoulder.

"I got you, bro. Just stay with me."

I didn't know if he was conscious, but I wasn't giving up hope. By then, the club had cleared out dramatically, so I was able to get around more easily. Cam wasn't light, so I wasn't able to move as fast as I hoped, but I was moving. I spotted Ariana sitting on the floor, covered in blood and crying.

"Ariana!" I called out to her.

I watched as she tried to stand, but something wasn't right. She was holding her stomach, and blood was just leaking out. *Fuck!* She had been hit too. I couldn't just leave her. I made my way over to her, still holding Cam up. I pulled her up and held her the same way I was holding Cam, but on the other side of me.

"Y'all stay with me. I'm going to get y'all to the hospital. Just stay with me."

I heard Ariana's breaths. They were short and faint, but I heard them, and that was what mattered. Cam . . . not so much. I didn't care, though. I was getting them to the hospital. We finally made it to where I had parked my truck, and I put them in the backseat the best way I could without causing more injuries. Ariana was alert. She was crying out in pain.

"Relax, baby. You going to be okay. Do me a favor. Talk to Cam. It doesn't matter what you say. Just talk to him and keep yourself alert for me, Ma."

She did as I told her. I jumped in the front seat, started the truck, and sped off. I didn't give a fuck about getting pulled over. This was life or death.

I swerved into a parking spot in front of the emergency-room entrance of Bronx Lebanon Hospital. My truck was crooked, but that shit didn't matter. I jumped out of the truck and rushed inside, returned to my truck with doctors, got Ariana and Cam on gurneys, and had them rushed inside. I stood outside the entrance and tapped my pockets, looking for my phone, but the shit wasn't there. I walked back over to my whip and looked inside it, but my phone wasn't there, either.

Fuck, man. I needed to call Skye.

I walked into the emergency room, hoping that the nurse at the nurses' station would let me use the phone. After explaining to her that I needed to contact the family of the two people I had brought in, she let me use the phone. I called Ariana's parents' house; luckily, the number was easy as fuck to memorize, and I was able to remember it. After speaking to them, I had to call Skye.

Matt

Niggas had got lucky tonight. My little homie Chris had hit my jack when he spotted Cam and Ty pulling up to Sin City. I'd been happy as fuck. I'd been keeping it low ever since I found out Cam had put a price tag on my head. I didn't even know how those niggas had found out about me. Miguel had me staying at one of his spots in the city until the Cameron situation was handled. But after those niggas had rushed out of there with all that heat, I was sure the situation had been handled. It was my time, and I was ready to claim what had been rightfully mine from the beginning. Only thing was, now I planned on taking everything, even Cam's bitch.

Skye

I was on my way back to bed, after waking up to use the bathroom for the fourth time, when my phone started ringing. I knew it had to be Cameron or my parents, because no one else would be brave enough to call me at that hour. I sat on the edge of the bed and answered the phone.

"Hello?" I answered, clearing my voice a little.

The background noise was loud as fuck, but nobody said a word. I removed the phone from my ear and looked at it strangely. Then I noticed that the number on the screen was not associated with anyone in my phone book. I was pregnant, aggravated, and tired! I was in no mood for the bullshit.

I placed the phone against my ear again. "Hello!" This time I shouted.

"Sis . . ."

It sounded like Ty, but I couldn't really hear through the noise.

"Ty?" I questioned.

I listened as the guy breathed heavily into the phone, sounding as if he was jogging. The background noise seemed to have decreased. I figured the caller was moving around to find a better reception so we could hear each other.

"Sis!"

It was now clear to me that it was Ty. Why the hell was he calling me? He was probably calling from the club, so that was why it was so damn noisy.

"Yes, Ty? What happened?"

The line went quiet. It seemed as if the longer we sat on the phone in silence, the more I panicked.

"Tyquan!" I finally barked at him.

"They shot them, sis. They fucking shot them. We're at the hospital. This is bad. Ariana will be okay, but I don't think he going to make it. They shot my brother, sis. They fucking shot him!"

I knew that Ty was speaking, because I heard him, but as far as knowing what he was saying, I didn't have a clue. The moment he had said, "They shot them," everything had gone numb and my mind had gone blank.

Why was this happening? As if enough bad shit hadn't happened recently. I had to get to the hospital. I needed to see him. This had to be a dream.

"Skye, are you there?"

Physically, I was, but emotionally, I was somewhere else. I'd say in limbo, because if I lost Cameron . . .

"What hospital?" I asked frantically, trying to keep it together. For the sake of my child, I had to.

"Bronx Lebanon."

I hung up the phone. My brain was saying, *Get up and put on clothes*, but my body wouldn't listen. I could no longer suppress the urge to cry, and I exploded. I let out a piercing scream.

"Why is this happening?" What am I being punished for?" I yelled out loud, not taking into account that Victoria and Mariah were sleeping.

I cried, and I cried hard. In between sobs I prayed. He had to make it. The thought of bringing our baby into the world without Cameron made me break down. Mariah and Victoria ran through the bedroom door and rushed to my side. At that point I was crying and repeating, "Why Cameron?" Mariah began to panic as she tried to calm me down so that I could tell her what was going on.

The thing was, I didn't know what had happened. All I knew was that we had to get to Bronx Lebanon!

Victoria walked into Cameron's closet and came out with a pair of his sweats for me. I was still unable to move, but she did the best she could at helping me put them on. Everything was moving fast. I was dizzy and couldn't really focus. I fought with myself to get it together and told myself that I could do this. If I had learned anything from Cameron, I had learned how to be strong. In that moment something hit me: whether Cameron made it through this or not, I would never be the same. In addition to that, I vowed that whoever was responsible for causing all the havoc in our lives lately now had to deal with me. I stopped crying and got strength in knowing that I had to protect my baby, this family, and my man's organization by any means necessary.

After I got myself together, Mariah and Victoria threw on clothes, and we headed to the hospital. When we walked into the emergency room, a feeling came over me. I felt it right there. Cameron was gone. Although I had this feeling, I still found myself walking over to the nurses' station, then demanding to see him.

"I need to see Cameron Carter!" I yelled at the nurse.

I felt a little bad for being nasty with her, because this wasn't her fault, but I was in no mood to be apologizing. *Fuck that.*

"Ma'am, are you family?" the nurse asked.

Was this bitch serious? Would I be in the emergency room at three in the morning, tryin'a see a nigga who didn't mean shit to me?

"What room?" I asked, completely ignoring her question.

She sighed. I was sure she dealt with shit like this on a daily basis, and you would think she would be a bit more compassionate.

"I'll get his doctor."

I watched as the ugly-ass nurse went to get the doctor. I looked around for Mariah and Victoria and saw them sitting with Ty, who was covered in blood.

I began to move my feet and head in their direction, until I heard someone call my name.

"Skye!"

I turned in the direction of the voice and saw Ariana's parents. I felt like shit. There I was, so worried about Cameron that I hadn't even asked about my best friend, not even once. I justified this by telling myself I didn't ask, because Ty had said she was going to be all right. Deep down, I knew it was still fucked up. I walked over to Ariana's parents and hugged her mom. She looked as if she'd been crying for days. Her eyes were so puffy, they looked to be swollen shut. Her father looked as if he was hurting, but he was barely keeping it together for his wife's sake.

"How is she?" I managed to get out.

Her mother was still shaken up and couldn't answer me. I completely understood that. Her father, on the other hand, was able to explain to me her condition. I was relieved to know that she was expected to make a full recovery. Although I was extremely happy that she was going to be okay, I couldn't really show that, because I was still 100 percent worried about the fate of Cameron.

"Family of Cameron Carter?" I heard someone say.

I turned around as I felt my heart sink to the bottom of my stomach. Mariah was approaching the doctor. I jogged over and caught up with her just as she reached the doctor's side. She was fighting back tears, and it seemed as if she was unable to get out her words, so I spoke up.

"We are Cameron's family."

The doctor's demeanor instantly changed. Sorrow fell over his expression. I said a silent prayer for my baby, and for the families of the people whom I was personally going to put under the ground.

As the doctor began to move his lips, I heard, "We did all that we could. I'm sorry. After surgery he slipped into a coma. At this point it is up to him. All we can do is wish for the best."

Victoria

As the words left the doctor's lips, it seemed as if time started to move in slow motion. *A coma?* That was all that echoed in my head. I desperately wanted to go stand with my mother and Skye, but I couldn't budge. It felt as if I was confined to that space right there in that instant. I didn't flinch, whimper, or bawl . . . nothing. I watched as Ty hurried over to Skye right after she fell to the floor and burst into tears.

With each of her sobs, my heart seemed to break into more pieces. Would Cam wake up? What about the baby? What about my family? We had just lost our father. Was this really happening? My mind raced as I thought of all the possible outcomes of this situation. Even if Cam did wake up, if it didn't happen soon, he would surely have to live with serious disabilities. I shuddered at the thought of him having to live like that. No question, I'd take that over death. . . .

"Not my brother. This ain't how it's going to go for him." I spoke out loud to myself, not giving a fuck if anyone assumed I was crazy.

After moments of being incapable of moving, I was finally able to get up and lug my feet over to where my mother was still standing with Cam's doctor.

I caught the tail end of what the doctor was disclosing to her. "Mrs. Carter, we just have to be optimistic. I know he's a fighter. After suffering eight gunshot wounds, with the majority of them in exceedingly life-threatening locations, we are fortunate to have him here at all."

If this doctor called himself consoling my mother, he was doing a weak-ass job. I guessed we had to respect his honesty about the situation, but damn.

"I need to see my son," I heard my mother say, which caused me to look at her oddly.

She'd been through a lot lately, and I felt like seeing my brother in the shape he was in would send her over the edge.

"Sure, Mrs. Carter. I'll take you to see him. But just you please," the doctor told her.

Oh hell, nah. It's not going down like that, I thought to myself before I interrupted the conversation sooner than my mother could speak.

"I'm going with my mother. She shouldn't have to face seeing my brother like this alone," I declared.

I could tell by the look the doctor gave me that he understood. He signaled for us to follow him, and as we started after him, I glanced back at Skye, who was now sitting on a chair, with her head in her lap.

I didn't know what to expect when I walked into Cam's room, but I prepared myself for the worst. As I moved toward his bedside, my knees got weak and I had to grab onto my mother for support. We were actually supporting each other, as she had given me the impression that her knees were about to give out too. What made it look particularly bad was all the tubes and machines that were hooked up to him, and the bandages. If we were able to take away all those things he would have looked as if he was sleeping peacefully. But there was nothing peaceful about that sight. I felt my mother's hand slither from my grasp, and I observed as she stood alongside the bed and rubbed Cam's hand.

"Baby boy, you are the strongest person I know. You got that from your father. You have to make it through this. We need you, Cameron. Please! I love you, son," she exclaimed between sobs.

Listening to my mother speak to my brother caused my tears to start streaming again. I didn't even try to restrain them.

The ride home from the hospital was awfully quiet. I drove, while my mom spent the entire ride back to Long Island gazing out the window. Skye was in the backseat, weeping. I understood the hurt my mother was experiencing, because Cam was her son. I couldn't imagine how Skye felt, though. Her sorrow was not only for herself. I was sure it was for her unborn child as well.

When we finally reached the house, everyone was emotionally worn out. I personally just wanted to lock myself in my bedroom until someone awakened me from this nightmare that I knew I was having. However, I couldn't do that. Instead, I went into my bathroom to shower. I wanted to sleep in my mother's bed with my mother and Skye, but when I got out of the shower, Skye was already showered and in her own bed. I didn't want to disturb her, so I opted to lie down next to her instead. Falling asleep was nearly impossible, because Skye spent hours tossing, turning, and crying. When she finally fell asleep, I wasn't far behind.

Skye

I fought to open my eyes. Because of the amount of time I had spent crying, they were puffy and heavy. Once they were finally open, it took a moment for me to grow accustomed to the light. I looked over my shoulder, praying and yearning for Cameron to be next to me, but to my dismay, it was just Victoria. I sat up in the bed and let out a lengthy sigh. I wanted to crawl up in the bed and cry until I couldn't cry any longer. However, I didn't have time for that. I thought about my parents and knew that I needed to fill them in on what had transpired. I looked over at the nightstand, spotted my cell phone, and seized it.

I dialed my mother's cell phone and listened as it rang three times before she finally answered.

"Hey, love bug!"

I wished I was able to return my mother's enthusiasm. I just couldn't muster up the energy. "Hi, Mommy. I just called to let you know what's going on. Cameron was shot last night, and he's in a coma." I stopped there, not only to allow what I had said to resonate with my mother but also to compose myself. I didn't want to start crying while trying to explain what had happened.

After her gasp from the initial shock of the news, she listened attentively as I told her about what had gone down at the club and about Cameron's present condition.

"Skye, I'm so sorry. How are you holding up? Mariah and Victoria as well? I really can't believe this has happened. Wow . . . Listen, I'm on my way to you," she stated, sounding just as sad as I was.

My mother had grown fond of Cameron, and although they didn't get to see each other often, they maintained an open line of communication, just as I had with Mariah before I came to staying with her and Vic. So I already knew my mother would be ready to come to me, but I had other things on my agenda.

"We are all as good as we can be at this point. And no, Mom, it's okay. You don't have to come out here. I'm about to head to the hospital. I'll keep you informed," I whispered, on the verge of crying.

We spoke for an additional minute or two before wrapping up our conversation. I laid down my phone and tried to mentally prepare myself for everything I needed to do today. I was ready to get up to start my day when my phone started ringing. I entertained the idea of ignoring the call, but to be sure it wasn't someone calling to update me on Cameron's condition, I looked at the screen. Good thing I did, because it was Ty. Our conversation was brief; he just gave me a heads-up that he was fifteen minutes away from the house. He was coming by to take us to the hospital. Ty didn't miss a beat, and that was something I really admired about him. He was really Cameron's right-hand, and he had shown how loyal he was since the day I met him.

After hanging up from Ty, I headed into the bathroom to wash my face and brush my teeth. When I returned to the bedroom, I looked through my things for something to wear. Getting dressed up wasn't an option today, so I slipped on a Victoria's Secret Pink sweat suit and a pair of Uggs. As I was slipping on my last boot, Victoria woke up.

"You okay, sis?" was the first thing she said as she sat up.

"I'm straight," I lied. Straight was the furthest from what I was, but I had to keep it together. "Ty will be here soon to take us to the hospital. I'm sure your mother is already up and dressed, so brush your teeth and stuff and get dressed."

I grabbed my cell phone and walked out of the bedroom, leaving Victoria to her thoughts. My intention wasn't to be rude, but I had a lot on my mind. As I was headed to the steps to go downstairs, Mariah was coming out of her bedroom.

She stopped in front me and embraced me. "It's going to be okay, Skye. We have each other."

I forced a smile on my face. "Yes, I know. Ty is on his way to take us to the hospital, and Victoria is getting ready. I'm going to wait outside for him to come."

I walked down the stairs and into the foyer, grabbed my coat off the rack, and walked outside. It was a typical December day in terms of the weather; it was freezing cold. Normally, I would have backpedaled back into the house to shield myself from the cold, but it was different on this day. The temperature didn't faze me, because I was numb. I paced back and forth as I went over my to-do list in my head. I was going over what I wanted to say to Ty when I saw his truck come to a complete stop in front of the house. I walked over and jumped in the passenger seat. There was no need for me to waste time, so I jumped right into what I had on my mind.

"Ty, hear me out. You're probably not going to like what I'm going to tell you, but this is how it's going down." I stopped long enough to make sure that I had his undivided attention. It was clear that I did, so I continued. "I want in. This organization is going to survive, and everyone responsible for us being in this predicament is going to pay."

I could tell he was confused as to exactly what I was telling him. There really was no other way I could explain it.

I went on. "I'm coming to you because you're Cameron's ace and I need guidance. This is new territory for me, but I'm capable. I'm not asking for your permission. This is basically a 'get down or lay down' moment." My last statement caught his attention, and he was finally ready to speak.

He said, "First off, not going to happen—"

I interrupted him. "Again, I'm not asking for your permission."

He shook his head from side to side and said, "Skye, I get it. You want revenge, and that's fine. But that is why Cam has a team. He got plenty of niggas ready to catch bodies over this shit. Let's not forget you're pregnant. Ain't no place in this business for you."

At that point I was pissed, and I let that seep through my tone as I continued to present my case. "Ty, if you don't want to have anything to do with what I have planned, that is fine. I'm just letting you know it's going to happen with or without you."

Ty had me fucked up. I was coming to him before I made a move off the strength of him being Cameron's best friend. I was a grown-ass woman, and I didn't need his permission to carry out my plans. I could sense that he wanted to continue the debate, but Mariah and Victoria were headed toward the truck. They had good timing, because I was tired of hearing Ty tell me what I wasn't going to do or where my place was. The worst thing a person could do was underestimate me, and I saw Ty was going to have to learn that I was extremely capable by me showing him that, since telling him was clearly not enough.

Ty

As I drove to the hospital, I couldn't stop thinking about the shit Skye had come at me with. Shit was a no-brainer with regard to whether I would let her go through with her plan or not, but she wasn't backing down. I was left with deciding whether or not to assist her or let her do the shit on her own. Either way, Cam would flip, but I figured it would be better if I was there to protect her and the baby any way I could, versus letting her fend for herself.

That was the moment I decided that regardless of the decisions Skye made, if I couldn't change her mind about them, I would just have to suck it up and roll with it. My loyalty to Cam extended to his girl and to his family as well. Before anything, I really needed to get her alone so we could discuss this shit further. I wasn't going to let Skye make decisions based on her emotions; that was the fastest way to find yourself in a fucked-up predicament.

As I pulled into a spot in the hospital's parking lot, I pushed those thoughts to the back of my mind. Right now I had to find the strength to get through seeing my nigga laid up in this hospital. Minutes passed after I shut off the engine in my truck, and still no one had attempted to make a move. So I knew I wasn't the only one who was dreading that we had to do this, but the thing was, we had to do it. I was about to get out of the truck when Skye started speaking.

"Mariah, I'm not Cameron's wife, so I can't make any decisions about his medical care."

I looked over at Skye. I didn't know where her speech was headed, but if she was about to fix her mouth to say some dumb shit, like "Take him off the machines," shit was going to get ugly in this parking lot. I didn't want to jump to any conclusions, so I sat back and let her continue.

"You are his mother, and I don't want to seem as if I'm stepping on your toes in any way, but I would like for you to consider having Cameron airlifted to another facility."

That shit caught me off guard. Where the fuck did that idea even stem from? I turned around and looked at Mama Mariah, and I saw confusion all over her face. If she didn't want to ask, I definitely would.

"Why, Skye?" I asked, focusing my attention back on her.

"Well, I'm glad you asked. Whoever tried to kill Cameron isn't going to stop once they find out he didn't die," she explained. "He's safer away from here, in a location that only we know of. My father's parents are doctors in Miami, and I'm sure they wouldn't mind signing off on any necessary paperwork to get him transferred. Victoria and Mariah would be relocating for the time being as well. So much is going on, and I want to keep you both safe, so I think it's best. You don't have to worry about the cost. I'm willing to pay all costs, including of the airlift and the hospital care. I just want him out of New York."

That shit made sense. Skye didn't know it was the Mexicans who were behind the hit, but she was right about one thing: those crazy motherfuckers definitely would not stop. I may not have agreed with what we had spoken about earlier, but the idea of moving Cam, I supported. Ultimately, it was up to his mother, though. We sat in silence, until Mama Mariah spoke.

"I can't argue with that, Skye. I can tell you care a great deal about my son and his family. However, you failed to mention you and my unborn grandchild in these plans."

Skye unsnapped her seat belt and turned to look at Mariah and Victoria in the backseat. Then she said, "Mariah, the baby and I will be fine. I promise you that. I have plans to go to Miami, but I will be back and forth due to the fact that my parents are here."

I knew what she had said was bullshit; she was not going to remain in Miami for the duration because she wanted to be in New York with her parents, but because in her mind, she needed to handle Cam's business. I couldn't front, though. My respect for Skye was growing by the minute. She talked a good game, and I hoped her actions backed that shit up. In this life, talking about shit only got you so far.

Skye

After explaining to Mariah my plans to have Cameron transferred to Miami, we headed into the hospital to see him. I couldn't really focus on much; my mind raced from one thing to the next. I knew I was taking on a lot of responsibilities, but regardless of how many things I took on, taking care of myself so that I'd give birth to a healthy baby would always be my priority. Everything else was secondary.

They allowed only two people into Cameron's room at a time, and I just wasn't ready. I needed a little more time to brace myself for what I would see. Mariah wanted to speak with his doctor, so Ty and Victoria went in to see Cameron first. I found a seat in the waiting area and sat down. As time passed, I started fidgeting and growing restless. Ty and Victoria hadn't returned from Cameron's room yet, so I went to visit Ariana. I walked into her room to find her sitting up in bed, staring at the TV, seemingly engulfed in the story being reported on the news. She didn't realize I was there until I was damn near close enough to touch her. I knew something other than the news report was on her mind. I was used to her always being alert, but now she seemed a bit distant.

"That news anchor must be announcing a sale at Saks or something, the way you stuck on the TV," I joked to get her attention.

"*Chica*, it's so nice to see you!" Ariana squealed as I bent down and hugged her.

I smiled. "How are you feeling, Ari?"

Her shoulders dropped a little, and her demeanor changed. "I've been better. I'm alive, though, so I'm grateful for that. How is Cam?"

Thinking about his condition saddened me. I wanted to change the subject. For some reason, I was dealing with the situation by just avoiding it altogether, which was why I still hadn't been to see him. She deserved to know what was going on, though.

"He's in a coma," I revealed.

I watched the look on Ariana's face: it went from shocked to confused to hurt in a matter of seconds. She looked at me as tears welled up in her eyes.

"I'm so sorry, Skye. I feel like this is all my fault," she said. I was interested to know what she was referring to, so I took a seat on the chair that was beside her bed.

"Sorry for what? What do you mean, it's all your fault?" I was totally confused.

I shifted in my seat as I listened to Ariana tell me about what had happened when she went out with Man that night after her shift at the radio station. Not only did I not know about her having drinks with someone that night—which was shocking, because we shared every-thing—but I also didn't even have a clue that she had an ex named Man. I felt a burning sensation throughout my body. I was furious, and I tried to suppress that feeling, but I couldn't.

"What the fuck!" I screamed as I stood up and slapped Ariana across the face. She was shocked. Shit, I was shocked myself. She grabbed the side of her face, her mouth still wide open in awe. I wasn't moved by that, so I continued to scream. "How dare you keep some-thing so important to yourself? Do you see where we are because of this beef with Man? Come on, Ari. I would have never kept something like that from you. We sup-posed to be girls."

Still shocked, Ariana said nothing.

I felt my anger start to surge again, and I knew that this time my actions could be much worse than a slap on the face. I wasn't trying to go there again, and I didn't want to stick around and listen to her tell me excuse after excuse as to why she hadn't shared the information she'd gathered that night, so I left the hospital. I didn't even go see Cameron. I blamed it on my anger at Ariana, but I knew it was more complicated than that. I just wasn't ready.

The good that came out of that hospital visit was that Ariana's revelation helped me realize how much I needed to solidify my plans and put them into action.

Ariana

Still in complete and utter shock, I watched Skye storm out of my hospital room. We'd had our share of disagreements throughout the years, but never had she put her hands on me. I had never done that to her, either. I didn't know what bothered me more: the fact that she had had the audacity to hit me or the fact that it was over a dude. I got that Cam's condition was touch and go, and I sympathized with that, but Skye and I had been girls for far too long to let this situation determine the fate of our friendship.

Then there was Ty. . . . The thought of him caused butterflies to flutter in my stomach. I slowly rubbed my belly, which up until last night was home to the baby Ty and I had lost. Last night the doctor had told me I lost a fetus, one that I had had no knowledge of. I had been doing the best I could since receiving this news to push to the back of my mind thoughts of what could have been and what no longer existed. Seeing as I didn't know how angry Skye still was at me, I couldn't predict her actions. I didn't know if she was going to tell Ty what I had revealed to her. What I did know was that if she did tell him, I would lose him as well.

I didn't know how I would ever get Skye to see that I hadn't kept the information from her or Cam to be malicious. It had been an honest mistake. And although I knew our friendship was worth too much to toss it away like trash because of this, I wasn't going to tolerate her putting her hands on me. I wasn't quite over that, and I didn't think I would be until I confronted her about it. I understood that she was experiencing a host of different emotions, but she had to have some self-control.

I was now beginning my own emotional roller-coaster ride, a ride that I had been trying to avoid at all costs. I had lost my baby, I was losing my best friend, and chances were, I would lose my boyfriend. I hadn't shed a tear since I felt the first bullet penetrate my rib cage, but I was overwhelmed with emotion now. I could no longer suppress the cries that threatened to escape, and I didn't try.

Skye

When I got home from the hospital, I was unable to make it past the living room. I was physically and emotionally exhausted, and I just needed a minute. I couldn't seem to wrap my head around how my life had changed so drastically in just a matter of months. I never would have envisioned myself being in a situation like this, but there I was. As if dealing with Cameron being in a coma wasn't enough, I now had to deal with the fact that Ariana had known about Man and Max's relationship but had decided to withhold that information for whatever reason.

I could have spent days trying to sift through my thoughts and all the events that had taken place to date, but what good would that have done? At this point all I could do was suck it up, put my big girl panties on, and thug through it. Remembering that I had left the hospital without giving Mariah, Ty, or Victoria a heads-up, I decided to send them a mass text. The last thing I wanted to do was leave them worrying about my well-being.

Hey, guys. Just letting y'all know I left the hospital and I'm okay. I just need some time to deal with my emotions. I'll be in touch.

After getting that out of the way, I decided to call my mother. I didn't know how I would get her to agree with what I planned on asking her, but I had to try. Her cooperation or lack thereof would ultimately determine how my plans played out. I needed her to give me my maternal grandfather's contact information. It was a long shot, and I knew that it would be like pulling teeth.

When I got my mother on the phone and explained what I needed, naturally, she was curious. I did my best to convince her that I just wanted to reach out to my grandfather so that I had as much support from my family as possible to help me through such a trying time. The timing of my request made her suspicious, and it took a lot of convincing for her to cave in, but ultimately she did. I was ready to set my plans in motion.

My maternal grandfather, Andreas "Poppy" Santiago, was the boss of one of the most powerful crime rings coming out of Central America—Panama, to be exact. When my mother was born, my grandmother gave my grandfather an ultimatum. He was to put the life of crime behind him or lose his family. Like most that lived that life, he found that it was not that easy to just give up his criminal endeavors. So one night my grandmother packed up and left with my mother and never contacted him again. She wanted to protect my mother from the very things I found myself experiencing, even if it meant she had to struggle. As far I knew, my grandfather tried to be in my mother's life, but my grandmother wasn't having it. Since my mother hadn't had a relationship with my grandfather, neither had I. But that was about to change.

I sat on the edge of the bed, glaring at my cell phone screen. All I had to do was press CALL, but I didn't even know where to begin. There I was, about to call on a man I had never even met, and for something so serious. I couldn't dwell too much on the fact that we had never met. At the end of the day, we were family, and either he was going to help me or he wasn't.

"Fuck it!" I declared out loud as I pressed CALL.

I listened as the phone rang, and after the third ring, I heard a smooth baritone voice say, "Who is this?"

My words got caught in my throat as I struggled to answer. "Hello. This is Skye. Am I spea—"

"*Nieta!*" he yelled, cutting me off.

My Spanish was a little rusty, but I was almost sure that *nieta* was the Spanish word for "granddaughter." Before I could answer, he continued to speak.

"To what do I owe the pleasure? Is everything okay with your mother? Is something wrong?" he asked, sounding extremely concerned.

"My mother is fine. I need to see you!" I didn't waste any time letting him know my sole purpose for calling.

"I would love that. When should I send for you?" he inquired.

"Today!"

I was taken aback when he didn't raise any objections but instead told me to give him a few minutes to get my itinerary in order and he would get back to me. Instead of sitting around, waiting for his call, I got up and packed. By the time I was done packing, my grandfather had called me back and had told me to head to JFK.

Skye

As I stepped off the plane in Colón, Panama, I felt a wave of nervousness invade my body. There I was, about to meet my grandfather for the first time and under such circumstances. I really didn't know how he would react to my proposition, but it was the only card I had to play at the time. I was doing what needed to be done. We needed a connect, and I needed someone other than Ty on my team whom I could trust. My grandfather was a businessman, and I was there on business.

After grabbing my bags and asking for directions, I headed to the parking lot, where my grandfather had promised a car would be waiting for me. I instantly spotted a short woman, who looked to be in her late forties, standing next to a black Yukon. As I got closer to the woman, I realized she was holding a sign that said SKYE. I swallowed my nervousness.

"It's now or never," I said in a low voice as I sauntered up to her.

She said, "You must be Skye. You're beautiful. You look so much like your grandfather. I'm Marisol." She spoke with a heavy Spanish accent.

"Thank you, ma'am." I smiled and hugged her.

She introduced me to the man that stood beside her, holding a back car door open. His name was Hector, and apparently, he would be my driver and security for the duration of my trip. That was cool and all, but I didn't have any plans to go anywhere. I was there for a sole purpose. Yes, I wanted to get to know my grandfather, but there were more pressing things that needed to be done. I handed Hector my bags and shook his hand before climbing into the back of the Yukon. Once my bags were stowed, Hector got behind the wheel and Marisol hopped in the front passenger seat.

Off we went, and twenty minutes later the car came to a complete stop in front of a beautiful villa. What made it appear more eye-catching to me was the vibrant Caribbean landscaping. As we exited the car and headed toward the entrance to the home, I took in the scenery. I could get used to this place. It was so serene. It was too bad I wasn't there on vacation. Maybe once everything blew over and was back to normal, I could bring Cameron and the baby here. Marisol gave me a quick tour of the villa. It was fabulous, from the stylish interior design to the amazing views of the turquoise waters of the Caribbean Sea. And the beach access had me. I was in house heaven.

"Skye!" Marisol called out to me, pulling me away from admiring the view of the beach.

"Yes, Marisol?" I turned to her, smiling.

"Your grandfather should be arriving any minute. Hector has put your bags in the master bedroom. Is there anything else you need at the moment?"

"What do you mean, he will be arriving? Where is he?" I was confused.

"He is coming from his home. This one here is yours, but he has countless properties. The moment you called and said you wanted to visit, he sent people to prepare this villa for you," she explained.

Why would this man have a house for me? He didn't know me from Eve. Before I could respond, there was movement in the front of the house, which immediately got Marisol's and my attention. I followed behind

Marisol and came face-to-face with my grandfather in the foyer. I knew it was him; my mother was the spitting image of him, and I was the spitting image of him as well. He stood about six feet tall and had almond-colored skin, small beady brown eyes, and long coolie hair that flowed freely past his shoulders. If I was correct, he was pushing sixty, but you sure couldn't tell that by looking at him. I saw good genes ran deep in my blood.

"*Nieta!*" he yelled, pulling me into an embrace.

"Hello, Grandfather." I smiled, taking in his scent. I knew the fragrance all too well. It was Guilty by Gucci, one of Cameron's favorites. I let out a sigh, thinking about him. I missed him so much.

"What's wrong? And please, call me Poppy or Pop-Pop. Grandfather sounds old." He chuckled.

We walked into the living room and sat down. He wasted no time bombarding me with questions. It felt as if he was trying to learn my entire life story right then. I didn't mind. I was happy to see that he was embracing me and really wanted to know who I was. I wanted the same thing. I always had. But I just couldn't focus on that right now. For one, I had to focus on the business at hand and then get back to the States as soon as possible. Cameron's condition could change at any second, and I would never forgive myself if I wasn't there for the change, whether it be good or bad.

After a few hours of talking and bonding, we sat down at the table in the kitchen to eat the delicious food that Marisol had prepared. She and Hector left Pop-Pop and me alone to talk. I felt it was time to mention why I was there.

"Grandfa . . . Pop-Pop," I said, catching myself.

He looked up from his food and grinned. "Yes?"

"I must tell you why I am here."

He looked at me as if his interest had been piqued. I took a deep breath before telling him everything, from the moment I met Cameron to the moment I found myself at this villa. I could tell from the expression on his face that he was digesting everything I told him, but I didn't stop there. I was on a roll, and I wanted him to know exactly where I was coming from before he decided to help me out or turn me down.

"I understand if you don't want to help me, but understand this. I'm not looking for handouts. I need to provide Cameron's men with work, and you got it. I'm willing to pay whatever your people pay. I don't want special treatment. If you are hesitant because you are my grandfather, I understand that as well. However, you should know that I will seek what I need from someone else. I came to you first because you are my blood, I know that I can trust you, and I know that you wouldn't steer me wrong."

He observed me intensely as I continued my speech. Once I was done, I sat back in my chair and sighed, feeling a bit of relief. I felt like a weight had been lifted off my shoulders. I had done a good job presenting my case, or at least I thought so. The ball was in his court now.

He smiled and sat up straight before speaking. "I admire your reasons for coming to me. It's very hard to find a woman who is willing to go down this road for their spouse. Cameron is a lucky man. I'm aware that you are new to this life that you find yourself entangled in, but I'm also aware that it is in your blood. I'll help you, if you do it my way. I get that you don't want special treatment, but it is my job to ensure the safety of you and your child. I will do that, but you must follow my instructions, Skye. That is the only way this will work."

I had to think about that. I mean, I knew his intentions were good and his heart was in the right place, but what I didn't know was whether following his rules would work for me. Those thoughts quickly passed. Who was I kidding? I didn't know shit about this life, and if following his rules would teach me everything I needed to know, then his rules it would be.

"Okay, Pop-Pop. Your rules," I said, surrendering, returning his stare.

He smirked. "I'm going to tell you what your great-grandfather used to tell me. While seeking revenge, dig two graves, one for yourself. He got that quote from Douglas Horton. My reason for telling you that is to get you to understand. I'm not allowing you to set out on a path of revenge. If you are taking on Cameron's business, you are taking on his enemies. They are now your enemies, and you're free to handle them accordingly, but to go into this with revenge on your mind would only put you in a bad position."

I nodded, completely understanding what he was saying, but at the same time plotting the death of each of the people who had wronged Cameron.

Ty

I was really starting to worry about Skye. I hadn't seen or heard from her since she hit me up that day when she left the hospital. I knew how badly she had wanted to see Cam, and I really couldn't see her leaving the hospital without seeing him for no weak-ass reason, like needing time to clear her head. It had been days, and still no word from her. I wouldn't be able to live with myself if something had happened to shorty. How the fuck would I explain that to Cam when he woke up? In the meantime, I kept myself busy by touching base with the other dudes on my team. I had to keep them calm. Work was getting scarcer, so they were starting to sweat.

Between speculating about what Skye was up to and handling business, I still made time to see Cam and check on Ariana too. She had got hit in her stomach, but no major organs had been struck, so she was good. I was thankful for that, because I couldn't even think about how I would manage if she was in the same condition as Cam or worse. One thing was for sure. Being in them streets was becoming a constant struggle. I had never had to worry before about where my next re-up was coming from. But my back was against the wall now. At this point, I had no choice but to go out on a limb and fuck with Skye and her plan, whatever that may be. What other choices did I have? I mean, yeah, it would be easier to just go out and find a new connect, but I would never jump ship like that. For one, I respected the game, and two, I respected my brother, Cam.

I hadn't really had the chance to discuss Skye's plans in detail with her, so I had no clue how shit would unfold, but I was looking forward to it.

Skye

I had been in Panama for three weeks, and it hadn't been a vacation in the least bit. Pop-Pop was adamant about sending me home fully equipped with a broader knowledge of the game. He schooled me from sunup to sundown. I felt like the little bit of sleep he did allow me to get was due to the fact that he knew I needed rest for the baby's sake. I couldn't complain, though, because the more time I spent with him, the more I became comfortable with my new position. He taught me how to shoot and told me everything I needed to know about white girl. I soaked that shit up like a sponge. There was no room for error in this business. The past few months I'd seen minor errors cause a few men's demise, and I wasn't going that route.

I spent the rest of my time in Panama with Pop-Pop, up at his estate. I had to be available at all times during my training phase. It was cool, though. I enjoyed being there. Aside from schooling me and making sure I saw a doctor, he spoiled me, and so did everyone who worked for him. I was starting to get used to it, and the day I was scheduled to return to the States came faster than I wanted.

"Princess!" Pop-Pop called, pulling me away from packing my clothes.

I looked up at him as he stood in the bedroom doorway. "Yes, Pop-Pop?"

"There are a few things I want to go over with you before I send you home," he said, walking toward me and taking a seat next to me on the bed. I stopped packing my clothes and gave him my undivided attention. "I know that you feel you can trust Cameron's best friend, and that is fine. However, your life is in my hands, so I would like to provide you with your own protection. Someone I trust wholeheartedly."

That didn't sound like a bad idea. I would never stop dealing with Ty, because he had proved himself to be loyal, but I didn't mind the extra muscle, especially if it was family.

"Who do you have in mind?" I asked.

"Hector, of course," he replied matter-of-factly.

I was cool with taking Hector. During the time I'd been with him here, I'd seen the type of man he was. Hector was definitely more than a driver and seemed to have no bounds in terms of how far he would go for my grandfather. I was sure having him around 24/7 would be beneficial, so I didn't have a problem with that at all.

"Okay. When can I expect him?" I asked, not expecting him to be heading back with me. Of course my grandfather had other plans.

"Hector will be leaving with you today," he responded.

I nodded at his statement. I realized that few things rattled me anymore. I had come to Panama very timid when it came to the game, but I was going back as a force to be reckoned with.

"You will have product waiting when you touch down. Hector will handle the pickup, but it's up to you to get it off. Do you understand me?" His tone was serious.

"Yes, Pop-Pop." I was wrong to think that this was the end of the conversation, because he went on.

"My understanding is that you have some buyers already. I assume they're clients of Cameron, which is good. I have a guy who was just down here a few weeks back, trying to work for me. He's from New York as well.

Jeff, I think his name was. I'll reach out to him to see if he still needs product. If so, you'll have another buyer."

Hearing the name Jeff sent alarm bells ringing in my head. That was Ty's father's name. I remembered Cameron saying he was in Panama, handling business. Was the world that small? If it was, I was thankful for that. I'd been thinking about how I would get to Jeff, and now my grandfather had just sealed his fate, and he didn't even know it.

I looked over at my grandfather, then smiled and hugged him. "That would be cool, Pop-Pop. Thank you for everything. I promise I will not let you down."

"I know you won't," he said before he got up and walked out of the room.

I went back to packing my things and prepping for the flight Hector and I would take later that day.

Matthew

I had fucked up when I thought all my problems would cease to exist once Cam was dealt with. For starters, Miguel and his team of hitters had lit the club up but hadn't even killed the nigga. Miguel didn't know how shit went in the hood, but I knew for a fact that if Cam was dead, the news would have been broadcast throughout the hood. All I could do was speculate on his condition and his whereabouts, but I knew he wasn't dead. He was probably lurking, waiting for his opportunity to strike back. I found comfort in knowing that he wouldn't show his face now that he knew the Mexicans wanted his head. I still had a chance to attain the crown. It wouldn't be an easy fight, but it was one I wasn't backing down from.

I had started to feel like fucking with them Mexicans was not a good idea. Like I had for most of my life, I was still living in Cam's shadow, and the nigga wasn't even in the picture. Instead of Miguel setting me up to do my own thing, he expected me to walk in Cam's shoes. I mean, it didn't really sound like a bad idea, but the problem was them young boys that worked for Cam ain't trying to fuck with nobody else. So there I was, stuck with a ton of work and struggling to get the shit off. A nigga even had to start traveling out of town to push the work, but even that shit wasn't working. I was spending more money trying to sell than I was actually making.

If something didn't give soon, I would have to add beef with the Mexicans to my list, and I wasn't trying to take that road. I was starting to feel like I had bitten off more than I could chew. Even if that was the case, I wasn't about to fold. I had started with one goal in mind, which was to be *that* nigga, and I wasn't stopping until I got there.

The past few days I'd been in Atlanta, handling a few business deals. I still had niggas out in the A to supply, but they were small time, and the amounts they were buying didn't even put a dent in the amount of product I had overall. It was becoming clear that tryin'a pull this off as a one-man show was no longer working. It was time for me to use my resources, the very few I had.

I sat in my whip outside my mom's house. I had just dropped her some money, like I did every time I was in town. As I thought about my next move, I found myself reaching for my phone and hitting Man. I didn't realize what I was doing until I heard his voice, along with Jay-Z's song "Tom Ford," blasting through the phone.

"What up, nigga?" Man asked before telling whoever was with him to turn the music down.

"Ain't shit, boy. What you up to?" I needed to see where his head was at before I stepped to him about joining my efforts.

"I'm in Connecticut now. I had to handle some family shit. I'm headed back to the hood tonight, though. You got any word on your boy?"

His question threw me off. I knew who he was referring to, but if anyone knew anything about Cam's where-abouts, it would be him.

"Nah. I know that nigga ain't dead, though," I replied, keeping it short since we were on the phone.

"Yeah, yeah. I feel you on that, but yo, we need to link up and shit." He must have sensed there was a lot more I wanted to say on the Cam topic.

I lit the blunt that I had rolled just before I left my mom's crib, and took a pull. "I couldn't agree more. I'm flying out in the morning, so I'll hit your jack when I touch down," I said, then took another pull.

"A'ight, boy. Stay up," Man said before ending the call.

I knew shit was going to get better. Man and I had a common enemy, and neither of us was afraid of going to war. Shit was about to get real, and I was ready.

Man

"Who was that?" The annoying female voice in my ear reminded me where I was and what I was doing.

"Bitch, chill. Why you so interested in my phone conversation? You pay my bill?" I barked.

There was nothing more annoying than a nagging bitch. I dealt with shorty only for the reason that she had access to things and people that I needed. If she wasn't whining about being in pain, she was nagging me about where I was going and whom I was with. I should have left her ass back in New York. I looked over at shorty and gave her an ice grill. I was silently daring her to say something stupid. She realized I wasn't in the mood for her shit, reached for the volume, and turned the music back up.

As she drove to the destination the GPS was directing her to, I thought back to the conversation I had had with Matt. I knew that nigga Cam wasn't dead, but I also knew it would be almost impossible to get to him now. At this juncture, I had a few ways of handling this matter, but I had to play my cards right on each of the leads. I no longer had an inside man, so my task had become a little harder. I wasn't sweating it, though. I had a nice number of niggas on my team who was ready to strap up and put in work.

That thought alone excited me. I lived for shit like this, the excitement of it all, and putting in work was what kept me going. I couldn't wait to get back to New York. After I got done with Cam's crew, that nigga would be sure to show his face. I knew the type of nigga he was. Him trying to be a hero and everybody's savior was going to be his downfall, that was for sure.

To think that just last year I'd been cool with the nigga. We hadn't been the best of friends, but he'd respected my space and I'd respected his. But then his pops had decided he wanted to expand into my territory. I was a businessman, so I'd seen that as a win-win for us all. Shit, Hassan had been moving major weight and had had an army behind him. I would have been a dumb nigga not to want to join that movement. I was ready! Hassan was feeling himself, though. Nigga felt like he didn't need me. He moved his boys in on my blocks, started taking food out of my mouth. That shit didn't sit well with me, and because of that, they all had to pay the ultimate price.

The shit with the Mexicans wasn't my beef, but when it came to wiping out those niggas, the more the merrier. The Mexicans gunning for the same group of people only helped my efforts. I was ready to get back to the hood, and niggas was about to see just how much Man was capable of. All I wanted to do was eat good and have all my boys eating too. I didn't think that was too much to ask for. It was cool, though. The sleeping beast was now alive and kicking. Ready to devour any and everybody who got in my way.

Skye

The first few days I was back in New York, I didn't reach out to anyone. I spent most of my time running around with Hector. He too was making sure I was prepared for everything. He took his time showing me how my product would arrive in the States, and he introduced me to key players in my grandfather's operation, namely, the ones that were located in New York, since they were who I would be dealing with. When I wasn't doing that, I was creeping up to the hospital to see Cameron. I had to creep because I wasn't trying to see his mother, Vic, or Ty, and I was lucky that I didn't. I wasn't ready to face the music about me disappearing.

Pop-Pop had a crib in Staten Island, and I had moved into it, following his orders. He felt too many people knew where I usually rested my head, and that wasn't going to work for him. I didn't mind that. I needed the space, anyway, now that I had a houseguest.

I was in the middle of stuffing my face one afternoon when my cell phone started ringing. At first I didn't budge, because, like I'd been doing since I got back from Panama, I was going to ignore the call. However, I suddenly figured it was time for me to come out of hiding, so I picked up my phone and glanced at the screen. Seeing that it was Victoria calling, I answered.

"Hey, Vic," I said, as if everything was all good.

"Don't 'Hey, Vic' me!" she bellowed into the phone. "Where the fuck have you been, sis! My mother and I been worried sick about you and the baby."

I felt bad. I knew how extremely close Mariah felt to her unborn grandchild, and it was selfish and unfair of me to just disappear like that. The visit to my grandfather's had been imperative, though, but I hadn't felt any of them would really understand that. So I'd opted out of discussing it with anyone.

"I'm sorry, little sis. I just needed time to get my head together," I replied. I paused for a moment. "You okay? Your mom okay?" I questioned.

"We're fine. Where are you? I went by your house and everything. Mom got the doctors to approve Cam's transfer, and now they need the paperwork from the hospital in Miami and the payment. She was going to cover it, but . . . I'll tell you when I see you," she said.

"I wish the damn doctors had told me that while I was up there. I could have had it all handled on the spot."

"You went up there?" she asked, as if me going to see Cameron was shocking.

As if the answer to her question was obvious, I said, "Of course I did!"

We spoke for a little bit more, and I promised her that I would stop by their house later on that day. I had to get with Ty. It was time for me to get rid of the work Hector had picked up two days ago. So after hanging up with Victoria, I immediately called Ty to set up a meeting. He was upset that I hadn't reached out. I had expected that. But once he calmed down, I talked him into meeting with me. I didn't have a chance to tell him what our meeting would be about, because we were on the phone, but I was sure he would be pleasantly surprised when he found out. We arranged to meet at my place in the city in two hours.

As I sat in the living room of my grandfather's Staten Island crib, I spent the next half hour mulling over what I would say to Ty when we met. Glancing casually at my Rolex, I realized that the minutes had flown by and that it was about time to head out.

"Hector, we need to be heading out now," I called, taking Hector away from cleaning his gun in the kitchen. It was his favorite thing to do in his downtime.

"I'm ready when you are, Ms. Skye," he answered.

I hated when he called me Ms. Skye. Yeah, he worked for me, but Ms. Skye made me feel extremely old. As I slipped on my coat, I thought about how things were going to be from now on. I was ready.

When Hector pulled up to my building, I spotted Ty's truck right away. I knew he would be on time. That was one thing I could always count on when it came to him. My grandfather had schooled me on the importance of being on time in this business, but I already knew that from watching Cam and Ty. I jumped out of the passenger side of my car and walked over to Ty's truck and tapped on the window.

"Wassup, little sis?" he said, smiling, as he stepped out of the truck.

"Nothing much, bro. Come on," I told him as Hector got out of the car.

I turned around and walked toward the entrance to my building, with both Hector and Ty on my heels. While we were all on the elevator, I felt this weird energy radiating off of Ty. I was sure it was because he was trying to figure out who Hector was and, more importantly, why he was with me. Hector was there to serve a sole purpose, which was to protect me, and that was why he didn't even acknowledge Ty as we stood in the elevator. He wouldn't do so until I properly introduced them. I planned on doing that, just not during our elevator ride. Both Ty and Hector had to endure the tension for a minute.

When we got inside my place, the guys headed into the living room to get comfortable, and I headed to the kitchen for an apple and a bottle of water. Even though I had just finished eating, the baby wanted more. The apple had to suffice until I could get some real food into my system. I walked into the living room, joining the guys, took a seat on my La-Z-Boy, and took a bite out of my apple.

"Ty, this is Hector. He works for me." I knew my introduction was weak, but I had learned from my grandfather never to offer too much information. Hector's position and how I had met him were irrelevant at this point in time.

I could tell Ty was curious but decided against saying anything. He just stuck out his hand and shook hands with Hector.

I continued. "Ty, what's going on out there?" I asked, referring to the streets. I needed to know who called themselves taking over, who was still on Cameron's team, and who we needed to eliminate.

Ty cocked his head to the side before answering me. "Ain't shit going on out there, little sis. We got work, but it's getting low, and the only other work that's circulating is some weak shit coming from the Bronx. I heard that the nigga Matt hooked up with the Mexicans, but he having a hard time getting his work off, because niggas are loyal to Cam. I really hope your plan is solid, because I promised my boys they wouldn't go without eating."

"They won't. I needed Matt as of yesterday, but we'll get to that. You need work, and I got it. I got fourteen bricks available right now. How many can you get off?" I said, jumping straight to the point.

I could tell that Ty was thrown for a loop. He probably had a million and one questions, but I just hoped he didn't ask them. I wasn't in the mood to have my methods questioned; I just wanted to get shit done and over with.

"Li'l sis, where the fuck you get fourteen keys from?" Ty replied.

"How many can you get off?" I repeated my question, completely ignoring what he'd asked me.

"Depends how much," he said, realizing his question wasn't going to get answered.

I smiled. "How much were you paying the Mexicans?"

"Twenty-two," he answered, glancing down at his phone.

I thought about it. I wasn't in this to make money. My job was to keep Cameron's business above water. I felt like Cameron stepping down was going to be his voluntary decision. Nobody was going to put my man out of business and sit around to enjoy it. Nah, not on my watch. I was paying close to nothing for the product, so charging cheaper than the Mexicans was still a win for everybody.

"A'ight. Fifteen," I said after doing the quick math in my head.

"What? Fifteen, you dead ass?" Ty looked at Hector. "You straight with that, Hector?"

"Whoa, Ty. Why you asking Hector? He not my connect, bro. I said I got the work. Don't question him about my pricing. I'm charging y'all fifteen a brick. While I got you here, I should let you know Mariah got the okay to move Cameron to Miami. I don't want Cameron's whereabouts discussed at all. You can let your boys know that he very much alive, and still in charge, but do not mention where he will be. Make sure you exchange contact information with Hector, and any concerns or inquiries you have regarding business, call him."

I felt like I had covered everything that I needed to for now. Then I thought of something I'd missed. "Oh, and you still haven't said how many you can get off," I noted, remembering he had never answered my initial question.

"We can manage all fourteen, as long as the product is A-one," he said, still looking shocked that it was me he was having this conversation with.

"By all means, and when you have the two hundred ten thousand dollars, contact Hector. He'll set up the meeting. And you are allowed to bring someone to test the product, unless you're into testing it yourself," I said, glancing at my phone, which was vibrating in my hand. It was my grandfather, and I knew that I had to take the call. "I'm sorry. I gotta take this, but y'all can discuss the details. I'll be back," I said. Then I got up and answered the call as I headed to my bedroom.

The conversation with my grandfather was brief. He had just called to check on me and make sure that everything was straight. After I assured him that everything was going well, he let me go. I headed back into the living room and found Ty watching ESPN, but Hector was nowhere in sight.

"Where did Hector go?" I said, breaking Ty's concentration on the TV.

"He went to make a phone call. So, are you going to fill me in or not, sis?" he said, looking me directly in the eyes.

As much as I wanted to confide in Ty and tell him about my visit with my grandfather and all that he had taught me, I just couldn't, especially not the way this team had been getting down. I didn't see Ty as the type to cross Cameron, so I knew he wouldn't cross me, but I just wasn't taking any unnecessary risks. Everything having to do with business was on a need-to-know basis

"No, Ty. The details don't really matter. I already told you I was going to make moves on behalf of Cameron, so just have my back, bro. That's all I ask," I said with sincerity.

"You don't have to worry about that, Skye. I got you. Whatever you're into or whatever plans you have, just think about the baby, a'ight? That's all I ask," he pleaded with me.

I nodded in agreement. That was nothing he had to worry about. My child was going to be okay. I wasn't trying to make a career out of this.

Ty and I talked a little more about my plans regarding the move to Miami before he left my place, leaving Hector and me alone. We hung around only long enough for me to whip up something to eat. My stomach was making a growling noise, and the baby wasn't trying to wait. After I ate, we too were on our way.

Man

It felt good to be back on my own territory, chilling with my niggas. Even better, being away from shorty. She complained nonstop, and I just couldn't get with that shit. I couldn't wait till this was all over and I was able to rid myself of her for good. I wouldn't be missing much. She was cute, but the pussy was mediocre at best. I had to laugh at myself, because I was a fucked-up nigga. I had sold shorty dreams, and she had bought them, just like the fiends I supplied my product to. Even if everything I let out of my mouth was complete bullshit, people bought it. I could definitely sell water to a whale.

The ringing of my cell phone brought me back to where I was and what was going on. I looked down on the screen on the phone and saw that it was Matt calling. That nigga must have really needed help, 'cause he'd been on my top lately, and it was low key annoying as fuck.

"What up!" My tone was flat, partially because I really didn't have an interest in becoming that nigga's ace. We could handle business together, but that was about it. So I was hoping this wasn't a social call.

"Shit, son, I'm in the hood. What you getting into?" he said.

"We on Van Siclen. Come through." The timing was good for him to come through. My niggas and I were planning on making a move on Cam's boys. Inviting Matt to the party would definitely let us know if he could back up his talk.

"A'ight, boy. Be there in fifteen," he replied, sounding excited.

This nigga needed some friends, clearly. I hung up the phone with Matt and directed my attention to my boys, who were standing around, kicking it, tryin'a rap at the group of chicks who were strolling past. We could holla at bitches another day; today our focus was on something else.

"So y'all with riding on them pussies today?" I asked, immediately grabbing their attention.

As expected, they were all ready. My crew may not have been the biggest, but they were definitely the most loyal. They would lay down murder game to any target on any given day. That was why I fucked with them the way I did. Today's target was some of Cam's men. It wasn't news when my little nigga Kevin told me Cam wasn't dead. I figured that much, since there had been no uproar in the hood. As much as I wanted to deny it, Cam was like a god in these streets to some niggas. If he had taken a bow, word of it would have spread like wildfire. Everybody knew he wouldn't show his face until the heat died down. I ain't have no intentions on letting it die down, though. I was bringing more heat.

I made sure they were all strapped, in case we needed to make a stop at our stash house to strap up, but as always, they were ready. I glanced down at my G-Shock watch every so often, thinking that if Matt didn't hurry his ass up, he was going to miss the party.

Ty

When I finally left Skye's crib, I was feeling optimistic. The news she delivered had put a nigga in a good mood. I knew for a fact how real shit was going to get if I couldn't get any product to my niggas soon, and there she had come up with fourteen keys, and for a low price at that. I just hoped the shit was on point.

I jumped in my truck and headed to meet up with my team at the crib we used for powwows in Brownsville. I needed to put them on game so they would be ready when I got the call from Hector. I was still confused as to who that nigga was and where he'd come from, but if he was helping Skye supply my niggas, he was cool in my book, for now at least.

When I got to the crib in the Ville, there were a few familiar cars parked out front, so I knew my niggas had arrived. I had figured they would get there before me, because they were hungry. The idea of having a new connect had them amped. I pulled into an empty parking spot and jumped out of the whip. As I approached the entrance to the crib, I got an eerie feeling. Something told me to turn around. Just as I did, I spotted a black truck slowly creeping up the block. Already knowing what it was, I hit the ground and pulled my nine out as shots erupted.

I heard glass shattering and car alarms blaring, but I couldn't lose focus. I rolled behind a tree and started busting back at the truck, and by that time I'd been joined by my niggas. We let off shot after shot, until the truck was no longer in sight.

"Fuck Man!" I barked as I stood up from the spot that had provided me cover. I looked around at my niggas, making sure no one had been hit. We couldn't take any more losses as a unit.

"Yo, Ty. You good, son?" JR asked as he walked up on me.

"Yeah. When is this shit going to end? These niggas need to die, real shit," I yelled as I paced back and forth, pissed the fuck off.

I couldn't waste time being mad or standing outside, venting. It was broad daylight, so I knew the boys in blue was going to be showing up at any minute. We had to get low fast.

"Sweep the spot, and roll out. Niggas can't be around when the boys get here," I said, giving orders that I hoped they would complete as quickly as possible. We couldn't afford any members of this unit being locked up.

I stood outside and waited till all my niggas were out and had cleared the scene. By the time I hopped in my truck and pulled off, I heard sirens. I needed to get my head together and get up with Skye as soon as possible, but first, I headed to Ariana's crib. I had kind of been keeping her at a distance lately. It hadn't been on purpose; a nigga just got a million and one things going on. She'd been on her distant shit too, going days without calling a nigga. I wasn't worried about that, though, as I needed a place to clear my head. Might as well run through her crib and kill two birds with one stone, I decided.

Skye

After my meeting with Ty, Hector and I headed up to the hospital to meet Mariah and Victoria. We needed to get the ball rolling on Cameron's transfer. I would feel much better once he was away from this city. When I walked into Cameron's room, I found Mariah and Victoria sitting beside his bed, watching the news. The news anchor was discussing a shooting that had taken place in Brownsville. Something was always happening in that neighborhood, so I wasn't too concerned about it.

"Hey," I said, making my presence known.

Mariah looked away from the TV and turned toward me. I could see that she was upset, but I just hoped she didn't want to discuss it right now. I wasn't in the mood, and it wasn't the time or the place.

"Hello, Skye," she said. Her tone was a bit cold and distant, but I'd take that over her questioning me about my whereabouts.

"I called my grandmother in Miami while I was on the way here, and she said she was going to fax the documents and release forms right away. Mariah, can you check with Cameron's doctor to see if he received them?" I said, taking Cameron's hand in mine and rubbing it.

I looked down at him and felt tears well up. I fought back the tears that were threatening to fall, because they weren't going to change anything and damn sure weren't going to wake him up. I had had my chance to cry, and I had taken it. It was all about getting shit done now.

"I'll go check with him now. I'll be back," Mariah said as she got up.

I was about to start talking to Victoria when my phone started vibrating. I looked and saw it was a text from Ty.

Yo, sis, meet me at Ari's crib ASAP!

I wondered what was so important as I slipped my phone back into my pocket. I knew that being in this position, I had to go there and see what was up. It was exactly what Cameron would have done. However, I was hesitant. I hadn't spoken to Ariana since the day we fell out in her hospital room. I was still trying to decide how she was going to pay for being so dumb. I didn't wanna strike out at her, because at the end of the day, she was like my sister, and I still loved her—probably always would—but she was going to learn today, that was for sure.

When Mariah returned, she was accompanied by the doctor. I was glad to hear that everything was a go and that Cameron would be transported to Miami in just two short days. All I had to do was keep everything under control until then. I figured I could manage. Since I had the news I needed to hear, it was time for me to finish up here and then head to Ari's house. I wrote a check covering all the expenses for Cameron's transfer, as I had promised, and gave it to Mariah. I wasn't the one paying for it, though. I had intended to, but my grandfather had covered this. It was his way of making it clear to me that he would do anything for me. I understood that before he even wired the money.

"Skye, will you be coming back to the house tonight?" Mariah asked me.

I lifted my head after giving Cameron a goodbye kiss and turned to her. "Not tonight. I have a few things I need to take care of. Tomorrow night I'll be there for sure."

I knew that wasn't the answer she was looking for, but it was the best one I could give her at this point.

"I have to get going, but, Mariah, I promise I won't disappear again. I'll call to check in, or I'll text you." I hugged her and walked toward the door.

"Wait up. I'm going with you, Skye," Victoria called after me.

I wasn't in any mood to debate with her, so I just let her come along. I didn't mind telling Victoria what was going on, because she had a clear understanding of this life. In addition to that, my efforts were on her brother's behalf, so I knew she would support them. We left the hospital and headed out to the parking lot, where Hector was waiting.

Victoria

I had a feeling that I just couldn't shake. Skye was up to something, and I planned on finding out exactly what it was, which was why I went along with her. When we got to her car, a Spanish man was sitting in the driver's seat, waiting. I so badly wanted to ask who the hell this man was, but I kept my cool. In due time I would have all the answers I wanted. I climbed into the backseat and thought about all the possible things Skye could be into.

When we arrived at our destination, no words had been shared at all between Skye and the driver. She calmly got out of the car, and I followed her. We entered a building and headed upstairs. We arrived at an apartment door, and after we waited a minute, Ariana answered. I was completely thrown for a loop when Skye entered Ariana's apartment without saying a word to her. I, on the other hand, embraced her. I hadn't seen her since she was released from the hospital, and I was happy to see her up and doing better since the incident.

"Hey, Ari," I said after I stepped out of our embrace. I walked past her. I spotted Ty sitting on the couch in the living room, with his head in his lap.

"Hey, Vic. How you doing?" Ariana said as I took a seat next to Ty and hugged him.

There was something about that hug, something about the way my body responded to it. I'd hugged Ty a plethora of times in my life, but none of those hugs had felt like this. It was electrifying.

"I'm okay," I said, forcing myself to shake off any thoughts about my and Ty's hug.

Skye's demeanor changed almost instantly. It was as if she was growing tired of the brief dialogue between me and Ariana. What the hell was going on? I decide not to pursue conversing with her. Instead, I sat back and observed what was going on.

"Ty, what happened?" Skye asked, standing in the middle of the living room.

"I went to the spot to tell my niggas the shit you put me onto, and these other niggas rode through and tried to air us out," Ty said, leaning back on the couch and massaging his temples.

That was something he did whenever he was stressed out. Why did I know when he was stressed out?

"You know who it was? Was this in Brownsville? Because there was a story about something popping off in the Ville on the news," Skye said.

"Nah, I don't know who it was. I put bread on Man and those niggas, though, because it's not really the Mexicans' style. And yeah, we were at the spot in the Ville," Ty responded.

"Get them all here now," Skye said, taking off her coat and laying it on the chair next to her.

Ty looked up at her, confused. Shit, I was too. I silently hoped she wasn't trying to fill in for Cam. I mean, I would respect that and love her so much for even stepping up, but she was pregnant. She had to know how much of a bad idea it was to get involved in this shit. I had to know what was going on. I had wanted answers before, but at this point I needed them.

"You sure that's a good idea, sis?" Ty asked as he held his iPhone in his hand, contemplating whether he should follow through with her orders.

"Skye, what he mean?" I asked, looking up at her, with confusion written across my face.

For the first time since we had arrived at Ariana's house, Skye sat. She let out a huge sigh before sharing what she had been up to lately. I could tell she was giving us only bits and pieces, and I made a mental note to have her fill in the blanks later. I was unable to hide how completely shocked I was. At the same time, a part of me understood. She was a real chick. I knew it was one of the reasons why I liked her, but in that moment it became so clear. She was really willing to go ham for the sake of my brother and my family. How could I not respect that? My one and only concern was the baby. The way she explained it made it sound as if Ty would be doing all the hands-on shit, but still any degree of involvement in this business had its risks. If she was willing to go to these lengths to help my family, I would go to the same lengths to be there for her and my unborn niece or nephew.

"I want in," I said, not realizing what I was saying until the words were already in the atmosphere.

"That's not going to happen. If something happened to you, I would never be able to face your mother or your brother, Victoria. Plus, once we get settled in Miami, you're going to school. There's a few colleges and universities down there, so you have a selection to choose from," Skye said.

"Skye, this is my family that you're risking your well-being to protect. It's only right that I join the effort. I'll stick by you and go with your flow, but I want in. If you're adamant about me attending school when we get to Miami, I'll do that too," I explained.

I didn't have an issue with going to school. In fact, I had actually been planning on getting into college before all this shit started happening. If my brother managed school and this business, I could too. Skye and Ty went back and forth about it for a minute, before agreeing that I could participate—as long as I shadowed Skye. I was cool with that. My main concern was the baby, since we had already lost my father and had damn near lost Cam. We weren't going to suffer any more losses if I could help it, so the closer I was to Skye, the better.

"Ty, make the call," Skye said, reminding him of what she had asked him to do before we had turned to discussing my participation in this effort.

He nodded in her direction, to acknowledge that he had heard her, as he punched buttons on the screen of his phone.

Ariana

I couldn't believe what I was hearing. Skye was really going through with this? I didn't know if it was really a smart idea on her part. What the fuck did she know about running this business? She was trying to be Cam's hero and was totally putting her well-being on the back burner. Don't get me wrong. I had a love for Cam and respected him, but Skye had too much going for herself to even get wrapped up in this mess.

I wasn't sweating that, though. Her decisions were her decisions. The part that had me pissed off was how Ty had been acting with her. He'd been at her beck and call, when I was the one who really needed him. I loved him, but I was glad I was getting a little attention elsewhere, because he just had been on some funny shit lately. I wasn't with that at all. Everything was about Skye. All the concerns were about Skye. I was tired of hearing that shit, especially from Ty. Since he stepped foot in my house, he hadn't even fixed his lips to ask how I was feeling. Just because I was no longer laid up in a hospital bed didn't mean I was feeling 100 percent. He wouldn't know that, though, because his head was too far up Skye's ass to take notice.

I stood back and observed, just shaking my head. We were all sitting in the living room, waiting for the guys that Ty had called over. No one was speaking; I guessed everyone was in their own thoughts. I figured that this was a good opportunity for me to pull Skye to the side and talk to her. If no one else would keep it real with her and tell her about the dumb-ass decisions she'd been making, I most certainly would. And I couldn't leave out the fact that she had come up in my place and hadn't spoken one word to me yet. I understood why she was mad, and I respected that, but I thought, *Really? Are we at that point? We can't even be cordial?*

"Skye, come here. I wanna talk to you," I said, gesturing for her to follow me.

When I saw her stand up, I turned and headed to my bedroom, and she followed me.

"Wassup?" she asked as she walked through the bedroom door.

"You sure you ready to go through with this stuff, Skye? This not you. It's not your life. You have so much more going on. Don't risk your baby's life by getting caught up in this mess," I said, trying to reason with her.

"If you called me back here to discuss my business, that's not going to happen," she said, looking at me as if she was bored with my presence.

If only she were privy to the information I knew, she would listen. You could lead an elephant to water, but you couldn't make it drink, I mused. If Skye wanted to fight Cam's battles, that was on her. I shook my head in disgust and attempted to shift the direction of the conversation.

"Skye, I'm sorry for what happened. I really am. Had I put two and two together at the time, things probably would have ended up differently. I hope you don't think that I had anything to do with it, because the only thing I'm guilty of is knowing Man. He is my ex, and we didn't end on bad terms, so us kicking it wasn't out of the norm," I explained.

Although she looked completely uninterested in what I was saying, it didn't take away from the fact that it needed to be said, so I continued. Whether or not she forgave me would be on her, but at least I could say that I tried.

When I was done talking, she nodded her head and said, "It's straight." Then she turned to walk out of the room.

What the fuck did that mean? She was dead-ass upset over this shit. If you thought about it, it wasn't even my place to get in the middle of the bullshit between Man and Cam. I would never involve myself in that type of shit. Cam was a friend because he fucked with Skye, and Man was my dude. At the end of the day, that was *their* beef. I had no place in it, and neither did Skye.

I shook my head, thinking about it, as I walked out of the bedroom and back into the living room. I walked in as Ty was holding open the front door, letting in the guys from his team whom he had called over. I thought about going back into my bedroom and letting them discuss whatever it was they needed to discuss without me being present. However, I felt compelled to see how this shit was going to play out.

Skye

I wasted no time getting to the point. I didn't even let them get settled in before I launched into my lecture. I tried to remain focused on what was at hand, even though something Ariana had said was dancing around in the back of my mind. I would have to address that later.

"A'ight, I'ma be as brief as possible, and hopefully, this conversation goes smooth," I said. "To my knowledge, you all respect Cameron, so you should have no issues with what I'm about to say." I paused to make sure no one had any objections so far, then continued. "I'm taking over for Cameron. Before y'all object, hear me out. I'm not tryin'a step on nobody's toes. Cameron is going to be fine, but in the meantime, I'm taking care of his business. Y'all need work. Ty got it. Treat me as you would treat Cameron, and we'll be cool. Y'all know I have the same views on family and loyalty as you do, because I'm here. So know that as long as y'all got me, I got y'all. We have the same goals—get money, eliminate the people that's been causing all the havoc. I'm not out here pretending to be no gangster or nothing like that. I'm simply covering for my man, as I would do if this was a legal Fortune five hundred company. Let's stick to handling business as usual."

I expected them to be rattled by my words. I was actually prepared to have Hector handle them on the spot if they got too crazy, but they seemed to be okay with the idea.

"Why you want to do this?" JR asked me.

I directed my attention to him before speaking. "Cameron's family gotta eat, period."

They all understood that. I could tell by their expressions that they had gained a new level of respect for me, as well.

"I got you, baby sis," JR said after hugging me.

Surprisingly, the rest of them followed suit. Ty was right: these guys really were still loyal to Cameron. At least for the moment they were. The way shit was going down, I was sure somebody was going to end up jumping ship before it was all said and done. For right now, though, at least it was going to be business as usual.

"Ty, where you got the work from?" one of the young boys asked him.

I didn't have to say anything or make any gestures, because Ty already knew what it was. I looked at him as if I, too, wanted to know the answer to that question.

"From some nigga Cam and I were discussing before all this shit went down," he answered nonchalantly.

I knew he didn't like having to lie to his boys, but he would do it if it was necessary. Well, he did do it, to ensure my anonymity and safety in case one of these guys got the bright idea to try me. As expected, his answer was on point. I didn't mind if these guys knew I was taking over for Cameron, but they couldn't know I was the connect.

We sat around for hours discussing how we were going to get ahold of Matt and Man. I was confident that this team of shooters was capable of getting the job done on that level. However, gunplay with the Mexicans was a whole different ball game. I thought about bringing my grandfather in on that. He had connections all over, so I was sure he could easily have the job done. I was going to try to handle it on my own first, but if I failed, my grandfather got me.

We were wrapping up our talk when I remembered something important. "If Cameron has any money on the street, get it to Ty tonight," I told the guys. "Ty, you can just drop it off with Mariah."

Surprisingly, Mariah didn't have access to all the money her husband had stored away at various locations. For security purposes, he had shared that information only with Cameron. The only money Mariah had access to was whatever was in her bank account.

They all nodded, letting me know that they had heard me and understood my instructions. If they continued to be this attentive, things would continue to go smooth.

I went on. "In addition to that, a team needs to head to Cypress and body whomever y'all need to. We need Man, and if he's not going to voluntarily show his face, smoke him out."

I looked directly at Ariana as I uttered the last part of my statement. She was gonna pay for being so fucking dumb. I just didn't know how yet. Those last instructions had the boys on go. I knew they were ready to send a message or two back to Man and his team. I had just given them the green light. It was only a matter of time before it would be slow singing and flower bringing for Man's people.

Victoria and I were no longer needed at this meeting. I had said all I needed to say, so we now said our goodbyes to the team and left to meet Hector at the car. I wanted a hot shower and my bed.

Ty

I was proud of the way Skye had handled the meeting with the team. I could tell the guys were too. If she kept handling herself the way she had been up to this point, she would definitely be a'ight. The guys and I kicked it at Ari's house a little while longer, just long enough to come up with a plan for Man.

"Who riding to Cypress with me?" I questioned, looking around at the dudes I considered to be family.

As expected, everyone was ready to ride. It was a job that could be handled by a handful of us. No need to have the entire team out on the same mission. We still had work that needed to be distributed. Business as usual, like Skye had said.

"Everybody don't gotta come, but I appreciate the willingness, though. I'll take JR, Bills, and Trey. Everybody else, resume your daily activities," I said while standing, giving them the cue that it was time to go. The niggas who were rolling with me lingered behind, while everyone else dipped out.

"You really gotta go right now?" Ariana said to me, finally breaking the silence she'd been under since we arrived.

"Not right now, Ma. I'll hit your phone later," I replied.

Ariana knew how things were going for us at that point. She pretended like she didn't understand why her wants and needs had to be secondary, but I wasn't the nigga that was going to keep reiterating the shit to her. If she didn't understand by now, she wouldn't ever. Shorty just had to live with shit. Her nagging forced me to expedite my exit.

Before heading to Cypress, we stopped by the East New York spot to switch whips. I wasn't driving my truck to put in work, because niggas could spot my shit on sight. We had numerous hoopties to use on our missions. When we got to the East New York spot, we made sure our clips were full, and grabbed extras. I made sure everyone threw on a vest as well. I wasn't trying to lose any more homies. After making sure all my boys were straight, we were ready to ride out. I tossed JR the keys to the 1995 Ford Taurus before jumping in the passenger seat. Not only was I the better shooter, but I wanted to be the one to light that nigga Man up. For that to happen, I couldn't be focused on driving. Getting us there and back in one piece was now JR's job.

When we pulled up to the block where the Cypress houses started, we found that the block was desolate. That was out of the ordinary, seeing that this was the type of hood where somebody was always on the street. Whether it be fiends, dope boys, or kids running around, somebody was always out. We were baffled, but we didn't give up. We drove around in search of our target or anybody who could carry back a message for us.

"Where are these niggas?" JR said, with a hint of defeat in his tone.

He had spoken too soon. As he turned the corner, I spotted a group of cats coming out of one of the buildings. Among the members of the group, I noticed Man. He was a short, pudgy nigga that rocked dreads, so it wasn't hard to pick him out of a group. My eyes created a red bulls-eye that began circling his head. Regardless of what was about to go down, Man was my target.

"Bingo," I said and nodded in the direction of the group of dudes, causing JR to slow down.

I didn't even wait till the car had come to a complete stop. I jumped out of the car, and Trey and Bills quickly followed my lead. We ran toward those dudes, letting off shot after shot. It didn't take long for them to return fire, but we didn't retreat. Between ducking and dodging, I kept focused on my target, and Trey and Bills handled the other three cats. I watched as Man's body got riddled with slugs from my twin .380 pistols. Only then did I feel satisfied enough to retreat to the car.

"Let's go!" I shouted to Trey and Bills over the sound of guns blasting.

We backpedaled in the direction of the car while still letting our guns go to work. Once we reached the car, we all jumped in at the same time. JR sped off and put distance between us and the crime scene as quickly as the hooptie allowed. The last scene that played over and over in my head as we zoomed through the streets of Brooklyn was of one of Man's homies on the ground, cradling Man's wounded body. It reminded me of the way I had held my nigga Cam a few weeks back. I prayed that, that nigga Man died on the spot. If he miraculously survived, I'd be back. It was nothing.

After parking the hooptie in the garage of our spot in the east, we switched back to my truck. I dropped my homies off at their respective locations before heading back to my crib. I contemplated going back to Ari's crib, but after all that, I wasn't in the mood to deal with her being on my back about how I been acting lately. I wanted to take a good shower and to be left alone for the night. Going home was my best bet, so that was exactly what I did.

Skye

The sound of the alarm woke me from slumber. I lay there for a minute, thinking about all that I had to do that day. I felt the urge to hit SNOOZE on my clock, roll over, and go back to sleep. I knew that was out of the question, given the length of my to-do list. I had a doctor's appointment, and I needed to get in touch with the Realtor my grandmother had given me the contact information for. The next day was the day that Cameron would be transferred to Miami, and since I couldn't be there to pick out a home for us to live in, I had to put my trust in a Realtor to find something for us. Going there and shacking up with my grandparents or staying in a hotel was out of the question.

I glanced at the time and realized I had to be at my doctor's appointment in an hour. I hated rushing in the shower, but it had to be one of them days. I headed into the bathroom, washed my face, brushed my teeth, and jumped in the shower. After taking the quickest shower ever, I slipped into a pair of True Religion jeans and a polo sweater. I was pissed at the limited number of sneaker options I had at the Staten Island house, but I settled for Bred 11s.

I headed downstairs, to find that Victoria and Hector were already dressed and ready to go.

"Good morning, y'all," I said as I slipped on my coat.

They said good morning back in unison before following suit and putting on their coats. With that, we were gone.

When we pulled up to my doctor's office, I had the butterfly feeling in my stomach as I thought about my baby. I couldn't wait to see my baby's face. I had spent countless moments wondering whether he or she would like Cameron and me. Hearing Hector's heavy Spanish accent brought me out of my thoughts.

"How long will you be here? I have to meet Ty to make the drop," he said, reminding me that today was also the day for him to deliver the first shipment to Ty. I really needed to work on being organized, because I found myself having a hard time keeping up.

"I totally forgot about that. Well, you and Victoria can go handle that. I will be heading to the hospital after this doctor's appointment to check on Cameron. I can take a taxi. It's not a problem. Just look after Victoria as you would if she was me," I said, directing my attention to Hector.

"Of course, Ms. Skye. Call me if you have any trouble," he said.

"Will do," I said as I climbed out of the front seat.

I strutted into my doctor's office. I was excited to check on the progress of my baby. I'd been making sure to eat right and get adequate amounts of sleep, so I prayed everything was still progressing as it should be. I couldn't take any more bad news.

Ty

When I awoke, it was still dark outside. In no way did I like to be up at the crack of dawn, and taking into account the type of night I had, there was no way I was leaving my bed just yet. We had guys on the team who handled business at these early hours, and I just wasn't one of them. But Hector had insisted on meeting up with me fairly early in the morning to drop off the work, so I couldn't linger in bed for very long this morning. Fifteen minutes later, I rolled out of bed. I showered, dressed, and left my crib before the clock struck 7:00 a.m.

An hour later, I sat with JR and Corey, one of the young boys we knew from the hood back in the day, in the little crib we had in the Bronx. Corey wasn't an addict, but he did like to do a little coke here and there, so we used him to test new product. He was hesitant now, because apparently, Man's niggas had been putting out some shit that had been dropping heads on the spot. Corey wasn't tryin'a die from the shit, but he trusted me.

While we waited for Hector, I thought back to when shit used to be smooth. We had rarely had issues like what had been going on lately. Before our current time of troubles, the biggest shit we had dealt with was little niggas tryin'a get the little product off on our blocks. We had solved that easily by putting them on. Everybody we fucked with respected the game and played by the rules. I still couldn't believe niggas would do the team dirty and land us in this situation. It hurt like hell that my pops was a part of that pool.

I hadn't seen him or spoken to him since the shit with Cam that night. I was sure he had heard that Cam got lit up, so I knew he would be showing his face soon. How was I even supposed to handle that? I knew for a fact that our relationship would never be the same, but he was still my pops at the end of the day.

The vibrating of my cell phone caused me to push to the side the thoughts that weighed heavily on my mind. I glanced at my phone and saw that it was a text from Hector. I pulled out my nine and held it down by my side as I walked to the front door. After the shit that had gone down at the Brownsville spot, we had to be on point. I looked back and saw that JR had his piece aimed at the door, ready in case shit went south. I took a quick peek out the window, and nothing seemed suspicious, so I opened the door.

There stood Hector. Realizing he was with Vic, I froze. I couldn't believe she had shown up with Hector.

"Fuck is she doing here?" I barked, grilling Vic so she would know how pissed off I was.

The deal was that we would let Vic help out and shit as long as she shadowed Skye. I looked Vic up and down and realized she was holding a nine down at her side.

"And she strapped? For what? Where Skye?" I asked Hector, not taking my eyes off Vic.

"Ty, calm down. And I'm strapped, in case something pops off. I'd rather be ready than have to get ready in the heat of the moment, right?" Victoria said, with sarcasm dripping from her tone.

"Skye is busy," Hector said, walking past me into the house.

"Cheer up, Scrap. Let's get down to business," Vic said, playfully slapping my chest.

I wasn't in a playing mood, though. This shit was getting out of hand. First, Skye up and decided that she wanted to be on some boss shit, and now Vic. I made a mental note to check Skye about this, though, because it wasn't a part of the deal.

Even though I wanted to be pissed, I couldn't help but admire how much Vic had grown up. She was a honey. She was five feet five, had a smooth honey tone, and rocked curly blond hair. Vic was on the slim side, but her ass was fat. She had definitely come a long way from thirteen-year-old, flat-chested, no-ass Vic. Twenty-year-old Vic was ready for this twenty-three-year-old dick. I had been feeling her since way back when, but it could never be more than that. She was like my little sister. Seeing her here, turned up, made me revisit my feelings, though. She was bad and had heart, and that turned a nigga on.

I couldn't focus too much on Vic, because Hector was ready to get down to business. He pulled out a pack and tossed it on the table. Corey tested the product and confirmed that it was A1, and even better than what we were getting from the Mexicans. Hector and I exchanged currency for the product. Shortly after that, he and Vic dipped.

"Yo, Ty, why you asked for Skye? How Vic know him? That's your connect?" JR asked, forcing me to realize that I had fucked up.

Skye didn't want the connect to be traced back to her in no way, and I had fucked up by asking for her. JR wasn't dumb, so he already knew what it was. I wasn't even going to try to play him, but I wasn't going to explain the shit in front of Corey, either. I paid Corey for his services and sent him on his way. Once he was gone, I explained to JR the little bit of information Skye did tell me. He was just as shocked as I was.

"Cam fucking with the right one, I see," JR said, giving Skye credit for the work she was trying to put in.

I had to agree. "It seems that way," I said.

I didn't want to stay on that topic too long. It was time to put our work on the streets. Time to let niggas know we were back. It was gonna take a lot more for us to fold.

Victoria

After dropping the product off with Ty, Hector and I headed back to the house in Staten Island. The entire ride, all I was able to think about was how Ty had looked at me. I'd caught him staring at me on several occasions before, but those stares hadn't been like the ones I received today. I could have misconstrued his looks, and they could have been totally innocent. I mean, I had shown up there with Hector without notifying Ty. That could have been the reason for his stares, and maybe he had been trying to assess the situation. I forced myself to believe that was all there was to it. After all, it couldn't possibly be anything other than that.

Putting thoughts of Ty aside, I contemplated asking Hector a few questions. I was still confused about how he fit into the equation and where he'd come from. I decided against quizzing him, though, because I trusted Skye and wanted her to know that she could trust me as well. If she felt there was anything I needed to know about Hector, I was sure she would reveal that information to me. I wasn't going to sweat it, not at this point at least.

Instead of trying to make sense of everything, I told myself to refocus my energy on learning more than I already knew about the business and getting in where I fit. No one knew how badly I wanted a spot in my father's operation. I had never had the chance before, because Cam had handled everything. Now it seemed as if the opportunity was finally presenting itself for me to step up. I respected Skye and had mad love for her, but at the end of the day, this was my family, my brother, my family business, and I felt like I should be running it. I knew I wasn't prepared for that yet, which was why I was going to learn everything I could from following Skye. And if Cam didn't make it—I prayed fervently that he would—I would be prepared and better suited to take over. Skye wasn't looking to be doing this forever, so I would kindly fill her shoes if the time came.

Once we reached the house in Staten Island, I made myself comfortable on the couch in the living room. I hadn't spoken to my mother since the night before, so I decided to call her. Her phone rang a total of five times, and I was ready to hang up, but she answered just in time.

"Hello?" She sounded groggy, as if she had been asleep.

"Hi, Mom. Were you sleeping?" If she was, I intended on letting her go back to sleep. Since Cam's incident, sleep hadn't come very often for my mother, so when it did, it was best that she took advantage of that.

"Yes, I lay down for a moment, and I guess I dozed off. I need to be getting up, anyway. Adriana is coming over to visit and keep me company." Adriana was Skye's mom. "Are you okay? And Skye?" my mom asked after clearing her throat.

"Yes, Mom, we are fine. I just wanted to check on you, that's all. I'm at Skye's house, waiting for her to come back from the doctor," I lied. Well, not really. I didn't know if Skye wanted everyone to know about us staying at her grandfather's house in Staten Island, so I just said we were at her place.

"Okay. I'm glad she is still finding time to check on the baby while doing whatever else she has going on. Please come out to the house today, the both of you."

There was no way I could tell my mother no, so I agreed to her request. "Of course, Mom. We'll be there," I replied before we said our goodbyes and ended our call.

I sat back on the couch and closed my eyes. I was exhausted, so I decided to take a quick nap before Skye returned from the doctor. I lay down on the couch in a fetal position and slowly drifted off to sleep.

Skye

The doctor's appointment went great. I was happy about that. The good news was much needed. The baby was growing at the rate he or she was supposed to and was healthy, and so was I. I couldn't ask for anything more. Hector and Victoria were going to meet me back at the Staten Island house, because I wanted to see Cameron after my doctor's visit. I hailed a taxi outside my doctor's office and was on my way to Bronx Lebanon. When I arrived, I said my hellos to the security guard in the lobby, who now recognized me, and then I headed straight up to Cameron's floor. I signed in at the nurses' station and sashayed toward his room. After entering his room and realizing he was not in his bed, I immediately went into panic mode.

No, God! Please no, I thought as I frantically searched the hallway for a doctor or nurse that I knew.

I found Cameron's surgeon. He explained to me that Cameron had been moved because he needed to be observed to ensure that he would survive the airlift that was scheduled for him the following day. I was upset that I couldn't see him now, but I was happy that it was only because of that. Thinking he was dead had me worked up and reminded me how unprepared I was for that eventuality. Cameron wouldn't succumb, though, because he was a fighter. He was going to bounce back from this. He had to.

Before leaving the hospital, I spoke with Cameron's primary doctor about the procedure for the next day. He advised me that only one person would be able to accompany Cameron on the airlift, and because we weren't married, it had to be Mariah. I understood that and was completely fine with it. I thanked him for his service and commitment to Cameron during his stay, and then I made my exit.

Catching a taxi to take me home from the hospital was a much easier process than catching one at the doctor's office. Cabs frequented the area because of the amount of business they received from people coming and going to and from the hospital on a regular basis. I slid into the backseat of my taxi and let out a huge sigh as the driver exited the hospital's parking lot en route to Staten Island.

Matthew

I had just jumped out of the shower when the vibrating of my cell phone caught my attention. I flopped down on the edge of the bed and answered the phone. It was a call from an unidentified number, but it could be an important call, and it was.

"Is this Matthew?" an unfamiliar voice said in my ear.

I was pissed at the fact that a nigga had the courage to call my phone and ask if it was me before even introducing himself. I was ready to end the call as quickly as it had started, but something told me not to.

"Yeah, this Matt. Who this?" I questioned, growing irritated.

"Not important. Just know I been working with Man on a few projects."

Already knowing what projects the caller was referring to, I was now interested, and the caller had my undivided attention.

"A'ight. So what you need with me?" I wanted him to get to the point and fast.

"Man and his boys was hit up last night. I don't have information on none of their conditions as of yet. I will after I make a phone call. He mentioned you to me a few times, and I wanted to know whether in the event that he is no longer able to complete his projects, you would be willing to step up," he stated.

I was hesitant, because I had no idea who this cat was on the other end of the line. But Man was my last resort in terms of having a team to help me wipe the hood clean of Cam and any nigga who did business with him. If I didn't have Man, I would be on this mission solo, and even though I would still do it, it would probably end badly for me. For the moment, there was Miguel and his crazy-ass goons, but getting rid of Cam's crew wasn't his concern. Miguel's purpose was flooding the streets with his work. This dude on the phone was my only other option, and if I didn't have Man and his boys, there was no way I could pass.

"Yeah, for sure," I answered, before fully understanding what I was getting myself into.

I almost heard the caller's smile through the phone as he said, "Glad to have you on board. I'll be in touch once I have more on their condition."

I heard a click, and the line went dead.

Skye

When the taxi dropped me off at the Staten Island house, I thought I was going to have the chance to grab some food and relax for a minute. Boy, was I wrong. When I walked into the house, Victoria told me that her mother had demanded our presence at the house on Long Island. I still intended to eat and snatch a quick nap before heading out there. That was, until she mentioned that my mother was going to be there. I needed to see her, so as quickly as I entered the house, Victoria, Hector, and I were heading right back out.

We pulled up to Mariah's house in record-breaking time. I was slightly disappointed with that, because I was in no rush to face Mariah, or my mother, for that matter. I hadn't seen my mother since before I left for Panama. Even though we texted frequently throughout the day, I knew that wasn't enough. Maybe under better circumstances, it would have been.

I staggered out of the car like a child who was on the verge of having a temper tantrum. I didn't want to face the music, but I had no choice. Victoria used her key and let us into the house. The aroma coming from the kitchen sent my appetite into overdrive. The house smelled like Thanksgiving Day. I didn't know who was cooking or what they was cooking, but I was ready to smash. Like the hungry pregnant woman I was, I followed the aroma right into the kitchen. There I found my mother over the stove and Mariah sitting at the table, drinking from a cup, which I knew contained tea, due to the fact that the kettle was still sitting atop the stove.

"Hey," I said, getting their attention.

"My daughter, how lovely is it to have the chance to see your face," my mother said with a hint of sarcasm in her voice.

"Get her, Adriana. I'm just thankful that it has only been a day or two since I've seen her, versus the few weeks she went MIA," Mariah said, taking another sip of her tea.

Oh no, I thought to myself. Mariah had opened a can of worms, and she ain't even know it. My mother had no idea that I had gone to Panama. She was the only person I made sure to contact daily to let her know that I was okay, but she still had no idea that I had been out of the country for a while. That changed quickly.

"Hello!" Hector said in his heavy Spanish accent upon entering the kitchen behind Victoria.

My mother looked at Hector oddly before turning off the stove and approaching us. I had no idea what to expect. To be honest, I hadn't even thought about how I planned on explaining Hector's presence.

"Hector?" she questioned, as if he seemed familiar to her, but she was unsure.

"Adriana!" Hector yelled before pulling my mother to him and kissing her on the cheek.

I didn't understand how they knew each other. My mother had never gone to Panama, as far as I knew, or at least not since she was a baby. Had Hector worked for my grandfather for that long?

"It's really nice to see you, Hector. I had no idea that you still worked for Father," my mother said. She spoke with a smile plastered on her face.

I knew otherwise, though. My mother was smart and had common sense, and she knew that Hector being here meant only one thing. I had indeed gone to Panama.

"Excuse me for a minute. Skye, come with me." My mother spoke without making eye contact with me.

I knew it was about to go down. I hung my head down and examined the tiled floor as I followed behind mother as she headed to the family room, where she proceeded to chew me up.

"Have you lost your fucking mind?" was the first thing that came out of her mouth.

I was taken aback. I had never heard my mother use such language, and more shockingly, she was using it with me. I knew the question was rhetorical, so I didn't bother answering. I let her continue her rant, which would surely go on for some time.

"What made you believe that going to Panama was the right thing to do? I should have known that your 'All I want to do is have my grandfather in my life' crap was bullshit. So what's your plan, Skye? You want to step up and run a fucking crime ring! You think you built for this shit?" She chuckled before continuing. "I bet Andreas told you it was in your blood, that you were born to do this, right?"

She had never referred to my grandfather by his first name. Regardless of the fact that they were estranged, she had always referred to him as her father. I knew she was mad. The tears welling up in her eyes told me her emotions went beyond anger. She was hurt.

"Your father and I bust our ass to give you everything and more, and this is our thank-you? You wanna throw away your life for what? For what, Skye?" she shrieked, getting closer to my face.

I knew that my mother would never put her hands on me, but her verbal lashing was intense. I felt as though she was slapping me around. I attempted to explain my viewpoint and describe what was going on without flat out telling her I was running the business. Although she knew I was, I would never admit that. Definitely not to my mother.

"I don't want to hear that shit, Skye. This is not the woman I raised. You trying to prove you're some type of ride-or-die chick. You could have proved that by being there for Cameron's mother and sister or, more importantly, by taking care of yourself and your baby. Or is that not even a damn factor? Wait till your father gets back from his business trip. I can't believe you. Go on, because I can't even look at your face right now. Go ahead, Skye!" By her last sentence, she was shouting at the top of her lungs, which caused me to tremble as I turned and walked away.

I ran up the stairs and went straight to Cameron's room. I fell onto his bed and buried my face in his pillow and screamed. My screaming was accompanied by enough tears to make a river overflow. I cried because I was in pain. She was right! Everything that had come out of my mother's mouth was completely accurate. This wasn't me. There may be a branch of my family tree that was built for this life, but I didn't belong to that branch. For the first time, I was admitting to myself that I was scared. The thought of raising my baby alone scared the shit out of me. I wasn't ready for that, and I wasn't ready to face the fact that we may possibly lose Cameron.

Taking over his business kept me busy. It didn't allow me time to think about the things that pained me, and that was what I wanted. I had no time to sit around and mope about the situation. Of course, I had the option to go back to school, but how focused would I be, knowing what was going on around me? Doing this was really the only thing that took enough of my attention to keep me sane. That probably would not make sense to anyone else, but it made perfect sense to me. So yes, my mother had hit the nail on the head with everything she said, but I wasn't going to stop. I couldn't. Doing this was giving me strength to deal with Cameron's condition. Otherwise I would just succumb to depression. For my child's sake, I couldn't do that.

I had already set things in motion, and like everything else I committed to, I was going to complete this task. I knew that my mother was irate, but I also knew that no matter what, she had my back. Right or wrong, my mother would stand by my side. If that wasn't the case, my decision would have been different. I couldn't imagine not having my mother in my corner. I knew that things between us would be rough until I completed this task and was back on the path she wanted me to be on. But as long as I had her, I was straight.

I didn't think I would be able to explain to anyone the vast number of emotions I was experiencing. The only one that was consistent and stood out was hurt. Everything was hurtful. Cameron getting shot, my mother's choice of words, the thought of my baby never knowing his or her father, and watching Mariah and Victoria feeling hurt. The only way I knew to deal with my hurt at the moment was by crying. I rarely had the chance to show my vulnerability, because I was busy being strong for everyone around me. I didn't have to right then, because I wouldn't judge my own self for showing a sign of weakness. So I let my emotions out. I cried tears I'd been holding in since Cameron was shot, drenching his pillowcase in the process.

Once I finally settled down, I remained in the room alone, until Victoria came and got me for dinner. When I got to the dining room, I was relieved to see Ty. I hadn't heard from him since I left Ariana's house last night. My mother had seemingly calmed down, even though I knew she was still pretty pissed. We all sat and enjoyed the meal she had prepared. I used dinner as the opportunity to discuss the plans for the next day. Mariah would be flying down to Miami with Cameron; and Victoria, Hector, and I were scheduled to fly commercial. Ty said that he was joining us. I knew that he would be coming, but I had just thought it would be later. I was ready to get out of New York, even though I would be returning regularly for business.

After dinner, I gave them the instructions provided by my grandmother, who was in constant contact with the Realtor. Mariah and Victoria packed a few things in preparation for the relocation. I didn't really feel the need to pack up my life, since I would be living in both states. Besides, Hector, Ty, and I planned on going shopping as soon as we touched down in Miami.

We sat around a little longer, solidifying our plans for the following day, before we headed to our respective homes. I talked Victoria into staying the night with her mother. Mariah didn't have a problem with me leaving, since I would be returning in a few short hours. Before I headed home, my mother expressed to me that she was in no way happy with how I was living my life, but I was still her child. She went on to explain to me that she had every intention of coming down to Miami every weekend. I knew that if that was her intention, it would happen.

On the ride back to Staten Island, I thought about what Ty had told me about his encounter with Man and his boys. There had been no word that he had died, so that was probably unlikely. Whether he was dead or not, Ty was sure that the work he had put in would have Man out of commission for a while. I was content with that and looked forward to the new chapter that Miami would bring. We would definitely see Man again, along with everyone else we currently had beef with.

Man

It was almost my time to be put under the dirt. Those bitch-ass niggas had really caught me slipping. I hadn't even seen that hit coming. Shit could have cost me my life. I hadn't been able to walk away, but I was breathing. This shit bag that was connected to me, along with the arm brace and the crutches, was sweet in comparison to dying. Most niggas who got hit like I had didn't survive to tell the story. I was down for a minute, but I wasn't out. And on the upside, the excessive amount of downtime I had helped me put a lot of things in perspective.

I had been spending a lot of time wondering who was calling the shots and pulling strings for Cam. I knew for a fact it wasn't that bitch-ass nigga Ty. He wouldn't have put in work like that if he was in charge. Couldn't front, though. I was thoroughly surprised and shocked when I found out it was Cam's bitch who had taken charge, but I was more surprised that ole girl hadn't slipped up yet and mentioned that piece of vital information. Having her nagging ass around was beginning to seem useless. I had a better chance trying my luck with that pig-ass detective. I wasn't ready to go that route yet. Finding out that it was a female who was running their show gave me hope. I shook my head, thinking about the day I found out.

I'd been chillin' in Queens, at my aunt's crib, trying to bounce back from the lead them bitch-ass niggas had pumped into me. My boys had been visiting me often and had been keeping me up to speed as far as the streets went. Shit I had heard so far wasn't nothing out of the ordinary. Cam's team still found a way to supply the hood, and Matt was still running around, trying to be that nigga. Nothing new on that front. One afternoon Kevin and I had got to talking.

"Boy, you not gonna believe this shit," Li'l Kevin said to me after taking a long pull on the L he had just finished rolling.

"What now?" I asked, irritated. I was tired of hearing the same shit. I wanted to hear about Cam losing every nigga on his team. The more time that lapsed, the more it seemed as if that would never happen. No matter what angle we hit, those dudes bounced back.

"I was in the Ville, visiting my shorty, and I ran into JR," he said, passing me the L. "You remember JR, right? He went to high school with us. Only high yellow–ass nigga rocking dreads back then."

I took a drag on the loud-filled blunt and nodded my head up and down. I knew exactly who the cat was. I had put hands on him a few times back in the day. Once he'd got the message that I wasn't to be fucked with, we were cool. Like all the other dudes we went to high school with, he'd thought I was soft. I was short and skinny, and dudes saw me as weak. My hand game was up there, though, so I never hesitated when it came time to fight. They said pussies solved their beef using guns instead of their fists. That was far from the truth when it came to me. I would shoot the fair with a nigga any day. I just knew better than to bring a knife to a gunfight.

"Yeah, well, he been fucking with Cam's team heavy and was rambling on about how he felt his manhood was being tested, because those niggas had him working for a bitch," Li'l Kevin told me.

Nothing he said stood out to me or even mattered, until he uttered that last part. Before I went jumping to conclusions, I needed clarification.

*"What you mean, a bitch? What bitch? His sister?" I
questioned, hoping it was her. If those niggas was dumb
enough to put a bitch in charge of their operation, they
had to be ready to hand over the reins.*

*"Nah, boy. Cam's girl. I think he said shorty's name
was Skye, or some shit like that," he replied.*

My cell phone ringing pulled me out of my thoughts.
Damn. I looked down and saw that it was shorty. I really
wasn't in the mood to talk to her. I was starting to wish
her man wasn't neglecting her ass, because he gave her
too much time to be on my top. I hit DECLINE on my
phone and started plotting the day I would meet this
infamous Skye. Although I'd given this old head my word
I wouldn't kill Ty, that bitch had to go, because he almost
marked me. I had to be sure to figure him into my plans
too. I had some time to get my plan right, because my
recovery would take some time. But I was sure that the
day would come, and when it did . . .

Skye

It had been five months since we relocated to Miami. I would be lying if I said things hadn't been extremely rough for me due to having to travel back and forth between Miami, New York, and Panama for business. I was holding it down and doing the best I possibly could at eight months pregnant. The beef between us and Man had simmered down a little since Man's near-death experience. The last we heard, he was laid up in a hospital, hanging on for dear life. I swear, Man had an angel, because he was definitely supposed to die that night. I wasn't sad that he hadn't. Would I be happy if the beef with him was over? Hell yeah, but at the same time, I knew Ty and the boys would definitely see him again. When they did, they would make sure he didn't live to see the next day.

In the time we'd been in Miami, we hadn't heard anything from or about Matthew and Miguel, but I knew better. They had to be on the sidelines, awaiting their opportunity to strike. If I had things my way, that time would not come. I wanted to get at them before they got at me. I probably would have had that accomplished already, but when I hit six months in my pregnancy, Ty and Pop-Pop forbade me from going to New York until I had the baby. I was good with that. I needed the few months of downtime. Having Ty in Miami was extremely helpful, because not only did I feel safe with him around, but he took genuine care of me, along with my mother.

She had kept her promise and came to visit every weekend. My father had also made it his business to come down as often as time permitted.

Although our relationship wasn't where it had been, Ariana and I were speaking and trying to rebuild our friendship. She, too, came to visit on occasion. She wasn't able to come as often as she liked, but that wasn't because of me, or her, for that matter. It was Ty who wasn't feeling it. I wasn't getting between them, because I had enough on my plate. For the next two months, I planned on kicking my feet up and awaiting the arrival of my and Cameron's prince. I had found out I was having a boy, and I was extremely excited. It was all Cameron had talked about having since he found out I was pregnant. I decided to name the baby Cairo, which was Cameron's middle name. I couldn't wait to see my baby boy and hold him.

I was busy reading the magazine *Vibe Vixen* when Ty and Victoria came strolling into the kitchen. I looked up just as Ty wrapped his arms around me.

"What's good, little sis?" Ty said, Then he stepped back from our embrace.

Ty and I had become closer than ever in the past six months or so. There was no way anyone could tell me that he wasn't my brother. At one of the roughest times in my life, he had stepped up and had been holding me down, and I truly did appreciate it.

"Hey, bro. Where y'all coming from?" I said, looking over at Victoria as she went into the refrigerator to retrieve a bottle of water.

"I took Vic to her school to meet her advisor. You good, little sis?" Ty said as he took a seat next to me.

"I'm fine. I'm about to head out. Hector is taking me and Mariah to the hospital to see Cameron. I'll call if anything changes," I uttered as I flipped the magazine closed and stood from my seat.

My mood had changed drastically during our time in Miami. I'd gone from vibrant and upbeat to sullen and depressed. Thinking about seeing Cameron in the hospital bed, unconscious, put me in a bad place nowadays. This didn't stop me from making sure I saw him as much as I could.

I heard Mariah calling me from the foyer, so I said my goodbyes to Victoria and Ty and went to meet her so we could be on our way. Although it wasn't one of my favorite things to do, because of how much it hurt, I still looked forward to seeing Cameron.

Victoria

That day was one of them days. I'd been having them a lot lately, and it seemed as if the more time that lapsed, the more I was losing faith. Cam wasn't going to pull through this. I felt as if we were making ourselves suffer. We were keeping him alive, despite no real indication that he would wake up. It was mentally and emotionally challenging. I wanted my brother alive and well, but if that was not going to happen, I didn't want to suffer the suspense anymore. I was tired of seeing Skye struggle with trying to see Cam often, handling the business, and taking care of herself for the baby. I was also tired of hearing my mother down the hall, crying herself to sleep every night. She, too, felt that it was over for Cam, but she wouldn't say it out loud, nor would she ever entertain the idea of taking him off life support. Neither would Skye. Deep down I knew I didn't want to, either, but I was just worn out.

I tossed the empty bottle of water in the recycling bin and headed out of the kitchen, leaving Ty alone. I staggered up the steps to my bedroom, took off my sandals at the door, and stepped onto the plush carpet. I was standing in the middle of my room, lost in my thoughts, when I heard a deep voice.

"What are you thinking about?"

I turned around and came face-to-face with Ty. I took a step back, and he took a step closer.

"Nothing. I just have a lot on my mind," I said, looking at him oddly.

"Talk to me." He reached out and rubbed my cheek.

I began to feel how I had felt back at Ariana's house when we hugged. His touch sent shock waves through my body, and it activated the magnet that seemed to attract me to him.

"We're going to lose him," I said softly, almost in a whisper.

"No we're not," Ty said, attempting to reassure me. "He been hanging on this long. Cam not gonna give up."

As badly as I wanted to believe what he was saying, I couldn't help feeling otherwise.

"What will we do without him, Ty?" I said as tears escaped the corners of my eyes.

Ty moved closer to me and used his index finger to wipe the tears away. He leaned down and placed his soft lips on mine. I was shocked, but I didn't want the kiss to end. Our tongues found each other and tangoed for what seemed like forever before Ty stood up straight, abruptly ending our moment. He kissed me on the forehead and gazed into my eyes.

"No matter what happens, you'll always have me, Victoria. You have my word," he said with sincerity.

He didn't need to tell me that; I already knew it. I just wondered if he would allow me to have him the way I wanted him in the moment. There was nothing wrong with trying, I thought as I went in for the kill. My lips found his once more, and they felt at home. We kissed feverishly, finally succumbing to feelings that we both had been masking for quite some time.

I fell back onto the bed, with Ty on top of me. Still kissing me, he reached down under my dress and rubbed my clit. While trying to control my breathing, I reached down and fumbled with his Hermès belt until it was unbuckled. Ty paused, and I looked at him, confused. I thought he had changed his mind, but he hadn't. He rose from the bed, stood at the bottom of it, and removed his Kenzo shirt, exposing his chiseled torso. I followed his cue and pulled my dress over my head and slid my thong off, never taking my eyes off him.

I slowly slid my left hand down my midsection and stopped at my now soaking wet, hot pocket. I fondled my pussy and, with my free hand, squeezed my breast. Ty must have been enjoying the show, because moments later, he pulled his briefs down over his piece, which had to be at least ten inches and stood straight up like a pencil.

I spread my legs farther apart, allowing Ty to have a complete view of the box he was about to have. He climbed in between my legs and grabbed my hand. Raising it up to his mouth, he slowly and sensually licked my pussy juice off each of my fingers. He smiled and flashed his gorgeous smile. I couldn't believe this was happening. I'd dreamed of this day for as long as I could remember, and it was finally here. I had no clue how long whatever Ty and I were starting would last, but I definitely was going to enjoy the ride.

He rubbed the tip of his dick against my pussy, sending my body into overdrive. Unbeknownst to Ty, I was a virgin. I had been holding out for *that guy*, and I had always known that guy was Ty. I didn't know if I should tell him I was a virgin or just let things flow. I felt my pussy widen as Ty guided his dick in.

"Your shit tight as fuck, Vic," Ty called as he continued to push farther and farther in me.

I couldn't respond, because I was on the brink of crying and was fighting hard to suppress my tears. The pain was unbearable; he was entirely too big for my virgin pussy. I guessed he sensed something was wrong.

"I'm hurting you?" he asked, sounding truly concerned.

I lied, "No, you're good."

"Why you lying?"

Damn, he was good. I put my arm across my eyes and said, "I'm a virgin."

He moved my arm, so that he could look directly into my eyes . . . more like peer through my soul. "Why wouldn't you tell me that? I don't want to hurt you, Vic," he said, pulling out.

"I want you, Ty, but I didn't want you to think I was some inexperienced young girl and not fuck with me."

He leaned down and kissed me gently on my lips. "You are inexperienced, but that's something I'm going to cherish. Don't be afraid or ashamed to share anything with me, Vic. I would never shit on you."

I smiled and kissed him. I had never seen sentimental Ty before, but I liked him. I pulled him down closer to me and reached for his dick. I guided it right back to its new home. The pain hadn't subsided yet, but gradually it did. And, boy, did Ty take me there. I was not sure exactly where *there* was, but I had arrived.

He grabbed both of my hands and held them above my head as he pumped in and out of me. The feeling was euphoric, and I didn't want it to come to an end. He released my hands just as I felt him slip out of me. I was confused, and I was anxious for him to keep going. He leaned over and planted soft kisses on my neck, then trailed down toward my chest. Ty stopped at my titties. After taking one in his mouth, he sucked it and bit down softly, but firmly enough, on my nipple, sending a ripple of pleasure through my body. Ty looked up and smiled at me before continuing to kiss me down my stomach to my inner thigh. He threw one of my legs over his shoulder and playfully nibbled on my clit.

Ty surprised me when he penetrated me with his tongue, causing me to let out a slow low moan. He continued to lick, suck, and finger my pussy in ways I had never imagined it could be done, causing me to experience my first mind-blowing orgasm. It resembled a seizure, the way my body shook violently.

"Tyyy!" I cried out.

At that point I was begging to feel Ty inside me again. However, he didn't give into my pleading that easily. Ty rubbed the tip of his dick against my pussy lips and pulsating clit, causing me to moan louder and harder. I begged for him to enter, and after a few more minutes of teasing me, he did, slowly.

"Mmm, Ty," I moaned out as he grabbed my waist and pulled me toward him as he went as deep as he could.

"Damn, baby. This pussy is so good," he called as he began to pump in and out faster.

He picked me up, with his dick still inside me, pinned me against the wall, continued to go in and out, deeper and deeper. In between moans, I softly bit his ear and scratched his back. Once again I experienced a body-shaking orgasm. Once my body calmed and stopped shaking, Ty walked back over to the bed and sat down, with me on his lap. I rode him as if my life depended on it. My ass bounced up and down as Ty squeezed and slapped it. I felt his dick about to explode, while I, too, was on the verge of having another orgasm. I bounced on his dick harder and faster. Just as he released his nut inside of me, I came all over his dick.

Ty fell back on the bed, and I collapsed on top of his chest. We were silent as we lay there, basking in the afterglow of our sex session. Our moment was interrupted by the ringing of his cell phone. I thought he would ignore it, but he didn't. I rolled over just as he reached for the phone to answer it.

"What up?" he said into the phone.

I sucked my teeth loud enough for him to know I was irked by this.

Ariana

"Now you answer your phone, Ty? Wassup with you?"
I was frustrated, and I wasn't afraid to let Ty know that.

"I been busy, Ari." He had the nerve to sound as if I was
bothering him.

"So busy that you couldn't call just to check on me, or
come visit, even if it was just for a day?"

I was so over Ty and his shit. First, he had just up and
left, following Skye to Miami. I couldn't be mad at her,
though, because he had had a choice, and he had decided
to go there. That was not even the punch line. I had
offered to put my job on hold and move there with him
so we could maintain our relationship. Skye and I were
working on getting our friendship back, so I didn't think
she would mind, but Ty had turned down my offer, giving
me the weak-ass excuse that he didn't want me to have to
uproot my life and leave my job. I could smell bullshit a
mile away, and Ty reeked of it.

"Yo, every time you call me, is this going to be the
dynamic of our conversation? Shit is getting old. I'll be in
New York in a few days. I'll stop by your crib, and we can
talk then," he barked.

The line went dead. I looked at the phone with con-
tempt. That boy really must have lost his mind, hanging
up on me like that. It was time for us to just dead this shit,
because I was tired of playing second fiddle to everything
else he had going on.

There was no reason why I was getting bent out of shape. I still had my side nigga. See, Ty thought I wasn't hip to the game. We hadn't fucked in I didn't know how long, so I knew he was digging in another bitch's pussy. Part of me wanted to say it was Skye's, but I knew Skye better than that.

I couldn't dwell on that shit, however, because I was supposed to go check my other nigga. Ty would definitely miss me when I was gone.

Ty

I had finally had my chance with Vic, and although she was a virgin, there was no denying that she had some good-ass pussy. With a little molding, her sex game was definitely going to be A1. I would be the dumbest nigga ever if I fucked up what me and her planned on building together. Not only did I never want another nigga tapping that, but I also couldn't ruin the relationships I had with Cam and Mariah. Hurting Vic was out of the question. The ignorant-ass phone call I had got from Ariana just reminded me that I needed to nix her and fast.

After putting my phone back on the nightstand, I rolled over and came face-to-face with Vic. She looked disappointed, but I really didn't understand why. I had no intention of asking her what was going on, until she turned her back to me.

"What I do?" I questioned, turning her around to face me once again.

"What happens now? You continue to mess with Ariana and creep with me? You think I'm going to be your side chick?"

I knew I shouldn't have answered the phone, but knowing Ari, she would have kept calling.

"Vic, you should know me better than that. I'm done with Ariana. I don't have ill feelings toward her or nothing like that, but it's just not what I want anymore. I would not have had sex with you if I wanted to be with her," I explained.

She said nothing, but I knew she believed me. Vic had no reason not to. I moved closer to her and pushed a strand of hair out of her face before leaning in to kiss her.

"I'm going to shower, and then I'm going to start dinner. You're welcome to join me if you want," she said, sitting up in the bed.

I didn't need to be invited twice. I got up and followed her into the bathroom.

Skye

We spent all day at the hospital, so by the time we made it home, all I had energy for was the shower. I stood in the middle of my shower, letting the high-pressure water massage my aching body. Cairo was kicking, so I stopped washing for a minute to massage my huge belly. I swear, if I didn't know any better, I would have thought there were two babies in there. I smiled as I felt his kicks, but almost instantly, the moment of joy faded and was replaced by sorrow. Cameron hadn't got to feel his son kick yet. How many other things would he have to miss? The shower gave me too much time to think, and I didn't want to, especially about that. I finished washing and got out. After slipping into pajamas, I headed down stairs to have dinner, which surprisingly, Victoria had prepared.

It was always good to have dinner with Ty, Vic, Mariah, and Hector. Regardless of what we were going through, we all still found a way to make each other laugh and smile, even if it was only for a short period of time. After dinner, Cairo had me ready to pass right out. I headed up to my bedroom and went straight to sleep.

I felt like I had been 'sleep for only minutes when I was awakened by the worst pain I had ever experienced in my life. I sat up in bed and grabbed my stomach. The pain subsided, so I took the opportunity to catch my breath. However, not even five minutes later, I was experiencing it again. This time the pain was joined by a gush of water. I started to panic as I climbed out of the bed. The pain was excruciating, and I didn't think I would make it down the hall, but I had to.

Taking baby steps, I finally made it to Ty's bedroom. I didn't even bother knocking. Under normal circumstances I would have, but I needed medical attention and fast. I was panicking because Cairo wasn't due for another month. I prayed he was early just because, and not because something was wrong.

"Ty!" I yelled as I tried to catch my breath. "My water broke."

He and Victoria jumped out of the bed and rushed over to me. I couldn't even focus on the fact that they were in bed together. I didn't have time. I would definitely address it at a later date. I was leaning in the doorway, trying to remain standing, while Victoria tried to calm me down. The pain was unbearable, and I just wanted to lie on the floor until it was over.

"A'ight, little sis . . . breathe. Let me get you something to wear, and we out. Vic, stay here with her," Ty said as he slipped on a pair of basketball shorts.

What the hell? I didn't need clothes; I needed a doctor. I really didn't care if I showed up at the hospital in shorts and a wifebeater.

"Ty, I don't need to change. Please just get me to the hospital!" At that point I was shouting.

Neither one of them had given birth, so they couldn't possibly understand the pain I was feeling. If they did, they wouldn't be standing there, dumbfounded, and looking at me.

"Vic, get Ma and Hector, and meet us at the hospital. Oh, and don't forget to call her parents. I'm taking her now," Ty said as he picked me up in his arms and headed toward the steps.

As he descended the stairs, I prayed that he didn't drop me. I was aware of the pounds I had gained, and I knew

I was heavy, but I was thankful that he didn't make me walk. When we got to his car, he laid me in the backseat, jumped in, and we were on our way.

When we finally arrived at the hospital after what seemed like forever, Ty ran inside and returned with nurses, who quickly got me on a stretcher and steered me to labor and delivery. Everything after that was hectic. Between my screams, Ty pacing back and forth, and Cairo not wanting to come out, I prayed and prayed. I hadn't been the best person these past few months, and I knew that I would one day have to pay for that. I just didn't want to pay the price with my son.

Four hours later, I was ready to push. After only one push, I had to give respect to every woman who had gone through this. I didn't think I could manage any more pushes, and I was ready to let them cut me open. Thankfully, I had Ty by my side, holding my hand and coaching me all the way. After six more long, hard pushes, I heard the words I'd been waiting to hear for months.

"It's a boy!" the doctor yelled just as Cairo gave the cutest cry I had ever heard in my life.

I allowed Ty to cut his cord, because he was Cairo's godfather. They showed him to me briefly before taking him to get him cleaned up and weighed.

The nurse called out Cairo's stats. "Ten fingers, ten toes. Eight pounds, six ounces. Nineteen and a half inches."

Hearing that he was healthy was all I needed before I closed my eyes and caught my breath. On what was supposed to be one of the happiest days of my life, I was sad. Why did Cameron have to miss this? I couldn't dwell on that for too long, because before I knew it, Cairo was being placed in my arms for the first time. I couldn't hold in the tears that were threatening to fall, so I let them out. I cried for a plethora of reasons: one, my son was the best thing that had ever happened to me; two, Cameron had missed this moment; and three, I was worried about him not being able to be a part of Cairo's life at all.

My and Cairo's mother-son moment was short lived. He was quickly taken away from me once more, since I had to be transported to another room. I wished I could have held him during the move.

The nurses got me cleaned up, then took me to the room that would be my home for the next few days. I waited patiently for them to bring me my baby. As soon as I was situated, Ty, Mariah, and Victoria walked in. I was happy to see them and glad that they had been there for me through everything.

"How are you feeling? Where is the baby?" Mariah asked as she stood on the side of my bed, rubbing my hand.

"I'm fine and—" I began but was interrupted by the sound of my door opening.

"Here he is," a bubbly nurse sang out as she pushed Cairo's bassinet over to the side of my bed.

Mariah took one look at him, and tears formed in her eyes. I knew it was because she saw Cameron in that little face. I did too. She immediately went into the bathroom to wash her hands so she could hold the baby. It was really nice having the family there, but I was glad when visiting hours were over and it was just me and my boy. Becoming a mom was the best feeling in the world. The moment I heard his cries, I knew that I would give my last breath for my son. After feeding and changing him, I watched over him like a hawk until he was knocked out. After he had fallen asleep, I spent a little extra time admiring my pride and joy. Then I finally gave in to sleep as well.

Cairo woke up a few times throughout the night, which was why when I felt myself falling into a deep sleep, I jumped up. I looked over in his bassinet, and he wasn't there. I hit the button that alerted the nurse that I needed her in my room. Although she took only a minute to get to me, it felt like forever. I wanted my damn baby.

"Ms. Lewis, are you okay?" she questioned as she walked through the door.

"No. Where is my son? No one informed me that he was going to be moved." I was pissed.

"I'm sorry. I thought they gave you a heads-up. Dr. Lewis, your grandmother, came for the baby a little while ago. Let me get her," she said before she turned and headed out the door.

As I started to get out of the bed, my grandmother came waltzing into the room with a wheelchair. She seemed so upbeat and happy, but where was my son? I started to speak, but she shushed me, then helped me sit in the wheelchair. She rolled me to the elevator, got me inside it, and then rolled me out when we reached the next floor. I noticed we had got off on Cameron's floor. I started to get anxious, and my heart began to beat extremely fast. I felt it pulsating through my gown.

When we got to Cameron's room, I was shocked to see that my parents, Mariah, Victoria, and Ty were present. I knew my grandmother had to pull some strings to have them all in the room together. The sound of Cairo cooing grabbed my attention. I looked around, but I didn't see him. I stood up out of the wheelchair and walked closer to Cameron's bed. I almost fell over when I saw that Cairo was in his arms and that his eyes were wide open. I had to grab on to Ty, who was standing beside me, in order to keep my legs from giving out beneath me. Was I dreaming?

Cameron tried to speak. "Sk—"

"Cameron, what did I say? Do not force yourself to do too much. Just relax. I know there is tons you want to say. We have a long road ahead, but we will get there," my grandmother said, cutting him off.

I looked at him and saw the tears welling up in his eyes. He looked the same, but I knew he was far from the same. I would do whatever I could possibly do to get him back 100 percent.

I glanced over at my grandmother. "Can we have a minute? Grandma, can you stay?" I stated before turning my attention back to Cameron and Cairo.

My grandmother waited while everyone exited the room, and then she walked up to me and signaled for me to sit down. I didn't want to leave Cameron's side, so I pulled a chair closer to the bed and sat where I had previously been standing.

"What's going on with him? I know you are not at liberty to discuss his condition with me, and yeah, I know Mariah wouldn't mind telling me what's going on, but I want to hear it from you," I said. "You've been handling Cameron since the day we got to Miami, so it's you who can tell me what it is and what it's not. Please, Grandma, and be straight with me. Whatever it is, I can take it. I just need to know what to expect moving forward."

I watched as she grabbed another chair and pulled it up beside me. Cairo was getting a little fussy, so I stood to take him out of Cameron's arms. Before I could, Cameron shook his head no. I hesitated but decided to sit it out and see if Cairo would calm down in a few, so I returned to my seat. My grandmother placed her hand on top of mine and began to speak. She explained that she expected Cameron to make a full recovery, but it depended on him and the people around him. He would have to go through vigorous physical therapy and speech therapy.

That was all I needed to hear. As long as there was a chance that he would get back to his old self, I would make that happen. I didn't care who I had to pay or how much it would cost; Cameron would receive the best care the state of Florida had to offer. Shit, if I had to have someone fly in, I would do that too.

After fully explaining his condition to me, my grandmother left the room, giving us some time alone with our baby boy. Cameron was able to speak, but his speech was a bit slurred. Nothing speech therapy couldn't improve. In an effort to minimize his stress, I did most of the talking. I told him over and over how much I'd missed him and how glad I was to have him back. I didn't want this moment to end at all. I smiled at Cairo, who was sound asleep in his father's arms. I stood over them and said a prayer. My boys needed protection, and I needed forgiveness. I leaned over and kissed Cameron. His cheek was damp from the tears that he thought I hadn't noticed falling. I had, but I hadn't said anything. I sat next to him, and we cried together.

The moment that I wanted to last forever came to an end when my grandmother returned to take me and Cairo back to our room. Cameron needed to have tests done, but she promised she would bring me and Cairo back to his room later.

"I love you and Cairo," Cameron forced himself to say as I got in the wheelchair with Cairo in my arms.

I was ecstatic to hear those words. Just when I had started to think I would never hear them again, I did.

"We love you too, baby."

Skye

I hadn't been home from the hospital for even a month before it was back to business. Although I wanted more time with my baby boy, I was happy when my grandfather called me and told me that I had to meet up with Jeff. After having his first offer rejected by my grandfather, Jeff was trying his hand again. Luckily—well, more like unluckily for Jeff—my grandfather had me working for him in the States and was able to accommodate Jeff's needs. I'd been waiting to catch up with him, and the opportunity had finally presented itself.

I had to make this trip as quickly as possible. My son was only a few weeks old, and I didn't feel comfortable leaving him. However, I had to. Who knew when I would get this opportunity again? I would be leaving Cairo with Mariah and Victoria, two people who I knew without a shadow of a doubt would not let anything happen to him. The only problem was Cameron. He had been released from the hospital and had been living at a rehabilitation center, and although he hated being there, I wasn't giving in. If he was to have fully functional legs again, he needed to be there. He would just have to deal with it. He was used to seeing me every other day, if not every day, and I knew he would get suspicious if I was gone too long. I wasn't ready to tell him all that had been going on. Even Ty agreed that it wasn't the right time to tell him.

"Ms. Skye?" Hector said, walking into the kitchen, where I sat at the counter, feeding Cairo a bottle. "I have spoken to your grandfather. What time will we be leaving?" he said, referring to our trip back to New York.

"Book the flight for as soon as possible. I would like to leave today, so I can see him in the morning and then head back here. I don't want to leave Cai for too long," I said, holding Cairo close to my shoulder to burp him.

"I understand. I'll let you know the time right away," he said as he turned around to do what I had asked of him.

At first, I hadn't really seen the point of Hector being around, but now with Cairo here, he would definitely be put to use. Whenever I had to run, I would be sure to leave Hector here to protect my son, in case something were to pop off. I was always good as long as Ty was with me, but this time I had to leave even Ty out of the loop. And I wanted to tell Victoria my current plans, but since I knew she was sleeping with Ty now, I decided against it. I didn't need for my activities to become pillow talk.

As if he had read my mind, Ty walked into the kitchen. "What up, sis? I overheard your conversation with Hector. I told him to add me to the itinerary. I wanna go check my niggas. Why you going out there, and why didn't you tell me?" he said, taking a seat next to me.

"I'm going to meet up with my grandfather. It's just to discuss some business plans, that's all," I lied.

Ever since I had told Ty that Andreas Santiago was my grandfather, Ty had opted out of every opportunity to be in close proximity to him. I didn't know that my grandfather's name rang bells in Ty's head until the day I told Ty exactly who he was. I chuckled as I thought back to that moment now. It was one of the many nights I had opened up to Ty about how I was feeling. I was dealing with a heap of emotions, and it felt good to have someone to share them with. Ty was always there.

"Your grandfather is who?" Ty said after I broke down and told him about my trip to Panama.

"You heard me," I replied.

"That's why your ass was so adamant about taking over this shit," Ty mused. "You got that nigga Poppy backing you up. That nigga got the power to kill a nigga just by looking at him too long. I had no idea you were his granddaughter. You like the Panamanian mob and shit."

He was so excited that his thoughts were all over the place and he was rambling on. I could tell he felt proud to be associated with me. I had gained some clout by being the granddaughter of Andreas Santiago, and although having this clout meant nothing to me, I had to admit it felt good knowing I was running with good company.

Cairo's crying brought me back to the present moment.

"Aw, little man. You tired? Come and let God-daddy lay you down and shit," Ty said, reaching out and taking Cairo out of my arms.

"Must you say, 'And shit,' to my boy?" I said, laughing at Ty.

Since Cairo was going down for a nap, I decided to take one as well. I knew that once I got to New York, sleeping would be the last thing I was able to do. It would be good to get a nap in before it was time to head to the airport.

Ty

I felt bad about lying to Skye. I couldn't have told her that I was going to New York to see my pops, because I didn't know how she would have reacted to that. It was like an unspoken thing between us, something that I wasn't trying to discuss. Truth be told, I didn't understand why I was even going to entertain what he had to say. I guessed because at the end of the day, he was still my pops. Me seeing him wouldn't change my ill feelings toward him at all, though. He had fucked up, and he knew that, but the least I could do was give him the opportunity to explain himself.

I laid Cairo down in the middle of my bed and placed pillows on all sides of him. Then I sat down next to him. That was my little nigga. The love I had for that kid had been instant. Maybe it was because since the day Cam had got shot, I had been mentally preparing myself to be the man in Cairo's life. I would have never replaced Cam, but I definitely would have stepped up and been the male that all young dudes needed while growing up. Thankfully, Cam was up and thriving, so now I just focused on being the best godfather I could be. That was cool with me.

My phone made a sound, alerting me that I had received a text message. I grabbed the phone before it had a chance to wake Cam up. I opened the text, which was from Ariana.

Nobody was going to tell me that Skye had the baby? I had to run into her mother in SoHo to find out. You been acting real different lately. Are you fucking her or something?

I put my phone on vibrate and tossed it beside me on the bed. I wasn't about to entertain the dumb shit Ariana was on. I would definitely be paying her a visit when I touched down, though. It was time I wrapped shit up with her, especially because I wanted to be with Vic. I had promised Vic I would. That was a promise I was keeping, no matter what.

I couldn't even pinpoint where Ari and I had gone wrong. I had really been feeling shorty at first, but something had changed. I had started feeling that she was being sneaky and shit, and once I got that feeling, I had started to lose interest. I wasn't a fucking detective, so I hadn't been about to search for clues about what she was up to or to try to figure out if she was keeping shit from me. It was whatever to me. I lay back on the bed now, rubbing my temples. Ariana really knew how to stress a nigga out. I used the time I had now to mentally prepare myself for dealing with her after I told her I ain't want any parts of her anymore.

Matthew

I didn't know why I was trusting this nigga. I had never met him and had conversed with him only once, and that was months ago. I had to suck it up, though, and take the risk. I ran it by Man, and he said the cat was cool, so I was going through with it. My nigga Man was doing much better now. He had recovered from some of the injuries he sustained when Ty and them hit him up. He was still walking around with that shit bag, though, so he was laying low. I didn't blame him for that. I couldn't imagine having to walk around while pissing and shitting into a bag. The thought of that shit was repulsive. At least he was alive, though.

The vibration of my cell phone caused me to shake my thoughts. I looked down at the screen on my phone and saw that I had received the text I had been waiting for.

Come in!

I got out of my car and walked in the direction of the house I'd been told to come to. As I walked up the front steps two at a time, I patted my waist, making sure my piece was securely in place. I'd been told to go straight in, so once I reached the front door, I twisted the doorknob, and as it should have, the door opened. Hesitantly, I stepped into the house and quickly looked left, then right.

"We're in here," I heard a deep voice say.

I took a deep breath and headed in the direction from which the voice had come. I walked into what appeared to be the living room, although it lacked the essentials. There were two guys there.

"Wassup, Matthew?" the taller guy said, extending his hand for me to shake it.

I returned the gesture and shook his hand. There was something familiar about this cat. I just couldn't place where I knew him from. I would soon find out. I shifted my attention to the other guy, who stood leaning against the wall. He hadn't said a word to me yet, so I already knew who the boss was.

"Thanks for coming through on such short notice," the familiar guy said.

I nodded my head. There wasn't much for me to say, seeing as I still had no idea why I was there in the first place.

"So I've heard through Man that we have a common enemy. Cam. Am I correct?"

I'd be damned. I knew exactly who this nigga was. All I could do was shake my head and think about how many people Hassan and Cam had pissed off. Niggas was jumping ship in their crew left and right. I smiled inwardly, knowing that if anyone had a way to get Cam, it was this dude right here.

"Correct," I said with enthusiasm.

He smiled and tapped the seat next to him, signaling for me to sit down. Once I did, he sat down across from me, then ran through a list of instructions he wanted me to follow the next day. Listening to this nigga's plan had me on the edge of my seat. I was ready, though. If this was the type of work I had to put in to ensure that I would be up next to run Brooklyn, then so be it. Miguel and his goons were interested in helping me achieve what I wanted. All he cared about was his work, which I was barely getting off. Between some cat in Jersey and my homie in the A, I got off enough work to make Miguel's money back and keep him off my back. I was still left with more product and less money. Shit needed to change.

"Follow those exact instructions tomorrow and we will be a'ight. Handle it right and there will be a spot for you in the army I'm building," he said before dismissing me.

The entire ride back to my crib in Canarsie, I thought about the last thing he had said. He had life fucked up if he thought I was agreeing to put in this work to be on his team. I was doing it because it benefited me. I refused to be a soldier on another nigga's front line. Now, once I earned my stripes and was running shit, he would be more than welcome to join my team. If he felt differently, we would definitely cross that bridge at the appropriate time.

Skye

Our plane got in at around two o'clock in the morning. Given that we had booked the flight at the last minute, that was the only option we had. I was up early in the morning, running on no more than four hours of sleep. I had to meet up with Jeff at nine, and if things went the way Hector and I had discussed, Jeff would be dead and I would be on a plane, heading back to Miami, by noon. Ty had already left by the time I was dressed and ready to go. Hector and I headed out right behind him, but not before I had the chance to eat.

While I drove us to Queens, where the meeting would be taking place, I decided to go over the plan with Hector again. There was no room for error. We had to get it right. There would be no second chance.

"Hector, remember the plan. I will be letting you out a block before the location, because I need him to think I am alone—"

He interrupted me. "Ms. Skye, there's no need to go over it again. I know what needs to be done. Don't worry. Everything will be fine."

I smiled, realizing he was right. Five minutes later, I nodded my head, signaling that it was time for him to get out of the car. Once his feet hit the pavement, I continued on up the street to the location where I was to meet Jeff. I parked directly across the street from the house. Before getting out of the car, I checked my gun, making sure it was loaded with a full clip. I opened the car door and stepped out into the morning sun. I was nervous and quickly wiped my forehead as I felt a bead of sweat forming.

I approached the house and knocked on the front door, and seconds later the door was opened. I knew that the man standing on the other side of the door was Jeff. He looked exactly like Ty, but older and with a beard.

"You must be Skye. Right this way," he said, pointing me in the direction of the living room.

I walked in the direction in which he pointed, and was floored when I came face-to-face with Ty.

"What the fuck?" I shrieked, spinning around and drawing my gun simultaneously.

"What the fuck you doing here, Skye?" I heard Ty say.

I couldn't focus on Ty, since I was now facing the barrel of Jeff's nine. However, I wondered the same thing about Ty.

"You thought you had me, bitch?" Jeff said, then let out a hearty laugh.

I was scared for my life, but I wouldn't let him see that. I kept my gun up and aimed the barrel directly between his eyes.

"You thought I wouldn't put two and two together when Andreas told me I would be meeting with you. Thank Cam for that. Your name seemed to come out of his mouth every time I was around the nigga," Jeff observed.

"Pops, this ain't her beef. Your issues are with Cam. Let her go," Ty pleaded with his father.

"Fuck out of here. Them niggas think they can touch any and everybody, and they thought they were invisible. Where Hassan's bitch-ass son now? His bitch about to pay for his sins," Jeff said in a condescending tone.

I heard a gun cock, but I didn't know if I would be seeing a flash next. I didn't move, though. Jeff wasn't going to make me fold. What followed the sound of the gun cocking shocked me.

"Pops, you know I can't let you kill her," Ty said, aiming his gun at his father.

"You would kill me over this bitch? Family over everything, Ty. You forgot that? What? You smashing this? Cam know?"

"You right, Pops. Family over everything," Ty said before I heard the blast of his gun and watched as Jeff dropped to the floor, with a small bullet hole in the middle of his head.

I looked back at Ty, who was just shaking his head. He had just murdered his father, for me.

"Ty," was all I was able to get out before he grabbed me and dropped to the floor as a shitload of bullets riddled the windows.

I wondered where Hector was, until I heard a machine gun return fire. I knew the machine gun belonged to Hector. If Ty and I had any chance of making it out of this situation, we had to move, and fast.

"Ty, get off of me. Let's go. That's Hector with the machine gun. He will cover us," I screamed above the gunshots.

Ty used his body to shield me as we maneuvered through the house to the back door. By the time we reached the back door, the shooting had ceased. We exited through that door, and as we crept around the house, we spotted Hector, who was looking at the mess that had been left behind. A second later I sprinted across the street, over to where I had parked the car. Ty followed me, and when he reached the car, I tossed him the keys, because I was in no way able to drive. All I could think about was what would have happened if Ty hadn't been inside that house. I also wanted to know who that shooter outside the house was.

Matt

"Fuck!" I screamed out loud as I jogged down the street, trying to making it back to my whip. Who the fuck was that nigga who was shooting at me? He had appeared out of nowhere and had fucked up my plans. After Jeff had told me that he had set it up so that he, Ty, and Cam's bitch would be in the spot at the same time, I had decided I had to handle shit my own way. Killing all those bitches at the same time would have saved me a lot of trouble. But that Spanish nigga just had to be there to spoil everything.

Once I was back inside my whip, I slammed my hands against the steering wheel in frustration. Nothing was going as planned. Man was still low, still bouncing back from his run in with Ty. At least that was the story he was selling me. But I was starting to think the nigga was scared. From this day onward, I was going to be out for myself. Fuck Man, and fuck them Mexicans. Everybody talked a good game, but nobody was producing any fucking results. I needed results. I *wanted* results.

As I drove home, I thought through all the things that had happened and came up with a new method. I wanted different results, so it was time to use a different method.

Skye

It had been two weeks since the shooting at Jeff's. Ty and I had decided that it was best that we keep what had happened from Cameron for the time being. No sense in getting him worked up when he was unable to do anything about it. Ty had also told me that Matt was the shooter who had been stationed outside Jeff's house. It was past his time to leave this earth. Keeping him alive had almost cost me my life. I wasn't trying to risk that again. I had wanted to talk to Ty about him killing his own father, but he hadn't wanted to discuss it. He had told me to bury all thoughts about it and not to mention it again. How could I let that go, though? Ty had saved my life and had had to kill the only flesh and blood he had left to do so. I would forever be grateful to Ty for that, and I just hoped he knew just how grateful I was.

In these past two weeks, it had been back to the drawing board for me. I was overwhelmed by emotion and stress. I felt drained. So much had happened in the past six months or so, and it had been so stressful trying to keep up with Cameron and his therapy needs, taking care of Cairo, and running Cameron's business—all at the same time. The way I looked at life had been slowly changing. The way I looked at myself had been changing as well, and that was the scariest part. I just needed to take a step back. I needed a break from everyone and everything. So I left Cairo in Miami with everyone, and I headed back to New York alone. To their knowledge, I was visiting my parents. It wasn't a lie, because I did go see them, but that wasn't my sole purpose for going to New York. I just wanted a break.

I spent my first day back at the mall, doing some retail therapy. Shopping was something that helped me relax and took my mind off of everything that was going on around me. I was glad when I pulled up to my building after my shopping trip, because I was beat. A nice bubble bath and a glass of wine were exactly what I needed. I grabbed the bags out of my truck and headed upstairs.

When I got to my door, a creepy feeling came over me. I knew something wasn't right. It was a gift I had picked up while working in this business. If you had a feeling something was off, nine times out of ten, it was. I dug down in my Céline purse and retrieved the .22 pistol that I had tucked away for emergencies. It was small and compact. It was definitely not my choice of weapon if I intended to do damage, but it worked as far as being able to travel with it.

I took the safety off my .22 as I let myself in the house. I almost regurgitated my lunch at the sight that was waiting for me. Ariana was sprawled across my foyer floor, beat up. Her eyes were swollen shut, she was half naked, and there were black and blue bruises all over her once smooth caramel skin. I could tell she was alive, although her breathing was faint. I didn't think to rush to her side, because instinct kicked it. I spun around, with my gun drawn, ready to shoot whoever was in my house. I was too slow, though, because a pair of huge hands found their home around my neck. The culprit relieved me of my gun and slammed my back against the wall. I tried to fight him off, but it was useless. That man had to be about 350 pounds of solid muscle.

I felt the air slowly escape my body, and I began to feel weak due to oxygen deprivation. All I thought about was my son. Would I ever see him again? The fucked-up thing about the predicament I found myself in now was this culprit didn't even have the decency to tell me why I was headed to meet my Maker. Suddenly, a voice came from the living room, stopping the culprit from choking me to death.

"That's enough, Jesus. Bring her to me."

The culprit, who I now knew was a guy named Jesus, removed his hands from around from neck and grabbed my ponytail. I swung at him violently and landed a couple of punches to his midsection, but he wasn't fazed. He dragged me into the living room by my hair and tossed me on the floor, at someone's feet. I looked up, and our eyes met.

"Miguel," I said, realizing that I was definitely going to die.

"Skye, Skye, Skye, you are a hard young lady to catch up with. Good thing I caught up with your friend out there. She didn't take much convincing to give up the information I wanted."

Miguel's voice was creepy and eerie as hell. I started to experience the same chills I had experienced when I first met him at Cameron's father's funeral.

"Fuck you!" I shouted.

If I was going to die, I wasn't going out like a bitch. He was not about to have me in my own house, crying and pleading for my life. Before I knew it, I felt wind, and then a hand crashed into the side of my face. After getting over the initial shock of Jesus slapping me, I jumped up. I grabbed the vase off my coffee table and slammed it on the side of Jesus's head, shattering the vase. He stumbled back and hit the floor.

"Hit me again, motherfucker!" I shouted. My adrenaline was pumping, and I was gonna fight until there was no life left in me to fight.

"All right, enough! Jesus, shake it off and get the fuck up!" Miguel ordered. "Skye, I'm not here to kill you yet, because I know Cameron is alive and in Miami. I'm also aware that you are now running his business. His debts are now your debts. He was due to pay me two million dollars, and it's now up to three. I will contact you when I am ready for payment. Please have it. If you don't, my next visit will be to Miami, and I'm going to be looking for Cairo."

Nothing he had said registered with me, because I had learned not to let threats faze me. That is, until he mentioned my son. How the fuck did he know I had a baby? And he knew his name at that.

"I told you, your friend was very cooperative," Miguel said, sensing my confusion.

I was going to kill Ariana. I didn't care that she had asked Jacob at the front desk to let her in my house with these men, but the fact that she had mentioned my son to Miguel was something else. Cairo had nothing to do with any of this shit. My worst fear could become a reality, and Ariana would be to blame.

Miguel made a few more threats, which I paid zero attention to, before he and his lapdog were on their way. Once I heard the door slam, signaling their departure, I walked back into the foyer. Ariana was sitting with her knees pulled up to her chest and was shaking. That bitch had the nerve to be acting scared. I had the urge to kick her dead in her face for being so stupid, but I decided against it. I had enough on my plate already.

"I'm sorry, Skye," Ariana said, looking up at me with eyes that were full of tears.

I looked down at her in disgust, and at that moment my mind was made up. None of the shit Ariana and I had been through in the past mattered. She was dead to me. This was the second time she had pulled some dumb shit, and I was through with it. There was no need for me to pretend to understand her or to even reason with her. Her days were numbered. I left her sitting there and headed to my bedroom to get her something to throw on. I returned and threw the clothes at her.

"You got two minutes. Get dressed and get the fuck out!" I said, leaning against the wall.

I stood there and watched as she got dressed and left. Once she was gone, I put away my gun and cleaned up my living room before plopping down on an armchair and calling Ty.

Ty

I had just left the rehab center where Cam had his physical therapy. I was in a good mood, because my nigga was doing much better. As expected, he was going to make a full recovery, as long as he kept up with the therapy. We all made sure that he did. I was walking toward Skye's whip, which she let me use while I was in Miami, when my phone started vibrating. I looked down, realized it was Skye, and picked up instantly.

"Baby sis, wassup? Yo, I just left Cam's PT session, and he doing mad good, sis," I boasted. It felt good to have some good news to share for once.

"I'm happy. I can't wait to get back and see him and Cairo. How's my baby? Where is he?"

I chuckled, because I knew before anything else was discussed, Skye was going to ask about Cai.

"He good, sis. He's at home with Ma and Vic. What's wrong with you? You sound like something is bothering you." I sensed that she was about to drop a bomb, but how heavy, though?

"Take the next plane back to New York and come straight to my house," was all she said before hanging up. That was the signal to let me know how important it was.

I didn't need to question anything. Baby sis had called, so I had answered. I dropped Skye's car back at the house and took a cab to the airport and was on the first flight back to New York.

***

It was late when I touched down, so I debated whether I should go to my house to crash and then catch up with Skye first thing in the morning or whether I should go straight to her place. I recalled the desperation in her voice during our phone conversation, and I figured she needed to see me right away, so I took a cab to her place. When I finally got there and she opened the door, right away I noticed a bright red handprint on her left cheek. My body temperature rose in a matter of seconds as I became enraged. I was ready to body somebody. Who had enough balls to put their hands on my sister?

"Fuck happened to your face?" I asked her as I walked through the door.

"I had a visit today," she said as we walked into the living room.

"From?" I was curious.

As Skye took a seat on one of the armchairs, I sat down on the couch and put my feet up on the coffee table. I expected Skye to pull my card about this, because she hated it, but she didn't. She had to be real upset. I sat comfortably as she filled me in on the events that had taken place that day. I couldn't believe the shit she was telling me: everything from Ariana knowing that Man and Max were working together to Ariana giving up Cam's and Cai's whereabouts to Miguel. How could one be so fucking stupid? It was evident that Ariana wasn't hip to our lifestyle, but at the same time she had common sense and chose not to use it.

I was relieved that Miguel had come through only to put fear in Skye's heart. She and I both know that shit could have gone south and ended bad for her. Skye must have played her cards right; that was really the only explanation I could come up with to account for the fact that she was still alive. Miguel and his shooters were

always on some "shoot first, and ask questions later"–
type shit. They had to be up to something. By the time
Skye was done putting me onto what had gone down, I
already knew in my mind what Cam would do about it,
but ultimately, it was Skye's call.

"What you want to do, sis?" I asked, looking over at her
for an answer.

"Kill Ariana. I'll handle the Mexicans," she said with a
straight face.

I didn't just hear her say she wanted me to kill Ariana.
Putting that aside, how did she think she could go toe-to-
toe with the Mexicans and come out of that in one piece?
Lately, I had been agreeing with Skye and letting her
handle shit as she saw fit, but this was on another level.
She wasn't ready for that type of war.

"Skye—"

She stopped me before I could even get my point
across. "Would you question Cameron's call?"

I didn't answer, because I knew where she was going
with this. She and I both knew that I wouldn't.

She nodded. "Exactly. So don't do it to me. Handle
Ariana ASAP. I'm going back to Miami in the morning.
I have some other things I need to do. I will handle the
Mexicans, Ty! So do not question that. Just do what I
asked." She stood and headed to her bedroom.

I had too much on my mind. The thought of having to
body Ariana and let Skye willingly sign her own death
certificate had drained a nigga of any energy I had left. I
lay back on Skye's couch and dozed off.

Skye

When I woke up the next morning, I lay in bed, gathering my thoughts. I just wanted my son. At that point, he was all that mattered to me. Protecting him was my job, and I would die doing it if I had to. It would be easier to just pay the Mexicans what they had asked for, but I knew it wouldn't stop there. Miguel had to go, and anyone else who got in my way would suffer the same fate as he did.

Realizing I needed to start my day, I grabbed my phone off the nightstand and searched for the Delta app. I needed to book a flight back to Miami. After booking my flight, I headed into the bathroom to wash my face, brush my teeth, and shower. When I got out of the shower, I saw that it was already 9:00 a.m., and my flight was scheduled for takeoff at 11:00 a.m. I had to get dressed and be on my way. I slipped on a pair of True Religion jeans and a True T-shirt. Nothing fancy. Just something comfortable for my flight. I grabbed my cell phone and noticed that I had a text from Ty.

Little sis, I'm letting you know that I left. I'll handle that and meet you back in MIA when I can.

I was glad Ty wasn't wasting any time, because I felt like enough time had already lapsed. I grabbed my bag and headed out to catch a taxi to the airport.

When my plane touched down in Miami, I headed to the parking lot where Victoria was waiting on me. I had texted her before I left New York, so she would be expecting me. I was glad she was on time, because I hated waiting. As I got closer to the car, I could see into it through one of the back windows, since it was rolled down a little bit. I saw my baby boy, and my mood instantly changed. Being around my son made me feel as if all the bullshit in my life was nonexistent.

Once I was at the car, I peered through the crack in the back window on the side where Cairo was in his car seat, and made baby sounds to him, causing him to smile. He was such a happy baby, and I smiled as I crawled into the front passenger seat. I reached over and hugged Victoria, but her face was expressionless.

"What's wrong with you?" I asked, looking at her as if she had lost her mind.

"What happened to your face?" she said, pointing at my face and reminding me that I still had the bright red hand impression on my left cheek.

"Nothing, sis." I said, brushing her off. I really didn't have a problem sharing the details of yesterday's events with her, but I needed this time to come up with an excuse for when Cameron asked me.

He still had no idea about my involvement in the business, and this red handprint on my face would be sure to raise some flags. Maybe it was time for him to know, and maybe I should have told him the minute he woke up from the coma, but how? I was glad that Victoria didn't press me to discuss the matter and left it alone. For the duration of the ride back to the house, I was in deep thought. Cameron was going to flip out.

Cam

I had become so accustomed to staying at the rehabilitation center that I didn't believe my therapist when
she said I was being released. I had thought that after
my hospital stay, I was going to be heading home for
good. I had had it all wrong. My moms and Skye had
wanted me to have round-the-clock therapy, so they'd
paid for me to live in the facility. I knew their intentions
were good, and I appreciated it, but a nigga wanted to
be home. And when I said *home*, I meant New York.

I still didn't have the slightest idea why we were in
Miami and how we had gotten here. Since I'd woken
up from the coma, everyone had seemed to be walking
on pins and needles. Conversation was limited, unless
it was about my progress or Cairo. Even Ty seemed as
if he was holding back from me when we kicked it, and
that was different, seeing as that was my nigga and we
shared everything. I definitely needed answers.

That was all I thought about as my therapist pushed
the wheelchair I was in out to the parking lot, where
my mother was waiting on me. I couldn't front. It was
nice seeing her, but I low key wanted Skye to be there. I
remembered her telling me she was going to New York
to see her parents, but that was days ago. I was sure my
mom had told her they were letting me go. I expected
her to be there and was a little hurt that she wasn't. I
would never openly express that to anyone, though. I just
wasn't that type of nigga. My therapist helped me into

the passenger seat of my mother's whip, took my walker from the intern, and put it in the truck.

That was when it finally hit me: I was out of that bitch. Leaving the rehab center was the first time I felt like I was really making progress. Being there had made me feel stuck. It was bad enough that I still couldn't walk without the annoying-ass walker. My speech was still a little fucked up too. Overall, I wasn't in a predicament that I could complain about. I was alive, and I had to be grateful for that. I may have missed seeing my first son being born, but having the chance to watch him grow up would definitely make up for that. I couldn't wait to hold my little man. It had killed me during my time at the rehab center to know that he was so close but at the same time so far away. Skye and my mother had brought him through occasionally to visit me, but it wasn't the same.

"I'm so happy we are finally bringing you home," my mother said as she leaned over and kissed my cheek before starting up the car and pulling off.

"Me too, Ma. When are we going back to the city?"

I was sure she was shocked by my question. I already knew that I didn't have clearance to leave the state, but I wanted to test my moms. I wanted to see how much information I could get out of her.

"Boy, don't be worrying about all that. You worry about getting back one hundred percent," she retorted.

She was smart. I smiled at her, just so we wouldn't have to talk about this subject anymore. For the duration of the ride, I sat staring out the window, reflecting on everything that had happened up to this point. When I first woke up, the incident that had landed me in a coma was a complete blur. I couldn't remember it for shit. That pissed me off, but my doctor promised that fragments would start to come back to me, and they did. I knew exactly what had happened and the identity of my assailant. Niggas really thought Miguel and them bitch-ass Mexicans were gods. He'd learn, but why did my little nigga have to cross me, though?

When we pulled up to what I assumed was our home, my mother got out of the car and walked inside. I attempted to get out of the car, but my attempt was futile. The "not walking" shit was mind blowing. A minute later, my mother returned with some Spanish-looking nigga, who helped me out of the car and into the house. I didn't say a word to him or to my mother. There was no point. I was sure whoever that nigga was, he had been told not to answer any of my questions. Everything was directed to Skye, it seemed, so I would be sure to get the answers I needed from Skye as soon as she came back from New York.

Ty

I felt like shit, knowing what I had to do. That didn't change the fact that it had to be done, though. Even though I wasn't feeling Ari on the level anymore, I still didn't want to kill her. Had she kept it one hundred with us from the jump about knowing that Man and Matt were related, a lot of this shit could have been avoided. Skye wanted her dead, so dead she would be. I still was shocked that it had come to this, given that they'd been best friends, and I hated to see how this shit had torn them apart. I knew that if Cam was able to make the call, he, too, would order someone to kill Ariana. I understood the reasoning. I just hated that it had to be me who did Ariana in.

After I stepped out of my truck, I jogged to the entrance of Ariana's building, trying to not to get soaked by the rain, which seemed to get heavier the moment I got out of the truck. When I got up to her floor, I paused by the elevator, getting my thoughts together. Would I say something first? Or would I just kill shorty and be done with it? I still had other shit to do, so I figured I'd just get this shit over with.

I walked toward her door and used the key she had given me to let myself in. She was expecting me, so it wasn't like I was catching her off guard and shit. To her knowledge, I was coming over to discuss our relationship and the prospect of moving forward. Shit didn't even sound like me, but whatever. As I walked through the door, I pulled my nine out. I wasn't wasting any time. I heard the TV playing in the living room, so I headed in that direction. When I got there, she was seated with her back toward me, so it would have been easy for me to pop shorty and go about my day. However, something in me needed an explanation. It wouldn't change her fate, but I needed one, nonetheless.

"Yo, Ari!" I barked as I inched toward her, breaking her trance as she watched the TV.

When she turned around, I watched as her eyes widened and her breaths got short as she came face-to-face with the silencer that was screwed on the tip of my piece.

"So you knew about Man and Matt but decided to let the shit slide? What were you even doing with that nigga? Y'all working together or some shit?" I barked, with my piece still aimed at her and my finger on the trigger.

"Ty, it's not like that!" she said, with eyes that begged me to let her live.

That just wasn't going to happen. I lifted my arms in the air and came down as hard as I could, forcing the butt of my gun to connect with her jaw. She grabbed her face and doubled over in pain as blood leaked from her jaw onto her carpet.

"My nigga could die because of you. I should've never dealt with you. Dumb-ass bitch." I didn't need to scream. I spoke calm, making sure each of my words cut that bitch deep, giving her something to think about while she was walking to the crossroads.

"Ty, please don't do this. I'm sorry. I've paid for not speaking up, in the worst way. I've lost so much," she cried out, pausing between words, trying to speak through the pain that was pulsating through her jaw.

"Bitch, you ain't lose shit yet!"

I raised my gun once again, brought it level with her head.

"I lost our baby!" was the last thing she was able to say.

The shit that had gone down at Ari's crib left me feeling a little fucked up. But at the end of the day, a nigga had to do what he had to do. As I buried my piece in the secret compartment in my truck, I buried all thoughts and feelings Ariana related. Before pulling off, I called my nigga and told him to handle the Ariana shit for me, and then I went about my business.

I had to check on my niggas to see if they needed any more work. I couldn't front. Since we started fucking with the shit Skye was supplying us with, business had been booming. Shit had calmed down on the beef front, but I knew them niggas were lurking and was going to slip up sooner or later, and when they did, me and my niggas planned on being right there to terminate those niggas' careers.

Skye

As we pulled up to the house after driving back from the airport, I got a phone call from Ty. I let Victoria go ahead without me so I could take the call. She had no idea about what had transpired between Ariana, Miguel, and me, and I wasn't trying to add explaining to her what had happened to my list of things to do. Once she was out of earshot, I answered the call.

"Sis, wassup?" He spoke in an upbeat tone.

I knew exactly why he sounded the way he did. I also knew that he was masking his true emotions. I knew that Ty had real feelings for Ariana, and that having to kill her had been a hard pill for him. She had been my best friend, so if anyone understood the mixed emotions, it was me. Contrary to what anyone else may have thought, Ariana had messed up one too many times. It had to be done.

"Hey, bro. You good?" I asked, genuinely concerned.

"Yeah. Just letting you know I'll be home tonight," he exclaimed, confirming that the job he had set out to do was complete.

We didn't speak much longer after that. Once I ended our call, I felt sick to my stomach. Never in a million years had I imagined that things would end this way between me and Ariana. I felt a pain in my heart for her parents. They would never see their daughter again, but at the end of the day, that was her fault. Shit, it was because of her that my son was now on Miguel's radar, not to mention that he knew where Cameron was. I had to shake the feelings I was going through. That was a reminder that I had a host of other things to handle, and that Ariana was just one less worry.

I stepped out of the car and opened the back door to get Cairo out of his car seat. As always, he had fallen fast asleep. Car rides had that effect on him. I cradled my prince close to my chest and strolled to the entrance of our home. I didn't even have the chance to close the front door behind me before I was bombarded by Mariah. She wanted Cairo.

"He's knocked out," I said, handing a sleeping Cairo over to his grandmother.

"He needs to wake up to see his daddy," she said as she turned to walk away.

I was puzzled. "Cameron is home?"

"Yes. I picked him up earlier today. He is in the bedroom. He's not really feeling like himself. He's frustrated. Go talk to him." Her voice trailed off as she disappeared up the stairs with Cairo.

I stood still, thinking about what she had said. I didn't think I was ready to deal with Cameron feeling helpless. I wasn't used to seeing him that way. It was okay when he was living at the rehab center, because I dealt with it for a period of time and then was on my way. Having to hear him complain about his situation every day was going to be a task. And also, I fully intended on helping him and easing the load, but it would still be another task, nonetheless. I knew I needed to go see him, but I was still hesitant because of the mark on my face. Nonetheless, I knew it was only going to spark a conversation that we needed to have. I took a deep breath and exhaled as I walked toward the bedroom we had set up for him.

Cameron

I don't even know what channel BET is on, I thought to myself as I flipped through the TV channels.

I was used to the Time Warner Cable channels back at home. The Miami shit was different. Just another thing to add to the list of reasons why I wanted to get the fuck out of here. Miami was a place I visited, but it wasn't where I wanted to live. I was ready to throw the remote to the other side of the room when my door opened and in walked Skye.

I had to smile, because she was still the prettiest girl in the world to me. Her body was still very much intact, even after just having a baby. She didn't even need to use them body wrap shits. As she got closer, I noticed the side of her face had a discolored area shaped like a hand. She was smiling, but the minute she detected the grimace on my face, her pretty smile turned into a scowl. If I had the ability to jump up, I would have, but since I couldn't, I struggled to plant both my feet on the floor and reached for the walker.

"You do not need to get up, Cameron," she said as she walked toward me.

She sat down next to me on the bed and leaned in for a kiss, but I turned my head, letting her know shit wasn't sweet.

"I can't get a kiss?" She cocked her head to the side, with a puzzled look on her face.

"Yo, what happened to your face, Skye? Don't make up some bullshit, because I'm not trying to hear it. Real shit," I said.

My speech wasn't one hundred, but she had heard me clearly. She shifted in her seat, and I watched her contemplate what it was she needed to say to me. All I wanted to know was who the fuck had put their hands on her. Everything else was irrelevant, to be honest. I didn't give a fuck about the circumstances. Nobody was putting their hands on mine without consequences.

Then Skye told me the whole story. I wasn't prepared the slightest bit for what Skye revealed to me. I was angry. I was aware that I should have been appreciative of the fact that I had a shorty that was willing to step up while I was down, but I wasn't. What she had been doing was careless and, to me, selfish. She hadn't been thinking about my son, whom she'd been pregnant with at the time that she started this shit, nor had she been thinking about his well-being now.

Whoever knew about her actions and had let this shit go down was definitely going to hear my mouth about it. Who the fuck thought it was a good idea? I would have preferred it if they had dismantled the business rather than had Skye run it.

Where the fuck was Ty during all of this? I thought to myself as Skye sat watching me, waiting for a response.

"You're not going to say anything?" she quizzed.

"Fuck you want me to say?" I stated, looking directly in her face, giving her a blank stare.

"Please don't talk to me like that, Cameron."

"What was the point, Skye? What you got out of this, yo?" I asked her, still not fully comprehending why she had taken this on in the first place.

"I did this for you, Cameron! Do you not realize that you would have awakened from a coma with nothing?

Your mother had zero access to the money your father had stored away. Oh, let me guess. You wanted me to sit back and watch her wonder how she was going to keep her lights on. Miss me with the attitude. I'm not even looking for a thank-you, but what I won't accept is your attitude. Because of me, when you're able to walk, you'll have a business to walk back to, if you so choose, and because of me, you have a team left! I did that! I handled your affairs, like I was supposed to. Did I enjoy it? Hell no! I wanted to walk away every minute of the day, but did I? No. And I wouldn't hesitate to do it again," she explained, attempting to get me to see it from her point of view.

She didn't get it, and I wasn't going to debate with her about it. I heard and understood everything she'd told me. It all made sense, but she didn't understand where I was coming from.

"We'll agree to disagree. I'm not about to argue with you over that shit. I'm up now, so it's over for all that, Skye. Bring me my son," I said, switching to a total different subject.

"It's not over. I have business to tend to. When you're able to walk, you can carry on with doing shit yourself. Unless you want to push your walker around New York City. If that's your plan, then be my guest. And Cairo is sleeping, so when he gets up, I will bring him in here," she exclaimed as she stood up to leave.

"What? You going to disobey what I'm saying to you?"

"Disobey? You are Cairo's father, not *mine*," she said before walking out of the room.

Skye

The argument with Cameron had left me in a very bad mood. I couldn't believe his reaction. I mean, I didn't expect him to jump up and down and praise me for what I had done, but I did expect a thank-you, or at least for him to say he understood. I wanted to feel appreciated. I didn't feel like that at all. He had left me feeling like everything I did was for naught, just like a kid who went above and beyond in school just for at least minor recognition from his or her parents, only to get nothing. That was exactly how I felt. I just needed to get a few more things done, and I would be done.

I walked upstairs to my bedroom. Since Cameron couldn't walk up the stairs, we stayed in separate bedrooms. I needed to be upstairs, close to Cairo's room. I guessed the sleeping arrangements had worked out this way for a reason, because the way things were, we would have been unable to share the same living space, anyway. I walked into the bedroom, mapping out my next move.

I had been avoiding the conversation that I had to have with my grandfather sooner or later. Things with the Mexicans were getting way out of control. I had told him that if things became too heavy for me, I would reach out to him. I'd been trying my best to handle this on my own, but I just couldn't anymore. After my encounter with Miguel, I knew that if I didn't respond with either the money or war, things would take a turn for the worse. I wanted out at this point and needed to seek advice from my grandfather about how to handle the situation. I needed to book a flight and get down to Panama. The only problem with that was leaving Cameron during this stage of his recovery, and I didn't want to go out of the country without my son. I knew that Ty would never allow anything to happen to him, but Cairo was my responsibility, and technically, so was Cameron, regardless of whether he wanted to be bothered with me or not.

I plopped down on my bed and searched for my grandfather's number. It was about that time. I found the number in my phone and dialed it. As expected, he answered on the first ring.

"Nieta!"

"Pop-Pop, I need to see you." I didn't waste any time getting to the point. I couldn't discuss anything over the phone, but I knew me saying that before anything else would put him on to how imperative this was.

"I know. I made plans to come to the States. I wanted to discuss other plans with you in person. I will be there in two days. Can you manage until then, Skye?" I heard the seriousness in his tone as he asked that question.

I felt as if I couldn't, but I knew that if I said that, he would be on the next flight out here. Obviously, he had other things to handle, which was why he wasn't schedule to leave Panama until two more days. I didn't want him to postpone his business to rush to my aid. I had to put my big girl panties on and hold shit down until he could make it to the States.

"Yes, I can, Pop-Pop. I'll see you then." I said, then ended the call.

It was normal for us to keep our calls brief. We didn't need to draw any unwanted attention to our phone calls. I hadn't had any run-ins with the law, and I was trying to keep it that way.

I lay back on my bed, with my eyes closed, and dozed off.

Ty

When I made it back to Miami, I was unprepared for the showdown that awaited me. My mind was still fucked up over the whole Ariana ordeal, and dealing with anything else at the moment was too much. It seemed like my life was like that Van Gogh painting *The Bridge in the Rain*, which was the embodiment of the phrase "When it rains, it pours." That was the way the cookie always shattered on my end.

When I got in the house, I went straight up to check on Mama Mariah. She was the only mother I had ever known, and it felt like she was my biological mother, because that was how she treated me. My mother had left me with my father right after I was born. I didn't know if there was more to the story, because my father and I had never discussed it. The fact didn't matter to me, because for as long as I could remember, Mariah had been the constant mother figure in my life. So making sure she was straight was always a priority for me.

Her bedroom door was open, so I walked straight in and found her and Cairo sleeping peacefully. I walked over to the side of her bed and kissed her forehead before backtracking out of the room. I went to check on Skye and found her in the same state. *Damn*, I thought as I headed back downstairs. I walked into the living room and spotted Vic sitting in silence, doing something on her phone.

"What up, baby girl?" I said, walking over to her.

When she looked up from her phone and saw it was me, a smile spread across her face. I bent down and kissed her before taking a seat next to her. We sat in silence for a minute, just enjoying being in each other's presence. We had decided not to announce our relationship until things got back to normal, but there was no telling how long that would take. It was cool, though, because we were in a good place.

"You know, Cameron is here. They let him go from the rehab center today," she said, taking her attention off her phone to address me.

"Word, I didn't see him in the room when I went to check Skye."

She pointed. "He in that room. He can't walk up and down the stairs, babe."

I had totally forgotten about that shit. I really couldn't wait till my nigga got back to normal.

"Let me go check him. I'll be back," I said, getting up.

I walked toward the room Cam was occupying. I knocked on the door and waited for him to tell me to come in before I walked in.

"Welcome home, nigga," I said, putting my hand out to give him dap. I was happy to see that my nigga was home.

He curved my shit and just nodded his head.

"Who pissed in your cornflakes, bro?" I asked, taking a seat on the edge of his bed.

"Son, how could you let Skye do this? What if something had happened to her? What if something had happened to Cai? I trusted you, Ty."

I knew he would feel that way. That was the exact reason why I wasn't trying to let Skye get involved in the business in the first place.

"Cam, she loves you, son. She did everything she did for you. I did what I needed to do, to make sure they were good. If I didn't help, she was definitely going to do shit on her own. Which would you have preferred?"

Knowing that the question was rhetorical, he didn't answer. I took his silence as a chance for me to tell him everything that had gone on since the day he was hit until this moment. He was shocked to hear the lengths that Skye had gone to. He didn't approve of it, but he respected it. Cam was a nigga, just like me. Full of pride, he would never admit that he felt good to have a shorty like Skye on his team. He let his fake anger do the talking, but I knew different, though, just like he knew me better than I knew myself sometimes. Cam was acting funny about shit because his pride was hurt. He was unable to do shit, so his girl had had to step up. I could imagine how I would have felt had it been me, so I knew how he felt. He would definitely get over it, though.

I left out what had happened at my pops's crib. The wound was still healing, and I wasn't trying to pick at it. I was hurting over that, but I knew I had had to do it. He'd gone too far. When I was in a better space with the situation, or whenever he asked me about my pops, I would definitely tell Cam. Right then just wasn't the time.

Victoria

Hector, Ty, and I decided to take a trip back to New York with Skye. She was meeting up with her grandfather to discuss business. I wanted to go along because I was in dire need of a new wardrobe. My first semester at school would be starting soon, and of course, I had to look my best. Ty wanted to come along because I was going, and because, of course, he wanted to check on his team. Hector was going in order to protect and serve, like always.

As soon as we got to New York, Skye and Ty both left to go handle some business, so Hector and I decided to hit up the mall. Hector wasn't gay, so he would be no use to me fashion-wise, and therefore, I left him in the parking lot, waiting at the car. I sauntered through the mall, going in and out of all my favorite designer stores. During the first hour of shopping, I couldn't help feeling as if I was being watched. I shook the feeling, because I hated being paranoid.

I continued about my business. But at some point, I became more alert and aware of my surroundings, because my gut was screaming to me again that something wasn't right. That was when I noticed him. I was in Bloomingdale's when I spotted him the first time, and I brushed it off as a coincidence . . . until I spotted him again in the Juicy Couture store. Matt was dumber than he looked. If he thought that I wouldn't recognize him, because I had seen him only a few times a long time ago, he had life and me fucked up. I never forgot a face, especially one that was sitting at the top of my family's hit list. I picked up a few things I really didn't want, and headed in the direction of the cash register. I had to purchase something because I didn't want Matt to realize I was onto his stalking ass.

As I waited on the checkout line, I texted, Hector letting him know what was up. He texted me back with a list of meticulous instructions to follow, and I followed them to a T. As I headed out to the parking lot, I noticed Matt was still lurking. I smiled inwardly and kept it moving. He was going to learn today that I was the wrong one. I strutted through the parking lot with Matt on my heels. He thought he was inconspicuous, but old boy needed a class in detective work.

I was approaching our car when Hector jumped out and put his paws on Matthew. It was like something out of a movie. Hector appeared from behind the van that was parked next to us, and I just saw his hands go around Matt's neck, and *bam*, Matt dropped to the ground. Hector assured me that he wasn't dead. He had put him to sleep. Hector threw him in the backseat of the car.

I knew exactly where to take him. I recited the address to Hector before calling Skye and Ty.

Skye

When I got the call from Victoria, I didn't know what to say. In a way, I wanted to be pissed at her for being so reckless, but at the same time, I was proud of her. She was ready to put in work for her family. We were all we had at this point. When I got the call, I was in the middle of discussing expanding the business and supplying the other boroughs with Pop-Pop. I was glad that her call had interrupted us, because I was totally against the idea. It strayed away from my purpose, but at the same time, I asked to be a part of this expansion, nonetheless. I had gone to my Pop-Pop for help, and he had been nothing but helpful since, and now he was coming to me for help in return, and I couldn't turn him down.

What made me agree to the idea was that it would be helping Cameron's business in the long run. Pop-Pop agreed that once Cameron was able to handle his own business, he would continue to supply him with enough weight to expand his business throughout the States. It was the job offer that Pop-Pop had given me earlier, and I had declined. However, since I had been successful thus far, I felt a little at ease with the idea of expanding to the other boroughs.

The only thing that didn't sit right with me was Pop-Pop saying we were going to pay the Mexicans, which was the issue I had wanted to discuss with him in the first place. I knew better and thought he should too. He explained that he knew it would be only a temporary solution, but it was one we need to act on while we still had our plates full with other things. I finally agreed, and he promised he would take care of it. He also said that ultimately, we would have to eradicate Miguel and his team, but he wanted me to focus on one set of issues at a time. If paying Miguel the two million in cash would make him fall back some, it was a good idea. The more he explained it, the more sense it made to me.

Pop-Pop wasn't pleased when I decided to cut our discussion short. Of course, he felt his needs trumped the needs of everyone and everything else. Normally, for me, they did, because I felt kind of indebted to him. He had helped me out when I really couldn't call on anyone else. That didn't change the fact that I had to get down to where Victoria had told me she and Hector were holding Matt.

It took some convincing, but I was able to shorten the meeting with Pop-Pop. I headed up to my bedroom and quickly switched into something comfortable. I smiled at the thought of Matt's demise being because of me. Who would have thought Matt would die at my hands? I surely hadn't. The thought forced me to smile. I jumped in my car and headed to Brooklyn.

When I pulled up to the location, a warehouse, I parked and ran inside. My adrenaline was pumping, and I was ready to see this nigga. He had been a little hard to get to at first, but finally, the time had come. Before walking into the spot, I made a decision. No matter what anyone told me or how hard they pleaded with me, Matt was not leaving this spot alive. I let myself in using the key provided by Ty. I already had my piece out and ready, in case something wasn't right.

I found Victoria and Hector sitting at the kitchen table, chopping it up, while Matt was bound to a chair, with what appeared to be a sock in his mouth. His presence enraged me as I stood directly in front of him. He looked beaten, but I didn't give a fuck as I slammed the butt of my gun against his head and watched him cry out in pain. Victoria and Hector were behind me now, laughing and calling him a bitch for crying. I wasn't focused on that, though. I'd been waiting for this moment for a long time, and I was going to make the very best of it.

I raised my gun to the point where it was aimed downward, targeting his kneecap, and pulled the trigger. Hearing the sound of his kneecap crack from the impact of the bullet had me excited.

"Now you will begin to feel my pain," I yelled out before spitting on him.

I raised my gun again, aimed at his other kneecap, and pulled the trigger. He fell over, still tied to the chair, and started squirming. I wasn't done, though.

"Don't die, Matt. You can't die until I tell you it's time," I said as my foot connected with his jaw.

I proceeded to deliver blow after blow to his squirming body. Under normal circumstances, my punches and kicks may not have had any effect on his six-foot-three-inch, 215-pound frame, but he was already in excruciating pain. I took advantage of that and continued to let my punches and kicks rain down on him.

Stopping to catch my second wind, I spoke through clenched teeth. "You feel that, bitch? It's what I had to endure for months because of the shit you did to this family."

I stood over him, with my gun aimed at his skull. I was ready to get it over with. Just as I laid my finger on the trigger, the door to the warehouse opened. My instincts kicked in, and I swiveled around and aimed my gun in the direction of the door. Then I realized it was Ty and JR, and so I switched my target back to Matt.

"What the fuck, yo?" Ty barked as he rushed to my side.

I was pissed off that Victoria had called him. We'd been through so much, and Victoria still seemed to doubt the work I was capable of putting in. She had had to call in reinforcements.

I turned around to face her. "You didn't think I could handle this shit myself?"

Victoria started to speak but was cut off by Ty. "Skye, we all are well aware of what you are capable of doing. She did the right thing by calling me, sis, but I just wish I had got here faster. This is not you. You're not a killer, Skye. Once you kill that nigga, ain't no coming back from that. You're a killer for life. I'm not letting it go down like that."

I was overwhelmed with emotion and started crying. "He ruined my family, Ty. Cameron almost died, and they lost their father because of this nigga!" I was livid, and my tears wouldn't stop falling.

Then I thought about Cairo. I was a mother! That alone was enough to calm me down a bit. No one could possibly understand how badly I wanted to finish this job, but I couldn't bring myself to kill Matt. I'd done enough sins these past few months that I would ultimately have to pay for, but murder wasn't something I really wanted to add to my résumé.

Ty walked closer to me and put his hand on top of my gun and slid it out of my hand. In one motion, he aimed it at Matt and pulled the trigger, ending his life instantly.

"You not getting this piece back, sis, but you can have the silencer, though." Ty unscrewed it and tossed it to me before he continued to speak. "Go ahead, though. I'll have this cleaned up, and I'll meet y'all back at your crib in, like, two hours. I'll stay the night there since we got an early flight," he said while he took out his phone. I guessed he was about to make a call to the cleanup crew.

It amazed me how Ty could take a life, then go on talking, like nothing had happened. I guessed he was accustomed to this. I was glad he'd stopped me, because this wasn't a part of my plan. I didn't set out to become a murderer, but then, who knew what I would do if my back was against the wall? That hadn't been the case with Matt, so killing him would have only left me feeling haunted.

Victoria and I left Ty and Hector alone with Matt's body as Ty waited for his boys to come through and do their job. Victoria and I jumped in my car and headed to the Staten Island house.

I was glad that Victoria didn't want to talk on the way to Staten Island, because I really needed that time to clear my head. I was happy Matt was gone, because he had been a thorn in my side since that shit went down last year, and now that chapter was closed. The story wasn't over, but I was making progress. At this point, I just wanted to get back to Miami, to my son and Cameron. I made a mental note to call as soon as we got in, to check on my boys. I knew they were fine, because I hadn't got a call telling me otherwise, but I still wanted to know how things were going. I wanted to hear my baby coo in the phone, and I wanted to hear Cameron as well.

Victoria

I thought Skye had become a different person since Cam was shot, but today she'd really shown up. She had really been seconds away from ending Matt's life. It was a good thing I had called Ty to give him a heads-up. More importantly, I was happy Ty had shown up when he did, because I didn't think Skye would have been able to live with herself knowing that she'd ended someone's life. I also didn't think that Cam would have ever forgiven any of us if we'd let her put in that type of work. Their relationship was on edge as it was. No fuel needed to be added to that fire.

When we got back to the Staten Island house, I decided to have a heart-to-heart with Skye. Given how much had been going on, I had never seen anyone stop to ask her how she was holding up, but she'd done that for everyone else. I owed her that much.

"I'm tired, Vic. I am physically and emotionally tired," she told me as we sat on the couch in the living room, eating a salad that I had quickly put together.

"You can walk away, sis. No one will hold that against you. You've done enough. You should be proud of yourself. If it means anything, I'm proud of you," I said, meaning every word.

I didn't think Skye received enough credit for the way she ran the organization. The team had gone from having almost no work on the street to flooding the entire city, the five boroughs and Long Island included. She had done it while never getting her hands dirty, although she was always ready to. She had done it pregnant, and now she was juggling it with being a mother. All the while being there for Cam. She deserved much more than the short end of the stick she was receiving.

"Walk away to what? Cameron and I are basically over. The messed-up part about that is he's the reason why I got involved in this in the first place. It was never supposed to go this far, Vic. Never, sis." She shook her head as her tears began to fall. She quickly wiped them away, but they continued to flow freely.

I could tell that there was so much more she wanted to say, so I let her. This was her chance, because throughout this whole ordeal, she had never really voiced how she felt about things and the emotions she experienced. I wanted her to know that I was her sister and that she could bare her soul to me. I would be there.

"I had my best friend killed because of this life, Victoria. My best friend! Ariana was my rib before I met your brother. I'm not blaming your brother, so don't think that. I am aware that it was my decision, but it was because I decided to take over for him. I had to commit, though. I had to walk the walk. I had to talk the talk. Now my best friend is dead. We could have talked it out, and I could have been understanding. Instead, I had her murdered. I watched Ty kill his own father and not blink twice. That was never supposed to happen. Jeff had to pay for what he did, but at the hands of his own son? It wasn't supposed to go that far."

I was floored when she revealed to me the murders of Ariana and Jeff. I had had no idea that she was carrying around that weight. I knew it had to be hard. It was hard for me, and I wasn't the one who had ordered or executed the murders. I moved closer to Skye on the couch and wrapped my arms around her.

She wept, and I didn't try to stop her. Instead, I repeated over and over, "I'm here for you, sis."

On the couch, wrapped in my arms, was where Skye stayed until we were joined later that night by Ty and Hector. Although they wanted to just rest tonight and head back to Miami the following day, I knew better. Skye needed to get away from this city and away from these memories, even if only for a little while. What she needed more than the aforementioned was her son. Before long, we were on the red-eye back to Miami.

Skye

Since we'd been back home in Miami, all I'd wanted to do was be with my son. Cameron and I weren't speaking, and we hadn't been ever since I told him I was going to continue to handle his business until he was capable of doing it himself. He didn't like the idea, and I understood why, but I just wanted him to be more appreciative of the fact that I did it for him. I continued to accompany him to physical therapy and speech therapy. I continued to take daily walks with him and Cairo, because his therapist had said that walking daily with his walker was needed. Even if Cam didn't acknowledge my presence, I did it.

On the days when his physical therapist came to the house to do water aerobics with him in the pool, I participated, just to keep him motivated. He was so close to overcoming these obstacles, but at the same time so close to giving up. I wasn't going to allow that, but he was making it extremely hard for me to be there for him. He was making me not want to be there. I was at the point where when it was all said and done, I wanted to leave. I wanted it to be over. I wanted to forget I had ever done the things I did. I knew it wouldn't be that easy, but it was what I wanted.

I would never keep Cairo away from his dad, because Cameron loved his son and did the best he could at being active in his life, but I was fed up with feeling unwanted.

I missed the Cameron before the incident, the one who was so loving and passionate. I hadn't even got as much as a kiss since he was released from the rehab center. I was over living like this and was ready to just put it all behind me.

Victoria

Skye had been going through a lot lately, and trying to sort through her feelings about the death of Ariana and the status of her and Cam's relationship was at the top of that list. I had to admit that she'd been tough through everything, but after spending all this time with her, I could see that it was starting to take a serious toll on her. I really wished my brother would notice and try to work through their disagreements, or at least try to see things her way. I knew my brother, and truth be told, I didn't think he would do that. He felt the way he felt, and he would definitely stand by that.

I had tried to make the load easier, but Skye had felt the need to take on all the responsibilities herself. I got that she wanted to be a superwoman, but she didn't have to be. We were family! She'd held us down the entire time my brother was in the hospital and the rehab center, but she hadn't let me do a thing for her in return.

"Hey, sis!" I said as I walked into Cairo's room, to find Skye sitting on his mat with him, watching him crawl from toy to toy.

"Hey, Vic." The tone of the greeting was extremely dry, but I chalked that up to her being depressed.

She had her days. Some were up; some were down. The only moments when she seemed genuinely happy were the moments she spent with Cairo. Like right now, she spoke to me all dry and shit, but as soon as she put her attention back on Cairo, she got chipper. I understood, though. Filling Cam's shoes was turning out to be a way bigger task than she had expected. It was more than she'd bargained for. The fact that she and Cam were still on bad terms also wasn't helping.

"I want to go out and get some air," I told her. "Can I take Cairo to the park?"

This was a long shot, because she rarely let him out of her sight, unless she was handling business, but she needed the break.

"Sure. Which park? And are you taking Ty?"

I was caught off guard by her asking if I was taking Ty. Although she knew about us seeing each other and didn't really disagree or agree, she just didn't mention it. I was good with that because I wasn't ready to discuss my feelings with anyone. I was afraid that they probably wouldn't agree with it.

"No. He's not here. He went to get a haircut. So just me and my nephew." I could see that she was battling with letting me take him.

"Okay, Vic."

I watched as Skye got up off the mat and picked up Cairo. As she walked over to me, she planted kisses on his cheeks. I loved watching her interactions with Cairo. She did her motherly thing effortlessly.

"Cai, be good with Tee-Tee," she said to him as she handed him to me.

"What you going to do while we are gone?" I asked her.

I already knew the answer, so I didn't even know why I'd asked.

"I'm going to go up to the rehab center to check on your brother. Hector took him earlier for his session, and since you taking Cai, I might as well stop by."

Exactly what I'd thought.

"Want me to get his bag together, or you got it?" she said as she smiled at Cairo, who was in my arms, smiling back at her.

"I got it, sis. Call me when you get to the center," I said as I walked over to get Cairo's baby bag off the rocking chair.

"I love you, Cai." I heard Skye say as she walked out of the room.

After packing Cairo's bag, I headed to the kitchen, made him a bottle, and then we headed out.

It was a beautiful day in Miami. While it was a bit hot, there was a little breeze, so I was straight. I opted out of driving just so Cairo and I could enjoy the nice weather. Plus, walking was good exercise. The park was packed today, as expected. School was out of session, so most parks and kid-friendly places were packed. As I walked through the park, pushing Cairo's stroller, I spotted an empty bench underneath a tree.

"Yes, some damn shade," I said out loud, as if Cairo could answer me.

Not only was the bench in the shade, but it was also away from all the kids who were crowding the playground. Directly across from the park was a track field. No one was occupying the track, and I supposed that was due to the heat. Once I was seated under the tree, I gave Cairo one of his bottles that was filled with water. I had to keep my nephew hydrated in this heat.

I looked at Cairo, who was drinking his water and dozing off. He was such a good baby, and he cried only when he was wet, hungry, or sleepy. Looking at him made my heart smile. We had been through so much, and Cairo was the constant happiness in our lives. No matter how bad things may have gotten at one time or another, having my nephew around always made the biggest problems seem small. I had watched Cameron struggle with trying to overcome his inability to walk on his own, and I knew his motivation was solely Cairo. Just as I was thinking about Cameron, my phone started ringing. I looked at it and saw that it was Skye. She was checking on him already, and it hadn't even been that long. *Typical Skye*, I thought as I slid my finger across the screen on my phone to answer.

"Sis, he is okay. We just chillin'," I said, getting right to the point.

She said something loudly in response, but I was unable to make out her words.

"Stop yelling, Skye. What happened?"

I heard her take a few deep breaths before she started to speak again. "Hector just called me, and Cameron was able to walk without the walker, sis!" She had excitement oozing through her tone.

As I fixed my lips to respond to her, I felt a hand cover my mouth with a cloth and press it hard against my lips. I squirmed, trying to break free, but it seemed as if the more I tried to fight, the weaker I became. Then everything suddenly went black.

Skye

"Hello!" I screamed into the phone, but in response, I heard only muffled noises.

The muffled noises ceased, and then I heard Cairo crying.

"Cairo!" I cried out as his crying began to fade, until there was silence.

Realizing that one of my most feared nightmares might be coming true, I went into panic mode. I shuffled around my bedroom, in search of my keys. I had to get to the park, where, I silently prayed, I would find Victoria and Cairo.

I finally made it to my car, and then I wasted no time putting the pedal to the metal. You would have sworn I was doing stunts for one of those *The Fast and the Furious* movies, the way I weaved through the streets. When I reached the park Victoria and I had frequented with Cairo, I parked the car and jumped out. My feet hit the pavement as I took off running. My first stop was the playground, but there was no sign of them there, so I continued my search. I noticed a huge tree with a view of the track field across the street. An ambulance had parked near the tree. I ran toward it. As I got closer, I saw paramedics loading a stretcher into the back of the ambulance. Running track in high school really paid off now. I caught up to the paramedics in the nick of time.

"Where is my baby?" I yelled in a panic when I caught sight of Cairo's empty stroller. "Please let me through!

That's my sister, and my son was with her." I pleaded with a police officer who had stopped me in my tracks and was holding me back.

"Ma'am, you can meet them at the University of Miami Hospital. There was no baby here when we arrived on the scene. This officer would be glad to give you a ride down to the hospital, where she would take your statement as well," the short, stocky police officer explained.

My world came crashing down, and I was now living the nightmare. My sole purpose for waking up every morning was now missing. I heard sounds coming from the police officer's mouth, but my brain wouldn't process the words. I slowly walked backward as the police officer called out to me. My concern was finding my baby, and I felt if anyone could give me answers, it would be Victoria. However, I didn't know her condition, but I would soon find out.

Although my knees were shaking and were threatening to cave in due to the weight of the world I was carrying on my back, I made it back to my car. I managed to contact Cameron, who was still at therapy with Hector and Mariah. They had to meet me at the hospital.

Cameron

That day was one of the many days I was thankful to have Hector around. Because of him, I was able to get to the hospital in record-breaking time. I was walking on my own but couldn't move as fast as I needed to, and I was still unable to drive. The entire ride across town to the University of Miami Hospital, I cursed and ranted out loud. I didn't have the facts. All I knew was that someone had knocked Vic out with chloroform and had taken my son.

"Not my fucking son!" I bellowed, causing Hector to look over at me.

"Mr. Cameron, we will get him back," he said, trying to reassure me.

His attempt was futile, and I didn't have the slightest idea about who would want to kidnap my son. Of course, my first thought was Miguel, but it wasn't his style. Kidnapping maybe, but he would have killed Vic. I stormed into the hospital's emergency-room department, with the look of death written across my face. I knew Vic would be fine, so my concern was my son. I prayed he was kidnapped for cash, because that was something I was willing and able to give up quickly if it assured Cairo's safe return. I spotted Skye sitting near the window, looking straight out at nothing in particular.

I hurried over to her. "Skye!" I said, trying to break her trance.

She wouldn't budge. I knew she had shut down, and I understood why. I wanted to do the same, but it wouldn't get us Cai back. I just knew we would get him back. There wasn't enough room for anything else, and the only outcome I was allowing was my son's safe return. Skye still hadn't acknowledged me. She should have known I wouldn't take that lightly.

"Yo, it's not the time to space out. You should be telling me who could have possibly done this, instead of sitting here, staring into space, looking lost. Nine time out of ten, this shit is your fault," I barked at her. I knew I had hit a nerve.

I didn't care at that point, because she needed to get it together if we would have any hope of finding Cairo. She jumped up out of her seat and pushed me, catching me off guard. I didn't budge, though.

"How is this my fault, Cameron?" she screamed, her tears flowing freely.

"Who knows, Skye? If you wasn't running around, trying to be a fucking thug, or whatever you called yourself doing, and were focused on taking care of my son, he would be home! I'm sure you made some enemies," I retorted.

"I didn't make enemies. I took on *yours*! You know what? Fuck you! I don't have to listen to you try to blame me for this. I did the best I could. Instead of pointing the finger at me, figure out how we are going to get my son back! After that, you can have this fucking life, because it don't mean shit to me no way! Just find my fucking child," she shouted.

"Fuck you too, Skye. Nobody told you to do the shit you did. Look where it got us." I knew that I was wrong for blaming her, and that I had cut her deep, but in the heat of the moment, I had lost it.

My son was missing, and someone had to answer for it. It shouldn't have to be Skye, because I knew she was a great mother, and I did realize she had held me down in ways that I didn't see any other female doing. But I wasn't concerned with any of that at the moment. I just wanted Cairo. My boy, my young king, was gone, and I had no clue where to even begin the search to find him. My frustrations toward Skye were due only to the fact that I was realizing how much of a fucked-up father I was.

Hector took Skye outside to calm her down, because we'd been approached by security. I stayed in the emergency-room waiting room until my mother came out and led me back to where Vic was giving a statement to the police.

Skye

Hector and I stood outside the hospital. He had me wrapped in his arms, and he was trying to console me as I cried. Why did this have to happen to my son? I knew I wasn't living right, but why did this have to be my punishment? Cairo was so innocent, and he had nothing to do with this at all. Who would use my child as collateral damage? Then, on top of that, Cameron had had the audacity to blame me. I had done nothing but try to be the woman he needed me to be when he needed it most, and he had thanked me by saying I had caused my son's abduction. Maybe he was right; maybe it was my fault.

My phone vibrating hard in the pocket of my shorts caused my thigh to twitch slightly. I was in no mood to converse, but thinking it could be someone calling in regard to Cairo, I answered.

"Hello," I said dryly.

"Skye, how are you?"

That voice sent me into overdrive. I wished he was in my presence, as I would have killed him. As much as I wanted to go off, I had to keep my cool and play by their rules to get my son back.

"Miguel, I paid you the money. What is it that I need to do to get my son back? Please don't hurt him," I pleaded, knowing that if that was his intention, my pleading would mean nothing. I had to try, though.

"I'm sorry, but I had nothing to do with that." He spoke in an even tone.

I would have preferred it if he was the one who had taken Cairo, because at least I would have a chance to do what he wanted in order to get my son back. Finding out that he had nothing to do with it only put me back at square one. Who could benefit from taking my son? I wondered. I had no clue, and I couldn't waste time conversing with Miguel. I had to find out.

"Miguel, if you don't have anything to do with the kidnapping of my son, why are you calling me? You got your money. We're done." I knew paying him the money was the easy way out. I should have just gone to war with them.

"That's where you are wrong. Your people caused us a great deal of trouble with Matt missing in action. Actually, I see you have a lot on your plate at the moment. I'll contact you when I'm back in the States. Do not have me looking for you, Skye. I promise getting your son back alive would be the least of your worries if you do," he said before ending the call.

Going to war with them really did seem as if it would have been the better choice. I had known the hostility wouldn't end. There was always something! I couldn't take it anymore. I had once held it together and had had it all planned out, but I was breaking, slowly but surely. Now not only did I have to focus on finding Cairo, but I also had to think about when Miguel would pop up, demanding shit from me. There was no way I was getting involved with him again. If Cameron wanted his organization back so bad, he could have it. Once I got my son, we were dipping and not looking back, because I couldn't deal with this anymore.

Everyone had been right from the beginning, Ty, Victoria, my parents, even Ariana. Why hadn't I listened?

***

Victoria was released from the hospital the same day, and although she gave a statement to the Miami PD, they were really unable to help us. We had nothing to go on, not one single lead. We spent most of the days following the kidnapping sitting by each of our phones, wishing and hoping for a call about Cairo, but none came. Ty stepped up and headed back to New York City to put his ear to the streets. All we could do was continue to wait around and hope for the best.

Ty

It had been a week since Cairo was taken, and I still couldn't believe the shit. Who wanted Skye this bad that they would go to this length to hurt her? I prayed they didn't hurt Cairo, and I knew in my heart we would get him back, because I wasn't stopping until we did. I just prayed they didn't hurt him. I been in NYC, trying to get some information, but no one knew anything.

I pulled up to the Waldorf and parked. I had been staying at Skye's crib since I arrived in the city, just in case the kidnappers called her there. It was unlikely, but we were running out of options. Before I could get out of my truck, my phone started vibrating. Without looking at it, I answered.

"Yo?"

"I have Cairo," a female voice answered

The voice sounded familiar, but it couldn't be. She wouldn't go this far. I shook my head as reality began to sink in.

"Ty, I don't want to hurt him," she said, forcing me to realize that this was real. This shit was really happening.

"Why?" I couldn't bring myself to say anything else.

She began speaking, giving me a million reasons why she was doing this. The shit didn't matter, though. Once we got Cairo back, the rest would be history. As she went on and on, I sat back and thought about the last time I had seen her. I had never thought my actions that day would come back around and bite me in the ass like this.

After hearing Ariana had lost our baby, I couldn't kill her. I couldn't stop myself from wrapping my hands around her neck and nearly sucking the life out of the bitch, either. But I stopped when she started to turn blue.

As much as I wanted to kill her, I couldn't. It was not like I loved her, but hearing she had lost my baby pinched at my heart. I watched as she regained her composure, and I listened as she pleaded with me. She explained that she had lost the baby the night she got shot. I felt guilty and fucked up that she had had to deal with the loss on her own. If she had told me, I would have helped her through it the best way I could have, but she was right. Way too much had been going on at the time.

By that point I had lowered my weapon and had made up my mind that I wasn't going to kill her. I stepped away from her as she sat sobbing on the floor. The damage was done, and there was no retreating from the place we found ourselves at in this moment. I had been sent to end her life, but I couldn't do that, either.

"Ariana, just get low. I got a homie out in Vegas who could help you start fresh. Skye wants you dead, and you know that given the type of shit she been on lately, she won't stop. I'll send you bread until you can get on your feet, but you gotta go. Don't contact your parents for a minute. Let them call Skye, worried. If they don't, she will get suspicious. I hate that it had to come to this, Ma, but this is all your doing. All you had to do was speak up. I'll contact my nigga and then get back at you with the details. Don't take anything," I barked, I prayed she followed my instructions, because if not, this shit wouldn't end well for either of us.

She nodded her head frantically while still trying to catch her breath. I said all I could and needed to say. I concealed my weapon and left.

"You stopped sending the money. How the hell was I supposed to live? Get up two million for me, and you can have the baby back, unharmed." Hearing her ask for a ransom brought me back to the situation at hand.

"Bitch, I should have killed you!"

To be continued . . .